WILLIAM
PETRICK

Published by Pearhouse Press, Inc., Pittsburgh, PA 15208
pearhousepress.com

First Printing: June 2020
Printed in the United States of America

ISBN: 978-1-7347119-3-6

Library of Congress Control Number: 2020940775

Cover and Book Design: Mike Murray, pearhouse.com

For Carol Billings

(1935-2018)

A BONE DANGLED ON A STRING FROM THE TAXI'S REARVIEW MIRROR. Dean stared at it as he might a corpse as he settled into the backseat of the old Chevy. The curve of the bone suggested a face; maybe a sliver of cheekbone. He knew enough about Haitian Vodou that the human relic was likely real and sourced from a family member of the taxi driver. Vodou followers used them as lucky charms, talisman to hold the ancestral spirits near.

The taxi driver squeezed behind the wheel and slammed the door hard enough to shake the car. He turned to greet Dean, his yellow, jaundiced eyes tired but friendly. The skin under those eyes sagged in deep folds like a bulldog.

"*Bonjou!* Where do we go?" he asked.

"Hotel Erickson," Dean answered. He didn't know what to expect in Port au Prince, but he was wary. He'd been following the recent reports about the unrest and the bloody, if isolated, attacks on the street by opposing political gangs. He'd gained the impression that the city was permanently on edge.

The driver took the bone between two, thick fingers and rubbed it like a rabbit's foot. The bone was left swinging lightly back and forth like a pendulum. Dean wondered if it was a ritual.

The car lumbered out of the dirt parking lot. It was a junker, a Chevy Bel Air from back when Detroit made cars as big as boats. It was a lounge inside and only getting hotter from the fierce, afternoon heat that streamed through the open windows.

"Can you turn on the air-conditioner?"

"Yes, yes. But it is broken."

The car bounced onto the two-lane blacktop that was the only road to downtown. The thick, brine-scented air blowing through his window was oddly comforting, reminding him of home. Not New York City, which he didn't think of as home, even after living there for two decades, but his boyhood home in the low country outside Charleston. He took a deep, grateful breath.

"You are a journalist?" the driver asked, making conversation.

The question felt both random and uncanny. Like the guy knew what he had been wrestling with for months before he even made the decision to travel to Haiti.

"Why do you think I'm a journalist?" Dean asked.

"Because the Erickson Hotel. All the journalists stay."

The Chevy slowed suddenly like a cruiser drifting into a crowded harbor. The heavy breeze stopped with the taxi. The other traffic rolled to a standstill. A line of old, used cars and small, beat-up Japanese trucks were panting and smoking in the haze.

Dean looked absently for the red light. But there wasn't one in sight. In fact, there were no traffic lights at all. There was no cop directing traffic either. No one could move. Dean worried they never would.

"Where is the Erickson?" The inside of the car had become a furnace. The thick humidity clung to his skin like plastic wrap.

"There." The taxi driver pointed at a white-washed building rising in the distance. A series of turrets resembled a gingerbread castle straight out of Disneyland. Tall, aging palm trees graced the entrance.

"Close enough"

"Yes, not far to drive."

"No, I am going to walk," Dean said. As soon as he pushed open the heavy taxi door and climbed out onto the boiling street, he had a feeling he'd made a mistake. It didn't help that the driver looked panicked. But he could see from the driver's wide eyes that he was fearful of losing his fare.

"*Map peye,*" Dean said. "I am going to pay."

Dean opened his carry-on and set it on the blacktop next to him. The angry sun was on him. He grabbed the envelope with his company's logo and ripped the end off, exposing a thick stack of crisp new Haitian g*ourdes* he'd been given as petty cash. It seemed excessive, enough to last weeks or more, not just a few days. He knew most people lived on little more than a dollar a day in Port au Prince and beyond.

As he sorted out the fare, he noticed a gaggle of school-aged children. They had appeared out of nowhere, streaming around the parked cars. They were hustling toward him like city pigeons chasing breadcrumbs. A young girl boldly took his arm holding the envelope. Her dark eyes, lascivious as a grown woman, locked on his. Dean yanked his arm out of her seductive grasp.

The young girl tilted her head and smiled at him. A sweet, coquettish smile. She went to touch his arm again, but Dean backed away, against the hot car. The girl nodded as if she expected as much from an old foreigner and turned away.

The muscled taxi driver suddenly leapt out and was halfway around the front of the car, his neck bulging. The gang of street kids bolted as if touched by an electric shock, scattering like a flock in all directions. Dean watched, dumbfounded. Then he searched for his overnight bag on the street. It was gone.

Dean stared at the empty spot, then searched around it. Surely he had moved it with his foot without thinking. But no, it was gone. He looked to the street where the children had slowed, attempting to disappear into the crowd. Dean bolted like a gun had been fired, sprinting after them. He thought he spotted the girl who had distracted him. But when he reached the broken concrete, she was nowhere to be seen. He peered through the crowd, hoping for a glimpse. They had somehow disappeared. Dean looked dumbly at a group of women in silk headscarves sitting on a blanket next to a neat pile of charcoal for sale.

The driver arrived alongside, breathing heavily. His wide nose was flared with anger.

"*Bouda kaka,*" he cussed in Kreyol. "Shitty ass."

"Kids?" Dean asked. "A gang or what?"

"*Sanguine,*" the driver answered. Street kids.

Dean remembered the look of the young girl. She was smart, focused—a girl-woman used to looking out for herself.

"*Mon sac,*" Dean said, pointing to where the sanguine had disappeared.

"They take your bag. Are you sure?"

At the airport, he had the hare-brained idea to put his passport, cell phone, and U.S. dollars inside the bag for protection and ease of travel. He had planned to redistribute everything once he was in the cab so everything was not in one place. But he'd forgotten about it.

"Can we get the police?"

"Police?" The taxi driver looked genuinely surprised.

"Yes, of course. I need the bag."

He felt the jaundiced eyes studying him.

"The traffic. It will be long for the police, too."

Dean felt the sun bore into his scalp. The goddamn heat was constant, lording over everything, an overbearing presence from the moment he arrived.

"I take you to police," the driver said. "Please."

Dean wasn't getting back inside that cab. He saw the engine was still running, the door wide open as they had left it.

"That's ok." He gave the driver the *gourdes* and made for the sidewalk again. He was quickly swept along like a log in a swollen river of arms, legs, and faces. The air reeked of urine, sewage, and sour human sweat. He dodged people as they rushed past, strikingly purposeful, intent on a destination. There was none of the doddering and tired wandering of the homeless or lost souls he was used to seeing on Manhattan streets. These men and women were industrious. But to what end? Jobs were as scarce as clean water.

Soon, the double turrets of the Erickson rose up ahead, framed by the iconic palm trees. Wide, cement steps led up a grassy incline to the lobby entrance. It was gaudy but with a raffish charm he liked. It had a history.

The gangly clerk checked him in with a cheerful, professional smile, not bothering to ask for his passport. He seemed to not notice or care that Dean carried no luggage at all. He was focused on the ledger, toying with a fountain pen. Like the old Chevy that had driven him to the city, the pen was yet another vintage object few had reason to use anymore.

"You are from New York, Mr. Dubose? We are very pleased to have you," the clerk continued, formally handing him a key. Dean couldn't remember the last time a hotel had given out a room key instead of magnetic cards.

"Your room is in the annex. We are full, yes? Small but *Tres prive*."

Overbooked with journalists? Dean wondered. He'd never thought he'd be in danger of sold-out accommodations.

"Any messages for me by chance?" Dean asked. He was due to meet his client and drive together to Coluers, the village in the high mountains where his work would begin.

"No, *monsieur*. No one."

Dean was relieved. He needed to solve his problem, especially the passport.

"Is there a police station near?"

"There is *problème*, monsieur?" The clerk looked concerned.

"My bag was stolen," Dean said.

"Ici à l'hotel?" The clerk's eyes widened with surprise and fear. He glanced around the empty lobby with an air of secrecy as though he suspected the culprit was in range, listening to them.

"No, out on the street," Dean said. The robbery replayed in his mind. He knew the police were unlikely to retrieve his things.

"The police station is across the street, monsieur. *Je t'accompagne*," the clerk offered. He came around the counter, ready to accompany Dean.

"No *merci*," Dean said, holding up his hand. What he really needed to do was get it replaced, quickly. The travel department would replace everything. They were skilled at backing up employees. Yet he was worried about how the rest of the office might interpret the incident. It would certainly ignite a new round of gossip, adding to those hallway murmurings he pretended to ignore, making light of his decision to take on the Haiti project. It was the kind of assignment even the most desperate newbies wouldn't touch. No one could understand why a senior partner would be so intent on traveling to the poorest country in the hemisphere.

Dean looked at the clerk without seeing him. He decided against the office. That left only his girlfriend, Cynthia. Beautiful, caring, overbearing Cynthia. It wouldn't be an easy favor. There was too much unsettled between them, not to mention she had also been critical of what she called his silly "jaunt."

"Sir?" the clerk asked. He stood patiently, waiting.

"I need to make a telephone call."

The clerk pursed his lips.

"Very good. We shall have that repaired soon."

"Repaired?"

"Within the hour, *monsieur*. There was a problem. Perhaps you can visit the café downstairs while you wait?"

THE CAFÉ WAS FULL, HUMMING WITH LANGUID CHATTER. Ceiling fans spun slowly in dank air that smelled sweetly of tobacco. Dean spotted a lone stool at the end of the plank bar. He slipped past the French-style café tables and elegant chairs packed with whispering guests. A few glanced at the *blan* with suspicion as though he were an intruder.

The lanky bartender was working the opposite end from where Dean stood, shaking a silver cocktail mixer like it was a marimba. He was enjoying himself. After he poured his creation into a glass tumbler, he started toward Dean, but was intercepted by another customer.

Dean waited for an opening to grab his attention. He distracted himself by admiring the Haitian art hung across the shadowed walls. They were bright, even in the subdued bar, with tropical colors—

tangerines and teals with crudely rendered cocoa bodies painted in a style popular in some of the Chelsea galleries in Manhattan. Avid collectors had become entranced with the simplicity of the paintings, equating the unschooled technique with honesty and thinking the apparent naiveté rendered them more authentic. The people lingering at the tables below them were urban, he thought, sophisticated, possibly European, dressed well and exuding a grace he liked and admired.

The bartender finally glanced his way with shrewd, knowing eyes. He had long, thick dreads that fell far down his back. Dean waved.

"R.J. will be over when he's ready. Save your arm," a man at the bar said. His narrow eyes peered from under thick eyebrows that gave him a fierce, bullish air. He had a narrow, brown face with a trim salt and pepper beard.

"R.J.?" Dean said. "You know him well."

"We've spent a bit of time together," the man said with an odd British accent, the kind often picked up in boarding schools there. Dean studied the pair of metal, SLR cameras displayed on the counter in front of him. They were decades old but gently used, more clunky museum pieces than the sleek plastic electronic cameras that were now common.

"You are familiar," the man said. He leaned forward, challenging Dean. "You were in Mogadishu, yes?"

Dean took a moment to remember the war-torn city was in Africa. CNN had put it on the map when the U.S. had sent in the Marines.

The rest of that vast continent, with many countries he struggled to name, wasn't on his company's client or would-be client list, and Dean's significant executive travel was usually trips to the moneyed coasts—the Mediterranean, the Hamptons, California—where the upscale resorts, hotels, and high-end retailers the firm represented set up shop.

"Somalia? Not me."

"No?" the man persisted. He wasn't the sort of person who entertained doubts.

"Haiti is a first for me in more ways than one." Dean turned to the man's cameras on display. "You always keep your cameras at your fingertips?"

"One can never be too cautious," the man said. "Things can disappear easily here, including people."

"I've discovered that."

Dean told him about the theft by the *sanguine.*

"I've seen them. What did you lose?"

"Everything. Almost."

"That's an impressive haul. How did they manage?"

"I helped them by putting my passport and money in one bag."

"I see. Well live and learn, I suppose."

"I suppose."

Dean's attention drifted back to the museum pieces. Classic Nikons. The metal casing was worn like an old bicycle part. There was a notch underneath that connected to the film roll inside. Kodak no longer made film and few labs bothered with developing it anymore.

"You don't shoot digital?" Dean asked, wondering what kind of journalist intentionally used outdated methods.

"I don't like them. It is too easy, too fast. Digitals only take snapshots, not photographs."

Dean was reminded of audiophiles who were turning away from digital and buying old record players to listen to music. People looking to have something more authentic as this photographer so clearly did.

"Ali," the man introduced himself.

"With Reuters. You?" He seemed to assume they were colleagues, covering the news.

"An agency," Dean said, intentionally vague because he liked being mistaken for a fellow journalist. He might have been an Ali if he had not left reporting.

"I was in Mogadishu a few years ago when your Marines came ashore," Ali said. "Thought you might have been in the pool with us there."

Dean was used to people mistaking him for someone else. He had good, even looks, but no feature stood out. His was the smooth, friendly face of a salesman. It was what he did, what he had become. He could sell an image or story about anything to any media.

"Haiti puts me in mind of Africa." Ali considered his own statement. "No, Haiti *is* Africa."

Dean remembered the tall woman in the flowing African dress he'd seen on the street, balancing a headdress of cartons piled high, the smooth, white eggs gleaming like precious stones.

"What are you covering here?" Dean asked. Normally, he knew better than to inquire, since most journalists were instinctively secretive about whatever they were pursuing. Some feared having their story scooped or compromised by a competitor.

"The Cite Soleil," Ali said as if it were obvious. "Like the rest of the pack."

Dean found it uncanny how so many reporters he had worked with, from so many different media outlets, invariably covered the same stories. The media was a group, chasing the unfortunate and the compromised like coyotes.

"We are all chasing *chimères*, yes?" Ali said.

"I don't understand."

"Chasing ghosts in the slums," Ali said, annoyed that he didn't get the play on words. *Chimères* was French for ghosts as well as the nickname for the gangs who fought in the slums.

Ali took a sip of his gold rum. He had only faint crow's feet at the corners of his eyes and none of the sag of aging underneath. Dean realized the reporter was younger than him yet still an accomplished journalist, what Dean might have been.

The lanky bartender appeared in front of them.

"Coke. No ice, please."

The bartender shook his head. "No ice ever. And no soft drinks. Mabi only."

"Mabi?"

"You'll like it. Healthy," he said smiling, and hurried to another customer.

"Mabi," Ali said, flashing a grin. "I have never see a *blan* order one."

"I didn't order it but looks like I'm getting one."

"Yes. Tell me, what do you think of the *chimères*?" Ali resumed. "Should those gangs have been routed? Do you attack your own people?"

Dean still didn't understand. But he held his tongue, not wanting to sound more ignorant.

"The United Nations invades the biggest, poorest, most desperate slum in the world," Ali said. "The result? No clean water, no sanitation, no services. Living worse than dogs and kept that way."

The bartender set a pint of murky brown water in front of Dean with one hand and poured more rum from a light amber bottle into Ali's tumbler beside it.

"It will take your thirst," the bartender said. "Trust me."

Ali and Dean watched him walk away in silence.

"The prime minister begs them. They want to free all of Cite Soleil from the gangs," Ali continued. "They go into the slum with tanks, yes, tanks, and their blue helmets. A war to root out the ghosts."

Dean found it hard to believe the United Nations would lead an attack within a sovereign country, especially against its own citizens. It just didn't happen. They were an international peacekeeping force, not a private army.

"Two days the battle," Ali said. "Many *chimères* were killed. Blue helmets, too." The journalist pressed his thin lips tightly together. Dean could see he was clearly disturbed by what he had witnessed. If he had seen worse, this battle had eclipsed it.

Dean studied the glass of Mabi. There were bits of herbs and other particles suspended in what looked like a murky tea.

"What do you report if not the invasion in Cite Soleil?" Ali asked.

When he was a young boy, Dean had a habit of smiling inappropriately if caught in the wrong, like fibbing. The odd reaction infuriated adults who perceived it as arrogance or defiance. They couldn't have been more wrong; the smile betrayed his own fear and nervousness. He tried to look serious and contrite because that was how he felt. But, somehow, like an actor misjudging his role, the look was all wrong.

"Is it a funny question?" Ali asked.

"I'm not a journalist anymore," Dean said. "I'm from the other side of the fence," he added. Most media professionals understood he was talking about public relations.

"Fence?" Ali asked. "I do not understand."

Many reporters he'd met secretly loathed public relations people as hacks pressing lies and propaganda, offering anything to anyone for the generous salaries they received for their story-placing efforts. All news was PR. Information was provided with an agenda, hidden or not, Dean thought.

"I'm on a story about an NGO, a charity," Dean said. He decided it was easier to act like a colleague than explain. Reporting was what he missed, anyway. It was a time when his life had meaning or at least some kind of purpose not centered around only earning a living.

"What do they do?"

"Grow trees," Dean said. "Miracle trees."

"They are miracles?" Ali smiled, hiding his small teeth.

"To the poor, yes," Dean said. "The entire tree is like a supermarket."

"I am not following."

Dean liked that their roles had suddenly, if briefly, reversed. Ali was not up on the news.

"The tree is edible. Packed with enough nutrition to feed a village."

Dean spoke with the same enthusiasm he'd felt since the beginning. Here was a magic bullet that could transform poverty and the quality of life in one shot.

"The seeds of the moringa even purify water," Dean said. "But that's still being tested."

Dean was thirsty, Mabi or not. He took a sip, the sourness enveloping his mouth. But as soon as he swallowed it, he felt better, revived. He studied the drink, deciding it reminded him of kombucha, his girlfriend's favorite beverage, which he usually avoided.

"Who sends you on this story?"

"Moisson," Dean answered. "A non-profit based in New York."

"They want to help Haiti," Ali nodded as if he'd heard this before.

Dean found himself taking a long drink of the Mabi. It was growing on him. Most importantly, it had a remarkable ability to slake his thirst.

"This place is a magnet for do-gooders," Ali said. "There was a Texan who rode into town a year ago."

He told a story about a wealthy man from Midland, Texas, who had been drawn to Haiti and wanted to help. He used his private jet for a scouting trip to see what he might do. Like so many of his class, he was reluctant to hand over any actual cash. He feared it would be lost to corruption.

The Texan decided he would add housing, since so many were homeless like the *sanguine* or lived in flimsy tin shacks. He would build the structures himself. He flew over construction equipment at his own expense and transported the heavy machinery to a spot up in the mountains, near the sea.

Ali paused to take a sip of the sweet rum.

"He wants to do everything," Ali said. "He got on his backhoe and was clearing brush, flattening the land, and he proceeded to drive off a cliff."

"What? Killed?" Dean was startled.

"Very much so."

The lights suddenly went out with a loud whine and a pop. Dean sat straight, pensive. The chatter around them vanished with the light but then quickly worked its way back like so many crickets chirping from a summer lawn. A Bic lighter clicked from behind the bar and the flame appeared in the bartender's hand. He lit a glass candle on the bar top.

"Like clockwork." Ali rested a hand protectively over his two cameras in the dim light of the candle.

"The power comes back?" Dean asked.

Ali shrugged. Power came and went throughout the city, every day and every night.

"So where do you go to see these miracle trees?" he asked.

"A village in the mountains." Dean was distracted by the sudden loss of power, reminded that he had not yet made the telephone call to Cynthia for help.

"Does the village have a name?"

"Coluers," Dean said.

Ali quickly looked down into his now empty tumbler. He picked the thick glass up before he realized there was only a film of rum on the bottom. His demeanor changed.

Dean stood up so suddenly he surprised both of them. His client had to have arrived at the hotel by now. He also felt a trickle of fear. What if Cynthia wouldn't help him?

"I have to go," Dean explained. Ali nodded and offered his hand.

"To your miracle trees?"

Dean nodded, worried the photojournalist might be mocking his story because it was far lighter and less important than war in the ghetto.

"A happy story," Ali said. "We need them."

They stared at one another in silence like competitors sizing up the opposition.

"Maybe you will go to see the Cite Soleil as well. To see for yourself."

"Why would I do that?" Dean asked.

"Because that is what we do, yes?"

Ali held up his empty glass in a toast to a colleague. Dean liked the feeling of camaraderie as well as the uncorrected assumption that he was a reporter. It made him feel good about himself.

Dean squeezed past the crowded tables where flickering candles now lit his way like votives in a church. He bounded up the stairs, expecting to meet the client. They had never met in person, only email. But Dean knew he was older, an accomplished attorney in Manhattan.

"Mr. Dubose!"

The clerk at the front desk was hurrying toward him as reached the top of the stairwell. He presented a note to Dean as if it were a gift.

"A message!"

Dean read the note, handwritten with the fountain pen. The handwriting was elegant and clearly legible. The nuns would be impressed. The note said there had been a delay on a connecting flight. Nelsen and other members of the board for Moisson were arriving tomorrow morning. They would leave directly from the airport for Coluers and meet Dean there.

"Something wrong, sir?"

Dean would need to hire a car but was sure he didn't have enough to pay for it.

"Is there a bus to the mountains?"

"*Mais oui*. Where do you go?"

"A small village."

"Have you ever ride in a tap-tap?" the clerk asked, looking skeptical. Dean shook his head. "You may be better served hiring a car and driver, sir."

"Next time," Dean said. "Where do I get it?"

DEAN RAN ALONG THE STONE WALKWAY TO THE ANNEX. The tropical rain fell hard, pummeling him like fists. When he reached his room, he stopped just inside the doorway, annoyed by the stale air and the cheap, damp carpet. It didn't seem that anyone had stayed in his room in months.

For a moment, he didn't know what to do with himself. He had no bag to empty, no shirt to hang in the open closet. The room itself wasn't much bigger than the walk-in closet. A tall candle flickered steadily from the counter alongside a tiny sink from the 1960s. He tried turning on the window air-conditioner, then remembered there was no electricity.

Dean took a deep breath, coaxing himself to relax and focus. It was all manageable. He would get what he needed and reset this trip. Dean found a smudged glass next to the sink and turned the old faucet to fill it with water. He was thirsty again. The Mabi had worked for a time. The water filling his glass looked clean. He remembered the warnings. So Dean set the glass down and cupped his hand, catching a small cold pool of the water, closed his eyes, and covered his flushed face. Nothing wrong with that.

He turned to find the rotary phone next to the bed. He needed to call for help.

Then, like a streak of lightning, he was reminded of the bracing truth of Cynthia's biting comment before he had left New York. They had been arguing about his decision to travel to Port au Prince. It was an embarrassment for an accomplished executive to assign himself a lowly errand, she insisted. Doing the work of a new, low-level hire was beyond foolish. He wasn't young anymore, either.

"Why are you going to Haiti of all places?"

"It's not about Haiti. It's something else."

Cynthia stared at him with her bright Irish eyes for an uncomfortably long time. They had been together over two years but moved into an apartment just months before. It was what she had pushed for, what she clearly wanted. Dean had been reluctant. In his mind, living together was a commitment just short of marriage, and he was far from feeling ready to tie the knot with Cynthia. Yet he found himself still admiring her beauty at moments like they had just met. But she couldn't have looked uglier when she tried to keep him from going to Haiti.

"You're that unhappy? Pining for the old days? I thought you were just in one of your moods. Maybe it's the birthday?"

"No, I don't care about that. It's only a number," Dean said. But he had been thinking about it often. There seemed to be more years behind him than ahead. The more he looked to the future, the more his life seemed to be receding in the mirror. Then, one morning, he learned about the Magic Trees.

"Don't go, Dean," she warned. "You're making a fool of yourself. Let someone from your staff go. You're too experienced and successful for this."

"I need to go."

"This is career suicide," she said.

Exactly, he thought.

Dean couldn't make the phone call in this heat. He spotted the wood door to the porch and hurried over to open it, relieved to feel the charged air as it flooded the room. Thunder boomed like distant artillery. He turned around and marched to the phone. Cynthia would send him whatever he lost, whatever things he needed. Clothes, money, a new cell phone. Overnight. But he also knew she would lord her faithful assistance over him, an example of how much he needed her, how she knew what was best. If every partnership has only a single leader, in this one it wasn't him.

Dean recalled the night they had met at an art gallery reception in Chelsea just after he switched out of newspaper reporting to take on a career track in PR, weary of the hand-to-mouth existence of a print journalist. He'd been confident about his life choice, even cocky about his planned corporate climb and the wealth to come. Dean was going to be a rousing success. Just inside the entrance was the dark-haired, refined beauty, surrounded by admiring men, summoning their attention with an easy smile and sweet laughter.

Cynthia was the blue-eyed queen from Main Line Philadelphia. When he boldly walked up to where she stood in a short black dress, Cynthia seemed amused but impressed, as if he were cutting in to take the next dance with her. He felt her immediate attraction, their mutual interest. But he also sensed Cynthia sizing him up, assessing if he was worthy of her time and status.

Dean put his finger through the metal hole on the dial, slowly turning the heavy dial to each number he knew without thinking. He waited for the call to go through, which seemed to take a very long time. He debated in his mind whether to speak with a casual air as if nothing had happened or to admit to the hapless robbery.

"Dean? Are you OK?" She sounded concerned, pensive. No trace of that argument before he left.

"I need some clothes—and money," he said.

"Already?" she answered.

"I got mugged."

"Robbed?" Her voice changed instantly.

He tried to tell everything that had happened on the street. There was a delay in the overseas phone connection that distorted the words, one falling on the other. He knew because she said please slow down. Frustrated, he stopped.

"Dean? Were you hurt?"

"No. I'm fine."

"You don't sound fine."

"It almost put an end to this mission before it started," Dean said.

There was a pause and an immediate change in her tone.

"Mission? It's a mission now?"

"Fact-finding mission. So?"

"Maybe it's a sign to turn around. Start over with something better than the hellhole you chose. You know that's almost the poorest country on the planet, right? I mean, I just don't get it."

"You have the address of the hotel I gave you?"

"Yes."

"Thanks, Cynthia. Thanks." He slammed the receiver down and jumped up to leave the room. He was done.

The downpour stopped as suddenly as it had begun. Dean strolled across the creaking, slat porch until he reached the wet railing. Light from the distant lobby spilled out in a fog, misting the surrounding palms and giant ferns. The close night air felt as soft as cotton against his tired face. He inhaled the cleansed air gratefully, surprised to smell a sweet, citrusy scent.

A lighter clicked behind him. There was a brief flame and the glowing red tip of a cigarette. The woman sitting in a caned chair took a deep drag. He could just make out the fine line of her nose and tapered chin.

"I didn't realize anyone was out here," he said.

A smooth stream of charcoal smoke escaped her. Together they watched the cloud disperse across the empty porch like it was a magic trick.

"Mind if I join you?" He felt the need for company. When the woman didn't answer, he took a seat anyway, careful to keep a distance. Dean leaned back on his chair and listened to the steady drips of water falling from the unseen leaves of the brush. The sound of traffic had returned in the distance.

"No mosquitos out here to feast on us," Dean said.

"They'll be back soon," the woman said. "They're just on break."

Dean liked her smooth, feminine voice that seemed playful.

"We don't have long then. What brings you to Haiti?" Dean asked.

"What brings me back to Haiti?"

"You're a native?"

"*Mwen se ayisyen*," she answered in Kreyol. "I was born out there, in the countryside."

The tip of her long, skinny cigarette glowed like a tiny ember as she took another drag. She exhaled the smoke into the planks below them.

"You're coming back from the U.S.?" he asked.

"You like to ask questions," she said.

"Always have. A trait I've never been able to control. Annoys a lot of people."

"I can imagine."

She laughed sweetly. The darkness beyond the screen began to fill with the familiar chorus of unseen crickets. He felt a lightness between them, the diffident wall of strangers sliding away.

"You're American?" she asked.

"A Southerner. Raised in Charleston, South Carolina."

"That's American. Charleston had a big slave market back in the day."

"Yes," Dean said, surprised by the reference. Most people thought of Charleston as a genteel, charming town with beautiful architecture.

"It's a tourist destination now," Dean said.

"The slave market?"

"As a matter of fact, the old market, too."

"I guess that's good."

He watched the smoke of her cigarette rise through her long fingers.

"What story are you working on?"

"What?" Dean was surprised again. The woman was smart, educated. He wondered if she might be the daughter of one of the wealthy families in Haiti. There were few, but each was very wealthy, a small elite society that went to the best schools here and abroad.

"You are a journalist. At least you sound like one."

"Yes, the questions. You know a few?"

"I do. But I like reporters."

"That's a relief. How do you know reporters? Work?"

She shook her head at his continued interrogation. The flash of a coy smile seemed to follow, at least he hoped it was one. It was difficult to be certain in the darkness.

"I work at an NGO, and journalists sometimes help us."

Dean wanted to ask more questions about the NGO, but he held himself back. He didn't want to irritate her.

"You are here on a story?" she asked. He watched her rub out her cigarette on the chair. She held on to the white filter like refuse she would take with her to dispose of in her room.

"I am. More than one," he said. Dean decided not to wade back into his PR assignment just yet.

"I have to go, I'm afraid," she said and stood up from the chair. "I have to get up early."

She looked down at him, her black hair falling past prominent cheekbones and a small, pretty chin.

"A pleasure," Dean said. "I'm doing a story about Cite Soleil."

"Are you?" she said, impressed. "I heard what happened."

Dean watched her walk away from him, down the creaking porch, until she stopped in front of her room door. As she pulled it to her, the light from the room cast her in a luscious glow.

"Good luck, reporter."

She waved her slender fingers as if she were playing piano keys in the air and closed the door behind her, taking the warm light with her.

Dean remained on the empty porch. He felt her lingering presence in the darkness. He looked at the closed door as if it held some mysterious meaning. A humid breeze brushed his face, feeling for a moment like a woman's hair. He realized he'd forgotten to ask her name.

DEAN SPENT THE NIGHT WIDE AWAKE. The theft still bothered him even as he was moving quickly to get things back in order. If he had just remembered to take his valuables out of his bag in the taxi or not hid them there in the first place, the trip would have started off smoothly. He would not be worrying about getting a new passport in the morning, which was essential ID. He was also angry with himself about his conversation with the photojournalist. He should have defended his Miracle Tree story and not allowed the Moroccan to bait him with the absurd idea to go and see Cite Soleil for himself. "It's what we do," Ali had said. Journalism was a profession Dean had abandoned. But why? Was it only the poor pay, the hours, the lack of status? Why do we leave things we love? He didn't have an answer.

In the morning, Dean made sure to arrive at the American Embassy promptly when it opened. He would be first in line. The trip would soon begin as he hoped it would. But when he arrived at the government building, there was no one around. The formal entrance doors, which were tall enough to allow a tall ship inside, were locked shut. Dean found a handwritten sign pasted on the stone façade next to the buzzer. The words were in French and apologized that the Embassy would not open until midday due to electrical failure.

Dean searched for another entrance. The shutters of the offices were boarded up and reminded him of a barracks. He could not find even a security guard. Dean understood he had at least two hours to wait. There was no sense going back to the hotel. He'd eaten a satisfying breakfast of scrambled farm eggs, fruit, and coffee. He could wander, sightsee landmarks like the Haitian White House. But then he remembered Cite Soleil and Ali's challenge.

The city streets and sidewalks were empty as his taxi sped toward the infamous slum. A few market women in loose dresses were setting up shop on tarps strewn over a barren lot. The sun was only just beginning to heat up. When the driver dropped him off, Dean could tell he thought the American was up to no good. A white foreigner didn't come to this part of town for anything but drugs.

"*Merci*," Dean said to the driver as he got out of the old Toyota. He pointed to another road across the traffic circle. "Cite Soleil?"

The driver's dark eyes looked swollen above his gaunt face. He nodded curtly and drove off the moment the door slammed shut in the quiet. He seemed anxious to escape.

Dean walked across the circle toward two white stucco walls that marked the entrance. He felt a jolt of adrenaline as he approached, excited and nervous to be investigating as a reporter. He felt alive in a way he hadn't been in a long time. In the still quiet of early morning, the neighborhood could have been mistaken for a low-rent district around Miami. The only thing that seemed threatening was the sweet stench of sewage.

Until he spotted the tank. At first glance, Dean mistook it for an abandoned truck. It was so compact as to be toy-like. But the thick, metal tracks and the long gun barrel were real enough. A blue-helmeted soldier in wraparound sunglasses leaned out of the cockpit, watching him approach.

Dean nodded in greeting. The olive-skinned soldier stared him down like a bouncer who wasn't going to let a *blan* stroll past into what some believed was the most dangerous slum in the world. Tourists like Dean, his stone face warned, needed to be protected from themselves.

"You are lost?"

The voice boomed through the dusty quiet. Dean, like the soldier, turned to find the source. A stocky, bald black man emerged from the other side of the tank. His barrel chest was thrust forward as he marched with the air of an emissary come to deliver important news.

Dean thought he looked like a monk with his smooth, round head and studied calm. The man broke into a warm grin.

"Where do you go? This is not a place for visitors."

"I've heard," Dean said and shrugged.

"I don't think you have."

"Well, I'm here."

"I see." Both were aware of the soldier who watched them through his dark sunglasses. He remained as still as a store mannequin. The monk spoke in Spanish to him, and the soldier nodded curtly, consenting for them to pass.

"Latin America?" Dean asked.

"The soldier is from Chile. I see him sometimes when I visit."

"Where are you are going exactly?" the monk asked. They walked side by side, Dean at least a head taller, his long arms swinging at his side.

"Just having a look," Dean said. "I heard about the battle."

"You are a reporter?"

"I'm checking up."

The cement road ended abruptly in the dirt. It was as if the builders had suddenly abandoned the project, fearing they could not risk going any further into the chaos. The wide, dirt lane ahead was also littered with a vast field of shanties splashed with clothes drying in the warming sun. The rank mist of charcoal smoke drifted above the trash where some residents were milling about.

"No more roadblocks," the monk said with evident relief. "So many people trapped by the *chimères*. Prisoners in their homes. Roadblocks of gunmen would not let them leave. But those are gone and that is a good thing."

As they walked past the shanties, Dean glimpsed an older, gaunt woman cooking over a small pile of the ever-present charcoals. Grease sizzled in her weathered, bent pan. Her skinny, barefooted son lounged alongside her, running his hand back and forth over the surface of the road as if comforting a sleeping dog.

"The smell makes me hungry," the monk said.

"This is your home?" Dean asked.

"No. I visit to say mass." He motioned toward a white shack on the verge of collapse far in the distance. A black cross was nailed to the facade like a store sign.

"A priest?" Dean said.

"I am Father Charles."

A rooster was crowing somewhere in the rubble ahead. Dean slowed as he spotted the water on a canal. It was slick and black, winding through the shacks like a slow, fat snake.

"I was a Catholic," Dean said.

"No longer?" The priest studied him with a wan smile.

Jesus, the Holy Spirit, and all the saints were distant memories to Dean, ideas learned in childhood that faded for him into agnostic adulthood. He wanted to believe in a higher power, a purpose behind the world. But religion had become literal, its teachings dogma, and he couldn't accept them.

"I was raised as a Catholic," Dean said.

"You will always be Catholic," the priest said. "It is the way. When you need Jesus, he will be there."

Dean stopped, looking upstream. Two children were playing at the water's edge with their dogs. But when there was a high-pitched squeak, he recognized the animals were not dogs but two small black pigs, burrowing their stub noses in the slop. The kids were searching for a glimpse of whatever was moving underneath.

"They want food," Father Charles said.

A warm, dank sea breeze wafted over them. The priest wiped away the sweat spilling from his thick eyebrows.

"You would like to see the church?" the priest asked.

"Your church?"

"We take a shortcut from this hot road."

Before Dean could respond, the priest bolted ahead of him, making a beeline for the tepid canal.

"Come," the priest said without turning around.

He was nearly to the water's edge but didn't stop or slow down.

"I thought you were going to the church," Dean called to him.

"I am."

Without warning, the priest plunged into the black water. But he didn't sink. He walked as if he were in mud, not water. He strolled further and further before pausing in the middle of the canal, standing upright on the black water as if it was an old mattress.

"Come, my friend."

"I don't walk on water," Dean joked.

"Perhaps you should try."

Further down the canal, the baby pigs squealed at a lump of garbage jutting out of the water, just out of reach. There was more refuse in the canal than water, Dean realized.

"The trash is bad, but it can be helpful," the priest said.

Dean took his first step and felt the syrupy water gel around his bare ankles. He could only imagine the bacteria and pollution bathing him. He took another step, searching the dark surface for a hidden gap that might suck him under the pool of sewage. He walked patiently until he was only a few feet from shore. He'd been lucky so far, he thought. Now he was close enough to jump over the water to safety. He readied himself, then his right leg plunged almost knee deep. Dean leaped. His shoulder hit the bank first, then he tumbled over himself. He was breathing hard as he sat helplessly in the mud.

"Are you OK?" the priest asked. "Why did you jump?"

Dean smiled. "I worried my luck was running out."

"It's better that you pray in times like that."

He caught up to the priest outside the entrance. There were pock marks in the cement façade of the church. Bullet holes from large-caliber weapons. The graffiti of war.

The parishioners were already inside. Dean stayed in the back, far behind the flimsy pews. He noticed that most of the churchgoers were women. Many wore the colorful, full length African dresses he'd seen in the city. Others wore cut-off jeans. They fanned themselves with scraps of cardboard trash. A barefoot girl with newly braided hair crouched next to her mother, clinging to her print dress with blackened fingers, humming to herself. No one paid Dean any attention or at least pretended as much.

Father Charles held forth at the makeshift altar and made the sign of the cross with his thick, calloused hand. He had slipped on a white vestment over his black shirt.

"In the Name of the Father, the Son, and the Holy Spirit," he began his prayer.

The liturgy followed in Kreyol and his congregation followed the scripture with rapt attention. Father Charles spoke too fast for Dean to understand, but the repetitions of phrases, the pausing for effect were apparent. The priest was a natural orator and rendered his people spellbound. Their faces brightened.

Later, when it came time in the mass to offer one another the sign of peace, a handshake or a kiss, the churchgoers embraced the Catholic ritual with enthusiasm. As Dean watched them hug one another, an older man in sagging jeans and a threadbare shirt suddenly offered his hand.

"*Lapè avè w!*"

"God Bless you, too," Dean said.

Water. The thirst came on like a sudden fever. He needed water. The humidity grabbed him by the throat. Dean closed his eyes for a moment. He was faint, dizzy. He needed water desperately.

Father Charles had finished mass and was strolling to the exit, draped in his white vestment, facing the exiting parishioners. He greeted most with broad smiles and boisterous hugs, as if they were family. Dean began to sway. But he waited until everyone had left. His dry lips were hardening, and his throat felt sore.

"Water?" he asked the priest.

"I don't. But I should. You don't look well."

"Water," Dean said.

"Yes, yes, my friend. There is a market over there." Father Charles motioned to a stall within a short walking distance. "But you must be very careful."

"Yes. I understand." Dean was annoyed by the repeated warning. He'd said it to Dean since they met at the entrance.

Father Charles looked at him skeptically.

"The water. Some will empty the old bottles, take the clean water for themselves, then refill from the canal. And sell. You understand? You must check the seal."

Dean nodded dumbly and turned around to walk to the street.

THE HOT, DIRT STREET WAS CROWDED AND HOSTILE. A steady stream of grim faces marched past, some glancing at him with disbelief. His eyes were tearing from the ubiquitous charcoal smoke and the smell of burning plastic and tires. A motorcycle roared past, its tailpipe bleating like an animal in distress. He stopped at the makeshift market the priest had recommended. They sold no water. But the young woman who ran it pointed him to another stall further ahead, beyond a blind corner. He backed away, unsteady on his feet. He looked up at the white sun glowering at him.

As soon as he turned the corner, the roar of the main road vanished. Ahead, a group of bored students loitered in his path. It took a moment before he recognized the objects that they toyed with were guns, assault rifles hanging from straps or barehanded like sticks at their side. A checkpoint. Dean was confused. The checkpoints that divided neighborhoods and terrorized the people who lived there were supposed to have been removed by the UN assault.

The attention of the boys went to him like a target. Their boredom vanished and they watched his approach in disbelief or amusement, he couldn't tell which. Dean considered just turning around and pretending to be lost.

"Hey *blan*," one of the boys called. A few others laughed, their voices crackling like wood. Dean slowed, then stopped at what he thought was a safe distance.

"Where you goin'?" The voice sounded like it was out of Brooklyn. The shirtless teen raised his dull grey weapon. His thin, muscular body was oiled in sweat. A bright silver chain hung from his neck like a dog tag.

"I'm a reporter," Dean said. His throat felt even drier. He willed himself to stay calm and not provoke.

"You missed the fun," the boy said. A few bitter laughs spread down the line of teenage soldiers. The rifle barrel remained pointed squarely at Dean's chest, but he tried to ignore it.

"You fought?" Dean asked. The quiet of the backstreet became unnerving.

"Why you want to know?"

All the boys were watching him closely now, fascinated by the stranger.

"The United Nations are peacekeepers. I have never heard of them attacking anyone. But that's what happened?"

"Peacekeepers?" The boy shook his head. "Peacekeepers don't have no tanks; you know what I'm sayin'?"

Dean let his arms fall to his sides. He wanted to look as defenseless as possible but not fearful. He took a step forward, testing the boys. The gunman's dark eyes narrowed slightly.

"There was no warning? They just came?" Dean asked. There was whispering among the gang. It ended with the boy with the gun nodding in agreement.

"How we know you a reporter?" he asked. "You got some ID?"

Dean couldn't tell the truth or pretend the press card was somehow left behind at the hotel. They wouldn't believe him.

"On my phone," Dean said. "Electronic. But I don't have my cell. And who else would come here by himself?"

The boy and his gang considered what he said.

"Come," the boy with the rifle said. "We show you."

Dean followed the group down the road, keeping a safe and respectful distance. None of the kids spoke. They walked around the deep puddles of rank sewage, past the shanties of tin and garbage and moved in the direction of the black canal. Dean was worried about being lured out of public view, but he had no choice.

The group stopped by a low mound of broken cement. They parted, making a lane in the middle for Dean. He walked down like it was a gauntlet, knowing there was no easy escape. When he came to the end, there were a cluster of flies swirling above the ground, and he smelled the shit and rank burned scent. But it wasn't until he caught the leader's furious eyes that he glimpsed the corpses.

They were bloated, roasting in the sun. The blood had dried on their faces and contorted torsos like syrup. They had been shot numerous times. He saw young children among the dead before he looked away.

"The peacekeepers," the boy said. Dean shook his head at the carnage on the ground.

"You tell them," the boy said. His thin face was drawn, his skin caked with dust.

"You saw this?" Dean thought there was the slim possibility that this was a kind of propaganda, a ploy to spin the event in the gang's favor. The boy-man took offense. His finger twitched near the worn, metal trigger.

"They live here. They die here by the UN," he said. "The UN try to kill us all."

The boy talked about the battle like a grizzled vet, describing machine gunfire, explosions, running, and firing back under cover. They were defending their territory and their homes from the invasion force.

"Why do you not write this down?" he asked, suddenly suspicious. Dean carried no notebook or pen and certainly no recorder.

"I can see. And I can hear," Dean said.

The soldier rushed toward him in fury. He raised his gun so that Dean could see the worn metal at the tip of the dark barrel. There was a flicker of the boy's dark eyes before the barrel swung up and away and he fired. Hot air blasted next to his head. Then he went deaf. The gang of schoolboys watched as he stumbled backwards and covered his ears. There was nothing. The mouth of the boy who fired the round was moving up and down and sideways. He was saying something Dean could not hear.

Dean closed his eyes, inhaling the sharp scent of gunpowder. He looked at one of his palms, relieved to see only sweat and not blood from a shattered ear drum. He tried to speak to the boy, to the *chimères*, but they were all backing away.

Dean spotted Father Charles standing in the road beyond them. He looked as if he were standing in a pulpit. He seemed to be scolding them with an outstretched finger. He was angry and animated. Dean could not hear what he was telling them. But they listened with growing impatience. They were talking to one another.

Suddenly, one of the kids pointed to the car in the distance. They turned as a group to watch it rumble through the entrance. The square, white sedan roared past the tank and soldier, kicking up clouds of dust behind it. Sunlight glinted from the protruding vintage grill and the familiar star.

The *chimères* looked as fearful as if they had seen a ghost. The fear caught on fire and they backed away in Dean's direction. But he may as well have disappeared. They hurried past him, breaking into a run.

The Mercedes slowed as it came closer. Dean saw the wide shoulders of two men stuffed into the back seat. They looked like thugs from a crime show.

"They are friends," the priest said. Father Charles had been watching him.

"You were not careful," he said.

Dean nodded his head in agreement, then realized he had heard the priest clearly.

"A close call," Dean managed to say.

The white sedan shuddered to a stop. Dust erupted around it, veiling the interior. As it cleared, Dean saw the guns. The men looked accustomed to using them.

The front passenger seat screeched open and a dapper, handsome black man emerged. He smiled brightly at Father Charles. His even teeth were movie-star white against smooth, taut skin and chiseled cheek bones.

"Poppy!" He saluted the priest in a jaunty, mocking way as if he were making fun of them both. He even had the charisma of a celebrity. "You're riding shotgun."

He glanced at Dean, just long enough for his sharp, observant eyes to size up the white American, before opening the back door. He squeezed into the back seat, joking with the others as he forced the broad-shouldered thugs to make more room.

"You need good stories to report," Father Charles said to Dean. "You must come to my village. The media report only on the misery, the problems. There are many. But there is another country if you look."

"They were afraid of the car," Dean said. "The *chimères.*"

"They are only children," the priest said. He grabbed the roof but let go as if he had touched a hot pan. He shook his hand to cool it.

"Where is your village?" Dean asked.

"In the mountains," Father Charles answered. "A village called Coluers."

Dean smiled in surprise. "I am going there."

Father Charles was already inside the car and didn't hear him. The white sedan lurched forward but, just as suddenly, the front window came down as the car stopped alongside Dean. He hoped they might offer him a ride. Instead, he met, again, the cool, analytical eyes of the movie star in the back seat. They feared him, Dean thought.

"My friend, for you," Father Charles said. He offered a plastic bottle of water. Dean hesitated to open it.

"It is good." Father Charles laughed. "And lucky that you are here to drink it safely."

Dean ripped the plastic top off the bottle. Water. Ice cold. He studied it like one might a rare jewel.

"*Bon vwayaj*," Father Charles said. "May God be with you."

Dean took a sip from the bottle, then chugged it, feeling the water wash relief to the pit of his stomach. He kept drinking, unable to slow down, nearly choking himself as the bottle emptied. He stopped, spent from drinking, and bent over to catch his breath.

He watched the white Mercedes reach the exit and wondered why a violent gang would fear a priest and his handsome friend.

THE WHITE MERCEDES GLIDED TO A STOP OUTSIDE THE BANK'S REFLECTIVE WINDOWS. The bodyguards got out first and took their positions with practiced efficiency. They held their weapons at the ready and waited for Herve, like soldiers expecting orders from their commanding officer.

"*Allez*," the taller one said, curtly. He pressed the butt of his machine gun against his side, the metal barrel pointed into the street, ready to fire. He peered into the wall of passing pedestrians with suspicion. Armed kidnapping and robbery were not uncommon in the commercial area near the banks.

Herve and Father Charles climbed out and were directed to the side entrance door. The bank was shut down and empty, but the glass door was unlocked.

"Why is it they want to meet me after all this time?" Father Charles asked. He feared they could be walking into some kind of government sting. Informants earned money, and no one would hesitate to capitalize if given the chance.

"They want to see the kind priest," Herve said. "That would be you, Poppy."

Father Charles was used to his partner's joking. They had been friends since childhood, and Herve had teased him relentlessly through their years at Academy Prep. Even then, the other kids looked up to Charles, treated him as both a leader and a confidante. Herve felt like his second in command even though he came from one of the most powerful families in the country.

Father Charles was surprised by his own reflection in the polished glass door of the bank entrance. His round face was fuller, heavier with age, and deep lines had been carved under and around his mahogany eyes. But for those inevitable manifestations of age, he was surprised he hadn't grown more haggard in the fifteen years since his ministry began.

As Herve often reminded him, they were left with little choice but to work around official channels to deliver children to new homes. It was illegal only in name. The government was corrupt, run by bribes, and the red tape in the United States could delay transfers for years. The orphanage didn't have years to wait for the official adoption process to play out. Children urgently needed to be clothed and fed.

Their unorthodox *methode* worked, thanks to Herve's talents. He knew business, he had contacts from his years at NYU. Father Charles assumed the responsibility of making the difficult placement choices. He pored over the handwritten letters from couples begging for children. Most were sincere and heartfelt, all pledged to treat the kids as their own. They were unaware that the calculus was in their favor, not the children. There were far more kids who needed homes than parents who wanted them.

In the past few years, the broker had changed the equation. Transactions were better, faster, with more children matched to homes in the United States. So many. But Father Charles had the list, always the list, if he needed to make contact, to check up on his children. In the end, the future was in God's hands, not subject to the vain strivings of men.

"Are you going in, Your Holiness?" Herve asked. He opened the door to the bank lobby with exaggerated care and showed the way with his open hand.

Father Charles ignored the sarcasm. He entered the air-conditioned bank, feeling the firm carpet underneath. It was the ordered calm of money. A youthful American in a blue suit and striped tie waited next to a glass office like an eager bank officer.

His blue eyes lit up and his face erupted into a broad smile as if the priest was an old, dear friend. Father Charles noted the broker's spotless white teeth, all perfectly spaced like Herve's. Fine breeding. The priest had long been wistful of owning such quality teeth. It was the ultimate mark of health and beauty.

"At last." The broker grabbed the priest's calloused hand. His grip was strong, his pale skin smooth as a young woman. Father Charles was intimidated by the man's confidence. His dark eyebrows were as carefully trimmed as his short, gelled hair.

"Charlie," the broker said. "We share a name. And a cause. May I call you Charles, Father?"

"You didn't kiss the ring," Herve said. He was standing just behind them.

The *blan* hesitated, not certain if Herve was joking.

"Your children, your system, are top rate," he said. "It's not like so many others here, I can tell you."

"Others?" Father Charles was surprised. He didn't know the broker was working with other orphanages, too, like a distributor. The priest didn't like it.

"Wanted to meet you," Charlie continued as if the question were unimportant. "I'm a secret admirer. Masterful what you have pulled off with your camp. May I say, we are grateful partners."

"My *camp*?"

"You care, Father Charles, and that's extremely important to us. Our clients have come to expect a human touch. The results speak for themselves," he said proudly, like a CEO reporting higher quarterly earnings.

"Who are the others you were referring to?" Father Charles asked. He was afraid of the answer. It was possible there were hundreds of other adoptions by less scrupulous orphanages.

"We have a number of clients," Charlie answered. "Not at liberty to disclose them. You understand."

"Fine." Herve clapped his hands together. He moved alongside his partner. "We all have business to discuss."

"Indeed, we do, Herve," Charlie said. "Please have a seat," he motioned to the empty chairs.

"I prefer to stand." Father Charles didn't like the man.

"Sure," Charlie said, cheerfully. "Whatever suits you, Father."

The American shifted from one tassel loafer to the other. He brought his hands together and folded them in front like he was set to begin a conference.

"There's none like you, Father. None. Which is why I want to propose a larger partnership." He smiled at Herve like a conspirator.

Father Charles felt as if he were being played, and his dislike of the broker grew.

"A partnership that will make us better and much wealthier," the American continued. "A win-win."

"You want to transfer more of the kids?" Herve asked. He knew, as everyone did, that not all of the children in the orphanage were true orphans without parents. In fact, many were not. They were poor and they were desperate.

"I do, Herve, I do," Charlie said. "There's demand. And the demand is for quality, the quality you deliver."

"How about going to the other orphanages?" Father Charles asked.

"You are the blue chip, Charles, simple as that."

"How much demand are we talking about?" Herve asked. He could barely hide his enthusiasm. More transfers brought more cash, more profit.

"It's time to up our game, right? We can make life better for all."

"Our game?" Father Charles asked. "You think this a game?"

"Not at all. I'm being too, how do you say it in Kreyol, *facile?* We are all very surprised by the sudden uptick in demand. But we're also excited by the opportunity it brings. So many lives given a new life. Am I right?"

"I like the sound of it," Herve said. "What do you think, Poppy? Time to step it up?"

Father Charles didn't answer. He couldn't. The business had taken a life of its own. He was not prepared for this kind of calculus. The kids would never be units of trade to him. It was a necessary evil, a bad to make a good.

"How many children do you have in mind?" Father Charles asked. He sensed Herve already knew but pretended otherwise. Father Charles guessed this meeting was not about meeting Charlie but about getting him to agree to a deal Herve had already cooked up. Father Charles wasn't going to play that game.

DEAN HURRIED TO THE PASSPORT INTAKE DESK. A squat, middle-aged woman glanced up at him with an air of boredom, then turned back to read her desktop computer. She had neatly coiffed black hair with a stern chin and wide, flared nose.

"*Pardon*," Dean said. "I have an emergency."

Her thick eyebrows arched with annoyance before she turned her attention to him. She stared at Dean as if she had seen a hundred *blans* like him.

"Oui, monsieur, may I see your passport?"

"That's why I'm here. It was lost. Stolen."

"DS-11," she said, handing him one form. Her sudden crisp English surprised him. "For the police report. DS-64 is the application for a new passport."

"What? Two forms? Can't this be expedited?"

The woman shrugged and handed him a worn yellow pencil. There were chew marks down the side.

"The form, *monsieur.*"

Dean looked in vain for a desk or surface to use. He knelt on the floor and turned the seat into his writing desk. He felt nervous, jumpy. He needed to get to Coluers, but each line of the form seemed complicated. He fought for focus through the remembered stench of the murdered corpses back in the slum. He saw the rifle barrel pointed at him, ready to blow his head off, knowing the *chimères* might have if Father Charles had not come to his aid. Twice now he had tempted fate. He left the taxi when he shouldn't have. He was robbed. He wandered into Cite Soleil.

Dean finally returned his completed form. The others waiting seemed maddeningly patient. Two very young boys watched him with intense, distrustful curiosity as they crouched alongside their mom. She looked at him as if he were a threat. Dean was getting more paranoid by the minute.

"Dean Dubose?" The question shattered the silence of the waiting room. Everyone looked at him. They seemed to expect that he would be served right away.

"*Le bureau.*" The woman at the desk announced. She pointed to a door at the far end of the room and raised her big, crescent eyebrows one more time.

When Dean entered the office, a slight man in a blue suit sat at his fine desk and grinned as though pleased to see an old friend. He had short, cropped hair and large, black plastic glasses too wide for his narrow face.

"Pierre," he said and stretched his arm across the empty desk for a welcoming handshake. His dapper suit, frayed at the sleeves, draped him loosely like a clothing mannequin. Dean felt as though he had wandered into a client meeting.

"You are on business." He had a smooth, resonant baritone and spoke without an accent. Dean guessed he had lived or gone to school in America, a fact that encouraged him. He lost no time explaining his predicament to what he hoped was a like-minded executive.

"Yes. This is unfortunate," Pierre said gravely.

"Unfortunate?"

"I am sorry that you have been the victim of one rogue element in our midst. Such a brazen act."

"Can I get my passport? I am traveling to the mountains today."

"Yes? You know that is where Haiti lives."

Dean didn't know what he meant. The mountains were the "real" Haiti?

"I'm late already. If I hadn't gotten mugged, there would be no problem."

Pierre nodded in a gesture of understanding.

"There is a fee for an emergency passport. And, of course, we must check your identity."

"OK," Dean said, uncertainly. He was almost broke. "But I need the passport to take to the bank."

"You have no driver's license from New York?"

"I told you. They took everything."

Pierre pursed his lips.

"I understand. This will take time. Is there anyone who might be able to assist you here in Port au Prince? A friend? A colleague?"

"I am meeting my colleague in the mountains. He could help."

"Very good," Pierre said.

"You don't understand. I am meeting him for work. We won't have time to get all the way back to Port au Prince."

"I understand. It is a difficult situation. Here we say *souri ou se paspò ou!* Your smile is your passport!"

"My smile is my passport? Are you kidding?"

"Wait. Do you have the fee?" Pierre raised his chin, almost in a challenge.

"The fee?"

"A replacement this quickly will be expensive, I'm afraid. But it will get the job done."

"How much?" Dean understood some, if not all of the fee, would be going to Pierre.

"One hundred dollars American I believe. I will check."

"You'll check?"

Pierre opened his arms as if to say the question of the fee was beyond his authority.

"You're American, Pierre?"

"*Oui monsieur*. From Boston. Time is money."

Dean pursed his lips. Corruption didn't have a nationality. There was nothing to be done. He would have to do without a passport—and the money that came with it—until it was time to fly back to New York. It meant he would be vulnerable if anything else went wrong. He hoped that wouldn't happen.

Hello is my passport, Dean repeated to himself, shaking his head at the absurdity of it.

"Good luck, Mr. Dean," Pierre said.

HERVE GUESSED THE BROKER WAS PLANNING TO REQUEST AT LEAST A DOZEN CHILDREN, DOUBLE THE AMOUNT OF THEIR USUAL TRANSACTION. Over the years, six was the most efficient and safest to process. His partner, Father Charles, would demand all the usual addresses and names to pretend he knew exactly where the orphans would live.

"Age you like?" Herve asked the broker. "Toddler, teen?"

Charlie leaned forward in his chair. The room hummed with the sound of the central air, one of the few buildings in the city outfitted with the expensive system and a private generator to run it.

"There are preferences," Charlie said. "I'm glad you recognize it. At the same time, we understand the, uh, circumstances of available supply."

Herve felt the priest glaring at him. He was always upset to hear his children spoken of in the cool language of mathematics.

"What sort of preferences?" Herve asked. "Teens. We have very good teens."

"Good as in breeding, beauty?" Charlie said.

"Of course, "Herve said.

"Good. This time, we are targeting thirteen."

"Thirteen?" It was one more than Herve expected. He loved it. Double the revenue. It would go a long way to improving the orphanage and his own lifestyle. He kept two residences and multiple companions, not lavish by elite standards, but he was feeling the pressure.

"We are prepared to offer one thousand dollars each," the broker said.

The *blan* was starting with a low bid like any competent trader. Herve recognized it. He loved haggling. As a child, he'd watched his father bargain skillfully with the changing roster of small farmers who sold the cane to be cooked for the family rum. His father always began with an impossibly low number just to get things started.

"Top of the line carries a premium," Herve said.

He noticed the dour look on Father Charles' face. He thought it comical. Herve knew his partner hated horse trading. In fact, Father Charles hated working with a broker for his orphanage. He wanted the old way when a few kids were handpicked. Back then, they would pore through applications and make minute evaluations based on the handwritten answers from prospective parents.

Poppy, Herve remembered fondly, was the model of responsibility. He treasured the parent histories, from race to income to age, evaluating each application with more discernment than any government. He scrutinized each pleading essay: "Why I want to raise a child." Poppy looked for meaningful clues about the character of the would-be parents. Herve always thought an adoption agency would have been lucky to have the priest's dedication.

Meanwhile, the *sanguine*—street children, impoverished children, problem children—all continued to flood into the orphanage, washing away the orphanage's supplies and its ability to care for them, threatening the operation of the orphanage itself. He and Father Charles were forced to increase the flow out into the world, arranging for more children to be adopted, but it only slowed the process, doing little to increase their income.

The American broker changed everything. Revenues were way up, but the selection process was changed. In the end, Father Charles accepted the deal. Herve understood his partner was focused on the kids. More money meant more kids saved, more to rescue. Father Charles expected the funds would be plowed back into the business of housing new children at the orphanage, nothing more. But Herve was a businessman, not a saint. Profit was his calling; capitalism his religion.

Herve took pride in his system and his strategy, both worthy of any shrewd CEO. His father would be proud, too, if he were still alive to witness his son's prowess. If the old man had seen this skill, his genius for transactions, he would not have handed control of the company over to Petra, his youngest brother, who didn't deserve it. Herve was certain the idiot would run the family business into the ground sooner or later.

"What level of premium are we talking about?" Charlie asked.

"Twenty-five hundred per head," Herve said.

"This is not what should be discussed. It has no place," Father Charles said.

The American seemed as surprised as Herve at the priest's apparent show of indignity.

Herve might have reprimanded his partner right there in front of the broker, but he was too practical and recognized an advantage. Poppy was creating urgency in the negotiation. It helped gain leverage. The whole operation depended on the priest and his flock, in the end, as the broker well knew. The priest would have to be placated or there would be no children, no deal.

"I understand," Charlie said. "I am sorry." He tapped the automatic dial on the screen of his iPhone. A Miami area code.

"We did not agree to this," Father Charles said. "Thirteen young girls? You think I do not know what this man wants?"

"Poppy," Herve lied. "He wants boys, too. Families want quality girls to raise. It's not China."

"I didn't hear any mention of boys."

"He has demand."

"Yes?" His partner was not convinced.

"You'll have the list, Poppy," Herve reassured him. After each transaction, he gave his partner a typed list with the names and addresses of every family. Father Charles was free to contact the new parents at any time to check up on his children. The priest never checked for accuracy because he never looked into the families at all. There was no time and, in the end, no genuine interest.

Herve snuck a glance at the American broker. He was getting approval from the higher up. There was always a higher up, always a bigger fish.

"I must tell you, Herve. Talking of the children this way." Father Charles shook his head in disapproval. "They are orphans not goats."

"This is business, Poppy. Business! This is the language of business."

The priest pressed his lips together, but that was the only protest. He seemed to accept the situation and had no appetite to fight back. Even when they were kids, Herve noticed that Charles avoided confrontation. He was a peacemaker, the kid who got guys to talk and lay down their sticks.

Charlie finished his phone call. "We'll go with the twenty-five hundred."

"I am sorry," Father Charles said, soberly. "I appreciate your work, but you must understand ours. I am not sure we have the children you would like. I cannot separate them in this way."

Charlie looked at Herve for confirmation. Herve jumped on Father Charles' words as the real start of a financial negotiation. The number of heads was being doubled on this deal, increasing the risk and the effort on both sides of the transaction.

"Final offer," Charlie said.

Herve leaned forward. "What Father Charles is saying is there are logistic concerns in our country. That is a large order to pass unnoticed."

Charlie waited for him to continue.

"We cannot depart from Toussaint," Herve said, naming the main airport at Port au Prince. "It is much more involved by necessity. We can accomplish it. At cost."

"Cost?" Charlie asked.

"A few dollars more per head," Herve said. "Keep authorities away. No problems. No publicity."

"Give me a number."

"Five hundred more. Each."

"Five hundred is a few dollars?" Charlie asked.

"Like buying insurance," Herve said.

"Insurance?"

"That's right. No one wants problems."

Charlie nodded stiffly. "Three thousand a head. That's it."

"Pleasure doing business," Herve said. He smiled at the *blan* trader, knowing how he was being seen. Sooner or later, most white men showed the same dislike and disdain. They could never see beyond the color.

"We are stepping it up," Herve said as he and the priest marched back to the car. Their bodyguards surrounded the Mercedes, checking the perimeter like they expected an attack at any moment. But it was quiet in the parking lot.

Father Charles waited for the door to be opened. One of the bodyguards acted as chauffeur, and the priest slipped into the soft, leather front seat without a word. Herve couldn't tell if his partner was angry or tired or both. The bodyguards joined Herve in the back seat. As soon as they backed out of the parking spot, Father Charles turned and spoke as though it had been something he had wanted to say to his partner all afternoon.

“I will need to see your list,” Father Charles said, sternly.

“Of course, Poppy,” Herve said. “As soon as it’s all finalized, you’ll have it in your hands.”

Father Charles looked out the closed window as the white Mercedes drove onto the crowded boulevard.

“Pétion-Ville,” Herve ordered the driver. It was the city’s most exclusive neighborhood, which sat high on a verdant hill above them. “We got a dinner rez.”

DEAN HAD JUST SWALLOWED THE LAST OF HIS WATER WHEN THE TAP-TAP CAME BARRELING AROUND THE CORNER. Passengers hung from thick ropes on the side of the bus like corks strung on a fish net. Dean waved away the cloud of acrid smoke that blasted out of the tailpipe as the tap-tap screeched to a stop. He was on his way to Coluers at last. His passport and cash would have to wait.

The passengers leapt off the ropes; others spilled out the back. A spray-painted mural on the side, below and above the windows, looked like graffiti from the '70s. The face of a black Jesus stared heavenward, his crown of thorns leaking crimson blood. Dean thought of the priest and how he had saved him from harm. If nothing else, Dean would look him up and thank him.

Everyone rushed to get on board as if a starting gun had just gone off. They bumped and bounced into one another like frantic commuters on a rush hour subway back in New York. The only thing that mattered was landing a seat or at least a space.

Dean looked through the windows for an open seat, but it was packed. The sour stench of body odor and urine wafted in the hot air. Dean involuntarily held his breath. The driver closed the folding front doors, let off the brake, and the tap-tap rolled forward.

Dean couldn't afford being left behind. He followed the lead of a young man in front of him who had grabbed one of the ropes and begun climbing. The bus belched more diesel fumes as it picked up speed, slamming Dean into the sun-beaten metal. He grunted in pain but chased the man's leather sandals as he clawed up the thick rope to the roof.

Dean hesitated at the top, straddling the edge of the tap-tap like a mountain climber as the bus bounced over the potholes.

"Jump now!" the man yelled.

Dean swung himself onto the pile of bags and supplies just as the tap-tap plunged into and over another small crater. Dean landed firmly in a niche between the luggage. He stopped, bewildered, and noticed the goat perched forward on the roof. Its dark eyes peered at him under floppy ears, its mouth making chewing movements as if enjoying a piece of grass.

Dean leaned back against a soft bag. This would be his seat for however long it took to get to the mountains. He had been warned that the bus moved slowly and stopped often. They were routinely overcrowded, mechanically unsound, and driven unsafely. But they got to where they were going.

"We are in the hot seat, my friend."

The passenger who had urged him to jump was smiling. He looked both strong and relaxed, like a surfer at the beach.

"I'm sure it will be," Dean said, squinting up at the white sky. "Thanks for the cue."

"*Rein de grave,*" he said. "Everyone needs a little favor to last the day. My name is Jerome."

Dean gave a nod in lieu of a handshake. He turned his attention to the passing neighborhood behind Jerome. There were collapsing shanties, ripped tarps propped up on poles made out of tree branches. Rotting trash spilled onto the broken concrete street from all directions like spilled dumpsters. The sickening, sweet smell was repulsive.

"Poverty is very hard to look at," Jerome said, following Dean's attention. "So better we all look the other way, yes?"

"Like nothing I've seen."

"If everyone witnesses, maybe there would be change."

Dean knew there was a wide and tragic gap between learning about a problem and acting on it.

"In Jacmel, there is poverty, too. But the beauty and the sea remain, yes? That is why it is my home. You will see."

Dean had heard that the seaside town was the jewel of the country. Tourists off the beaten path came for the sea and the beaches and a few expensive resorts desperately trying to rival their Caribbean neighbors.

"Not going that far," Dean said.

The tap-tap picked up speed as it finally reached the edge of town. Tropical brush and the occasional palm tree appeared alongside the road like stage props. A heavy breeze swept over him and cleansed the stench. Dean took a deep, grateful breath.

"Where do you go?" Jerome asked.

"A village in the mountains."

"Yes," Jerome laughed. "Where in the mountains?" He leaned forward, his hair whipping across bright, inquisitive eyes. When Dean answered him, Jerome grew excited.

"I have heard of Coluers," Jerome said. "They get much American money."

The road climbed quickly, the tap-tap aggressively engaging blind curves. The driver blasted his horn at each bend, warning the oncoming traffic. But he stayed in the middle of the lane, which meant a head-on collision was almost a certainty. But not a single car or truck passed them.

"There are strong *lwa* in the hills there," Jerome volunteered. He was looking at the distant mountains, one bare, treeless summit falling on another like the heads of tired, bald men.

"Devil spirits?" Dean asked.

"You know about Vodou," Jerome said. "But *lwa* are not devils. They are young spirits, they only live for themselves, not others."

"There are plenty of young *lwa* where I live," Dean said. Himself included, he thought. He did little for the lives of others.

"Here, too," Jerome said with a smile. "But the young spirits grow old like people. And learn to live for others."

They rounded a summit far above Port au Prince and its harbor, driving past a paved overlook where a bare-chested artisan stood guard over rows and rows of steel drum sculptures and candy-colored folk paintings. No one else was around.

"I should sell my work here," Jerome said.

"To who? There's no one to buy it," Dean said.

"They will come one day," Jerome said. His cocksure, blind confidence in that eventual end was impressive.

"You're an artist?"

"I sell in Jacmel. But the tourists do not come as they did. Too much violence. She has been neglected by the world. Even her own people. And *Bondye* is too busy."

"God is too busy?"

"God is elsewhere," Jerome said without judgment.

The bus stopped. A father and his girl stepped out of the back of the bus and walked away. Beyond them was a towering view of the green harbor and the muted brilliance of the Caribbean beyond. A thin, grey and yellow mist drifted above it, dimming what would have been a majestic vista. The air pollution disappointed them both. The tap-tap dropped into gear and continued its strained climb.

"What do you do here in Haiti?" Jerome asked.

"To see some miracles," Dean joked.

Jerome waited, amused.

"Miracle *trees*. A project near Coluers that can help your country."

"You are reporting on it?"

"More or less. It's financed by a client."

Jerome nodded as if the answer made some kind of sense to him.

"So many travel here to profit from Haiti," Jerome said after a time. "Funny, yes? The relief peoples, the missionaries, the governments. But Haitians? Not so many."

They passed a pothole the size of a bomb crater. The road was littered with gullies from the downpours. Without trees to stop or slow the water, tropical rainstorms washed down the denuded hills, taking dirt, stones, and gravel with it. A moonscape was left in its place. A century of deforestation had savaged the countryside.

An hour later, they reached a dirt plateau. Hand-painted road signs popped up like clumps of weeds on the side of the road. French-looking town names were written on the tall, narrow stalks, their tapered ends pointing in all directions. Dean searched the jumble of script for Coluers but didn't find it.

The bus rumbled off in the direction of a town marked Leogane. Dean looked to Jerome, who was now dozing against a pile of luggage and tightly wrapped contractor bags, eyes closed to the sun and dust.

"Jerome?" Dean asked. The surfer opened his eyes. "Are we still in the direction of Coluers?"

Jerome nodded without opening his eyes. Relieved, Dean sat back.

"Why do they call the trees miracles?" Jerome asked. He was watching Dean, deciding something.

"They provide a lot of nutritious food. Big seed pods, leaves, branches, everything."

"You eat the whole tree?"

"More or less."

Jerome opened his eyes.

"Does it taste good?"

"I don't know yet. They say it does."

"Everything tastes good when you are hungry."

Later, the tap-tap was rolling down the main street of a large town. Houses, storefronts, and food stops lined the wide, prosperous-seeming avenue. The bus lurched to a stop near an open-air town market, a collection of canvas-topped stalls, separated by crude wood fencing. There were hundreds of shoppers, strolling through like it was the mall.

"Come. The bus driver is taking a break," Jerome said and swung over the edge of the bus and made his way down the rope. Dean followed.

They strolled together like old friends toward the busy outdoor market. The stalls were mostly goods, not food, except for an umbrella cart that had a pile of raw, red slabs of meat piled high. Flies buzzed around the bloody meat, darting in and out of a shaft of sunlight that leaked through the ripped canvas.

"There are sweet spirits," Jerome said, nodding with approval.

"The flies?"

"No. The feeling, my friend. It is the feeling."

"Doesn't feel too sanitary," Dean said.

Next to the meat stall, two women sat alongside a small stack of charcoal. They chatted between themselves, oblivious to the shoppers, who showed little interest in the few briquettes anyway.

Dean watched a thin old man in a striped madras shirt, sleeves rolled up. He crouched next to his lime-green cart, sewing together a torn tennis shoe. There were more shoes scattered around him and spilling out of the cart. He worked with the seriousness and concentration of a craftsman.

"He's repairing old tennis shoes?" Dean asked.

"Cheaper than new ones, yes?"

Jerome turned his attention to the market bustling in front of him. He spotted a towel in the dirt piled with a half dozen sandwiches made with baguettes.

"*Pan!*" He acted as if he couldn't believe French bread was sold here. He hurried to the husky *ti marchan*, a market woman, who sat alongside. She wore a loose sundress, bursting in myriad colors. Jerome asked her about the *pan*.

"You like?" he called back to Dean who was just catching up to him. Jerome didn't wait for an answer. He gave the woman a handful of *gourdes* and she handed him two of the sandwiches. Jerome turned to Dean.

"For you," he said.

Dean held the sandwich in front of him like a specimen. He could not tell what was between the crusty baguette, torn by hand, not sliced.

"Is good," Jerome said after he'd bitten off an end. "Very good. Better than trees."

"Funny," Dean said. "What's in it?"

"Butter," Jerome said. He took another hungry bite and chewed happily as though it were full of cheese or meat or something more substantial.

Dean spotted the camera pointing at a small clump of red meat on one of the tables of the *ti marchan*. He was surprised to see the thin salt and pepper beard on the Moroccan. He was crouched low to the ground. Dean heard the clicks of the camera shutter go off in rapid succession. What an odd coincidence, Dean thought.

"Going to say hello to a friend," Dean said. He assumed the photojournalist he'd met at the bar was long gone, traveling back to Miami with his assignment complete.

"Ali," Dean called as soon as the photographer paused between takes. It took a moment before the Moor's eyes lit with tepid recognition. The photographer looked trapped, holding onto his camera like he'd been caught with stolen goods. There were plastic canisters of film attached to his shoulder strap like ammunition.

"Good to see you. You're working up here?"

"Yes," Ali said curtly. He checked his camera settings as though the aperture and shutter speed suddenly needed attention. He flicked the metal switch, and the body of the camera whined as he advanced a few frames of film.

Dean was confused by the journalist's cool reception. They were colleagues.

"Great market," Dean said, trying to guess why he was being kept at a distance by the photojournalist.

"Very busy, indeed."

Ali clearly had no interest in conversation. They said goodbye in the awkward silence that seemed to stretch for a long time. Dean caught up to Jerome, who was listening to the market woman as she gestured toward the mountains beyond them.

"The *ti marchan* say the *pan* is made where you are going," Jerome said.

Dean remembered his client telling him about new plans to build a bakery as a compliment to the Miracle Trees. Clearly, it had already been built.

Dean looked to the sandwich in his hand. He put his nose close to the edge of the bread and inhaled. It smelled of yeast and charcoal. He took a small and cautious bite through the dark crust. The salt and cream of the butter swirled inside his mouth.

"The bus is leaving. We must go."

Dean glanced behind him as he walked to the tap-tap. Ali was taking close-up pictures of the meat pile, its thick blood glistening in the sun. Dean remembered how Ali had become quiet and evasive, his mood markedly different after learning Dean was travelling to the town of Coluers. Dean hadn't thought too much about it at the time.

THE TAP-TAP SHUDDERED TO A STOP IN THE MIDDLE OF NOWHERE. Dean got up from his perch on the roof of the bus and searched for the village of Coluers. All that could be seen were mountains upon mountains, the color of blue jeans in the late afternoon light.

"*Es tu directione,*" Jerome said, pointing to the intersection they had just passed. The single dirt lane plunged down the barren hill and up again. On the crest, Dean spotted the lone, towering tree. A squat, white building hid underneath, scaffolding rising alongside. There were cinderblocks piled high on the top plank.

"That's the entire village?" Dean asked.

"You were expecting Manhattan?" Jerome smiled. He was incurably happy.

They grabbed one another's hand, linking thumbs, and pulled each other close. Dean felt a genuine bond even though they had just met.

"You must try to see my home of Jacmel. It is close."

"If I can, I'll look you up."

"I pray to see you again, my friend."

After the bus rumbled away, Dean hiked down the silent road toward the big tree and the only manmade structure visible for miles. Across from the squat building, a garden of baby banana trees was taking root on the brown hill. The banana leaves fluttered like a herd of elephant ears.

There wasn't a sign to mark Coluers. The white patchwork of cinderblock and brick stood alone with a commanding view of the blue hills. He spotted a lone rooster poking along the road. A warm breeze whistled faintly. Dean smelled the new concrete as he approached the cinderblock building. There were patches of construction dust alongside the bare scaffolding and a weathered vat the size of a bathtub next to it. The construction work looked as though it had stopped abruptly, without warning.

Dean was relieved when he saw an older woman next to a make-shift clothesline. She was adding more laundry to the rope that was already sagging under the weight of wet clothes.

"Pardon, Madame," Dean said.

The woman froze, her arm suspended in midair, and eyed him fearfully. Her thin dress fluttered in the hot breeze.

"Hello, reporter." The words came from the direction of the building.

Dean recognized the voice before she appeared out of the dark shade of the entrance. It was the NGO woman from the hotel.

"Did you meet the *chimères*?" Her blue eyes were startling. He'd never seen anything like them on a person of color. They were regal like her strong shoulders, lending her an air of majesty as if she were descended from an ancient monarchy.

"I met them," Dean said, made nervous by her beauty. He hadn't been able to see her before. "But they weren't ghosts."

"And you survived to tell the tale," she said, her lips hinting at a smile. "Most *blans* would have been afraid to go there."

"Count me in on that one. It wasn't bravery; it was boredom."

The older woman standing by the clothesline was a rapt audience. She held a pair of wet pants, water dripping into the dirt alongside her bare feet.

"I didn't think I'd ever see you again," Dean said.

"Small country," she said.

Dean remembered she was returning home to Haiti.

"This is where you grew up? Coluers?"

The woman strolled toward him. One foot turned inward as she approached, which had the effect of making her gait more languid as her small hips swayed to compensate for her uneven steps. It was girlishly awkward and suggestive at the same time.

"You're here to investigate me now?"

"Yes," Dean said, smiling. "And your miracle trees."

Her bare arms were sinewy and muscular. They looked like someone who was accustomed to hard, physical labor. It seemed odd for a woman who otherwise carried herself with the elegance of good breeding, of money.

"How do you know about them?" she asked, surprised.

"They brought me to Haiti."

The woman at the clothesline slapped the wet jeans she had been holding over the taut rope. The sound echoed over the silent hills. As she turned away, Dean spied her smiling.

"I didn't ask your name," Dean said.

She raised a delicate, wide eyebrow with amusement.

"Grace," she said. "Grace Mouzon. I don't believe I know yours."

Something mysterious and fleeting passed between them. It was as if the barometric pressure had suddenly changed from an approaching front.

"You look like you could use some water," Grace said.

"Water?" Dean repeated. He didn't know why. "I haven't had anything to drink since Port au Prince."

"That means yes?" Grace asked, amused.

Inside the community center was a small dining hall with a handful of long communal tables and metal chairs. They turned into the kitchen, gleaming with a stainless-steel sink and propane range.

"How did you get here? I don't see a car," Grace said, handing him a bottled water. Dean went to twist off the cap, but the seal was broken so he hesitated.

"The tap-tap," Dean said.

"Don't worry. I filled the bottle," Grace said. "Most *blan* get a driver."

"Nothing wrong with a bus."

Grace laughed, silver earrings jingling from her earlobes.

"I am just taking a break from the bakery. But I have to return. I will see you later?"

"Bakery? You make the baguettes?"

"You are surprising, Mr. Dubose. How do you know about the bread?"

"Call me Dean, please. I tasted them at the market in Leogane. With butter."

"Did you like it?"

"Good. I mean, great."

Grace nodded with satisfaction.

"A pleasure to see you again, reporter."

Dean watched her saunter away, entranced again by her odd, girlish gait. She soon was climbing the road that went up the hill from where he had come. Dean realized the tap-tap had passed the bakery, but he had been looking in the other direction, searching for this tiny village.

There was no sign of his client who he was supposed to meet. He looked at the space around the building to see if he had missed a parked car. But there was only the warm wind kicking up the dust and the echo of Grace's light steps in the distance.

THE WAITER APPEARED FROM BEHIND THE PATIO TORCHES WITH TWO WHITE BOWLS AND A CLOTH FOLDED OVER ONE WRIST. He set the first course in front of them, the soup *jounou,* with a flourish. He paused, silently checking to see if the men were pleased, then backed off into the darkness.

Herve and Father Charles picked up their heavy, silver soup spoons and slurped the peppery pumpkin. A touch of *creme* had rendered the puree even more silken.

"They are many children," Father Charles said. "So many."

He looked over the manicured privet that walled off the patio. A few street kids wandered like skinny feral dogs just beyond the reach of the restaurant lights. They knew to keep their distance.

Herve paused before sipping the orange soup from his spoon. He swallowed.

"We have talked about it enough," Herve said. "Please."

Pétion-Ville was perched on a hill far above the squalor of Port au Prince's slums. The black leaves of the tree-lined neighborhood rustled softly in the night. The sweet smell of jasmine and honeysuckle drifted over the empty streets. For both men, it was the familiar aroma of home, the streets where they had been escorted by armed guards to and from the academy they loved and, in equal measure, hated. It had been a difficult, privileged school, and they were expected to do more homework than they believed was necessary. Still, most of the teachers were kind and deferential, even afraid of the elite's children, and never pushed their students so hard as to get complaints.

"All girls," Father Charles said, shaking his head. "Bodies."

"Do we have to talk this bullshit?" Herve asked and took a shot of the bourbon he had ordered. Father Charles watched in an angry silence. Herve would never change. He did not even make a pretense of caring, like so many of the elite did.

He was a Frenois, after all, raised with the help of servants in the family's luxurious comfort, trappings of three generations of the lucrative rum business and sprawling distillery. Herve had grown up expecting to do whatever he pleased, good or ill. Many of their classmates at the academy were the same. Yet there was little awareness among them that their precious lifestyle or education was unusual. Everyone they knew lived the same way.

Father Charles suddenly called to the waiter. He shuffled over and bent down close to hear the priest. The waiter looked surprised and worried when the priest whispered his request.

"Our arrangement will allow the orphanage to flourish," Herve said. "We need the bodies. The children. Like a shark, Poppy. Stop hunting and you're dead."

"We are not sharks," Father Charles said. "Why do you talk like this?"

"Poppy. You take these kids in like stray cats and expect The Lord to care for them. Well, The Lord may do it in the next life. In this one, they need money. You need money. We need money. This is how we get it."

Herve slammed the cafe table with his fist. A few other diners glanced their way.

"This country, Poppy," Herve said. "We didn't choose it."

Herve pressed the dark, protruding vein on the side of his forehead, glaring at his friend.

"Only one pair of eyes looking down on us, checking our welfare. The black head of a vulture, Charles."

"Stop it," the priest said. "You are speaking nonsense."

The waiter withdrew their soup bowls and retreated as silently as he had arrived. But at the last moment, he nodded to the priest that his whispered order had been carried out.

"You and me know there gonna be more orphans until this country has another revolution," Herve continued. "There will be more than ever to take care of. More and more and more. I know that. You know that."

Father Charles watched the bread being handed out to the children outside the fence. They grabbed the baguettes with a fierce desperation that saddened him. So many hungry children.

The older kids came out of nowhere. They knocked down the younger kids with their fists and arms, ripping loaves out of their hands. Father Charles was instantly sobered. He should have known better than to hand out food without planning.

Herve continued. "There's gonna be more mouths to feed and more clothes to buy. You gonna need more shacks. I mean bunk rooms. More wood, more water. Now you will have the funds we need."

The priest wanted to quit the arrangement. He would find another way to support the orphanage.

The struggle in the darkness erupted into a loud fight. Yelling and crying echoed over the staid patio.

"Who gave them food?" Herve said, exasperated. The priest closed his eyes for a moment but didn't answer.

The waiter reappeared with the main course. A plate of roasted *Griyo Cabrit* was set in front of Father Charles, the fried goat meat surrounded by golden slices of lightly fried sweet plantain. It smelled of hot oil and the spicy pickled onions that were part of the *pikliz* piled on top. His hunger grabbed hold of him.

Herve watched his own plate being set in front of him. A large grilled lobster sat on a throne of grilled conch pieces with a mélange of vegetables, smelling of salt, spice, and the sea. *Lanbi Boukannen.* Father Charles knew it was his favorite. He could eat it for breakfast, which Herve sometimes did.

The commotion died down and it was almost quiet again. The older boys were eating the bread, the younger at their knees as they stooped, snapping up small chunks thrown to them by the ravenous boys.

"*Bon appétit*," Herve said.

They had been like brothers in school. Studying together, afternoon soccer, chasing the willing girls. Herve was a good man and wanted, in the end, what he did. But Herve was also a businessman first, a neglected son who wanted to make a mark in the world like his father.

Father Charles finally followed Herve's lead, picked up his fork, and plunged into dinner. They ate greedily in silence. Father Charles ignored the children. There was nothing to be done. Herve paused, cracking the spine of the lobster.

"Think of it. They will have a better life, better than here. They will not starve. They will be educated. The girls will grow to be fine young women."

Father Charles was surprised to find he had already eaten most of the *cabrit*, the sweet plantains cooling and untouched.

"Do we really know what will happen to the girls?" Father Charles asked, as if this were a new question, not one he had repeated over and over again.

"You will have the list, Poppy. As always. A longer list. That is all."

Father Charles felt guilty. He had never actually written to any of the families. He was fearful of upsetting them or getting any in trouble with immigration. The sound of a police siren floated in the distance.

A commotion erupted yet again at the fence. Bread had been delivered and had set off new fighting among young and old *sanguine*. Father Charles stared in shock and disgust. They should not have delivered even more food. It was fuel on a fire.

The dark neighborhood suddenly flooded with sirens and the flash of Morris lights. The police jumped out of their cruisers and ran to the struggling pack of children, wielding long nightsticks. Father Charles heard the first crack of bone and the explosion of screams as the children tried to scatter.

Herve turned slowly to watch the riot. A few of the younger children were dragged toward the cars, crying, desperately trying to escape. A policeman delivered a blow across a teenager's skinny back and he crumpled to the ground.

"You had them give out the bread," Herve said. "Didn't you? Now you can see what happens when you get sentimental."

Father Charles felt unmistakable relief when a gang of the young children eluded the police and escaped into the darkness. Electricity was precious, even in this wealthy enclave. The open doors of the police cars leaked the only light. Shadows of children were herded into those back seats like ghosts.

"We should return to Coluers now, Poppy." Herve stood up.

THEY ARRIVED IN WHITE LAND ROVERS LIKE A UNITED NATIONS CONVOY. Dean watched as the boxy, high-roofed cars rumbled to a stop in the dappled shade of the tree. The board members filed out slowly, carefully stepping onto the floorboard before landing in the dirt. A tall woman in a white cardigan sweater unfurled a matching umbrella to protect her greying hair.

"Pungent!" she said as if she had accidentally plunged into a field of manure. Just behind her, a stout old man laughed warmly.

"Mae, you'll come to love this as much as I do." He wore a broad-brimmed Panama hat and rimless eyeglasses that reflected the shadows of the waning sun. Dean recognized his client from the picture on the internet.

Dean delayed greeting him so he could watch the group. They were members of the Moisson board, the group that funded the tree project and that Nelson, as CEO, led with unbounded enthusiasm. The group, Dean knew, were a mix of bankers, social workers, and religious volunteers. Nelson had invited them to Haiti to see the trees for themselves. They not only helped to run the organization but did most of the fundraising.

"Need help with those bags?" Dean asked. He'd been surprised they came in expensive cars and carrying nice luggage. He was reminded of the privileged but generous people whom he met at lavish fundraisers in Manhattan.

"You're here!" Nelson called out to him and showed a gregarious grin. The other board members halted behind their leader's round, aging shoulders. Nelson extended his strong hand, tattooed with age spots. His blue eyes were amused, set off by the white hair of his eyebrows.

"I am sincerely impressed you've come to see our trees and let the world know." Nelson hesitated before answering Dean's offer. "We could use some help unloading if you don't mind."

He handed Dean one of the heavy suitcases.

"Lovely country, isn't it?" Nelson asked. He pulled two more sacks out of the trunk. Both were filled to the brim with carrots and squash and food wrapped in white, waxed paper. "How could anyone not fall in love with it?"

"They might be pressed to swoon over Port au Prince," Dean said. "But it's beautiful out here in the mountains."

"The city has its charms, too," Nelson said.

After bringing the bags inside, Nelson ambled into the kitchen and returned with a bottle of water in each bear-like hand. He offered one to Dean before chugging his own.

"It is great to finally meet face to face, Mr. Dubose," Nelson said, wiping his wet lips. "I am surprised that you offered to come here to help us."

"You shouldn't be."

"But you are a partner, an executive. In any case, we are very grateful. You can help us so much."

Grace slipped through the open door. A red handkerchief, dusted with flour, was tied tightly over her dark hair. Her gaze was dazzling.

"Grace is home!" Nelson said. He went to hug her.

"I'm a mess," she said. "A smile will have to do. But I wanted to welcome you!"

"I have not seen you in so long. Too long."

"I see you've met our reporter." Grace slipped her slim arm in Nelson's, then turned them both to face Dean.

"You know, Nelson dreamed of being a journalist when he was younger so he's going to be jealous of you."

"That's true. I did want to be a reporter at one time," Nelson said, beaming at Grace. "But my life took a turn. I like being a lawyer."

"The reporter is staying with us, Nelson, so I expect we'll all have a chance to talk later. At dinner?"

"Well of course he's staying with us," Nelson said.

"Do you need anything?" Grace asked, looking vaguely confused.

"We're good," Nelson said. "A relief to be off the road. Enough bumps to rattle my kidneys."

"At least it isn't the rainy season," Grace said. "I'll be back. Have to keep going. Make yourselves comfortable."

"Why is she calling you a reporter?" Nelson asked after Grace had walked out and headed back to the bakery.

"I don't know," Dean said, although he guessed it was because he didn't try to correct her back at the hotel.

"No matter. I'm going to boil some good Haitian coffee. Would you care for some?"

DEAN STEPPED OUT OF THE COMMUNITY CENTER AT DUSK. He looked in the distance at the light fading over the bald peaks. So many trees had been razed to make charcoal that the once lush mountains were dry as a desert. The scale of the destruction was overwhelming. But Dean sympathized with the fact that many citizens had little choice. People needed the lumber for shelter, for fuel. He hoped the planting of Moringa trees might one day spur the reforestation of the countryside. It was another miracle those trees could deliver.

Dean turned his attention from the sunset to watch a boy slouched on his mule as they rocked their way up the steep grade. The boy held a stick high in one hand, ready to urge the animal forward with a slap.

The mule moved stoically up the steep grade at its own pace. The boy spotted Dean and smiled, then plodded past, the stink of the mule left behind.

The simple, earthy immediacy of the boy, the sunset, the cotton-soft breeze comforted Dean. He felt oddly at home even though he had never set foot in the country before. He sat down in the cool dirt at the side of the road, crossing his legs.

He was reminded that Cynthia loved sunsets, especially on the Hudson River near their apartment. It was one of the few situations where she stopped and relaxed. She thrived on being busy, cabbing it to appointments and meals, texting furiously. He was happy to be away from all that.

Dean heard voices, punctuated by easy laughs, drifting into the approaching darkness. China plates clinked like cymbals. The board of directors was gathering for dinner inside.

Dean stood up and wiped the dirt off his pants. Inside the center, everyone was gathering around a long table. The chatter and laughter were loud, amplified by the bare cement and sparse furnishings. He spotted Grace, the natural center of attention, talking with Nelson.

Dean walked around the long wood table set with the old, used china. Ceramic bowls of steaming rice dirtied with dark beans were set in a row. In between were platters of blackened nubs of meat and tureens of cooked vegetables. Everything smelled to him like cabbage and strong vinegar.

"How did the bread come out?" Dean asked. He searched the table for the French baguettes.

"The generator died," she said. "No oven for the bread."

"Out of fuel?"

"I don't know. With a fresh mind, I can look at it tomorrow."

"I can help," Dean offered. He understood how generators worked from his grandfather, who got them going after the seasonal hurricanes that often came through the low country.

Grace appraised him, her bright eyes calculating.

"Yeah? Do you know about them?"

"I'm a country boy at heart. Used to play with them as a kid."

"Charleston, yes. You told me," Grace said.

Dean took the only open seat, next to a nun. The nun's name was Marie. She was tall with silver hair that bobbed just above narrow square shoulders. Her kind eyes were the color of cinnamon.

"Have you eaten food from the moringa before?" she asked. Someone handed her a plate of what looked like butterscotch-colored beans, dirty rice, a spinach salad and peppery green beans.

"I'm not big on vegetables," Dean said. "And definitely not trees." In fact, he was a complete stranger to vegetables. He liked his burgers and chicken, avoided salads, and usually left any broccoli on the plate. He also had a weakness for fried food, especially catfish and any version of a potato.

"You're in for a treat," the nun said.

The small mound of beans, on closer inspection, looked like a cross between small peanuts and large seeds. The smell of red pepper and vegetable oil wafted off the dense coating of sauce. The aroma of the spices awakened his hunger, but he wasn't looking forward to actually eating the food.

"It's a miracle," the nun said with a sly smile. "And there is more nutrition than you might find in a steak dinner."

Dean stared at the moist rice and the peppery beans, some of them mashed from mixing. He thought it looked like warmed-over seconds.

"We are so happy a journalist has thought enough of what we are doing to travel here. Thank you."

Her maternal eyes shined brightly. Sister Marie reminded him of the Franciscan nuns who taught him in grade school. They wore black habits, loose-fitting blouses, and long skirts that stretched to their clunky black shoes. Their tightly fitted habits masked their femininity. Sister Marie seemed like a kind aunt.

"Well," Dean said, "there will be journalists visiting here to report on the trees if I do my job right."

Everyone had served themselves and was waiting.

"Oh Lord," Grace began, bowing her head humbly. Her loose, dark bangs were streaked with flour. "We are grateful for all your kindness and love, for this moringa you have provided, for the help you have given so we might help others."

A murmur of approval swept the room before everyone grabbed their silverware and dug in. Dean started with the spicy mound of beans. They tasted like boiled peanuts, mush, and fiber.

"Seeds of the tree," Sister Marie said, observing him carefully.

"Wow," Dean said. He moved on to the greens, the leaves of the moringa. They tasted like steamed spinach.

"Good?" Sister Marie asked. She had taken only a small, delicate forkful of rice.

"Healthy," Dean said, nodding appreciatively.

"Those are the pods. People call them drumsticks."

"I like drumsticks," Dean said.

The spice blew up his mouth. It was hot, sweet, and tasted faintly of horseradish. He reached for the water.

"There's moringa root mixed in there," the nun said. "Ground up like mustard seeds."

"First time eating a tree," Dean said. When he learned of the miracle trees, he hadn't given much thought to people actually eating one, especially himself. He should have, he thought.

"Won't be your last," Nelson said from his seat next to Grace. Dean never lost track of where she was sitting. He stole glances of her during the meal. He loved the way she tilted her head away from Nelson, her blue eyes taking him in as if he were the only person in the world.

"No cooked bark?" Dean said, joking. If they had it, he wasn't going to eat it.

"The bark is toxic," Nelson said. "But when used properly, a strong antibiotic."

"Medicine for infections?" Dean asked.

"You bet," Nelson said. "It's the tree that doesn't stop giving."

After dinner, they went to a smaller room in the center with a makeshift bar. There was local rum, whiskey, and a local beer. The nun made some herbal tea, offering some to the group, which Dean happily accepted. Nelson offered him a shot of rum as well.

"I'm good," Dean said. "I don't drink. Not on the job." He added the last part because he didn't want to say he had been clean for years.

"You take your work seriously," Grace said, lounging on a metal chair next to Nelson.

"When I have to," Dean said. "But I like to have fun, too."

"Do you?" Grace smiled. "Not much nightlife in Coluers."

Dean took his mug of tea from the nun and thanked her. He found Grace still watching him.

"How about you?" Dean asked. "You're not drinking anything. But you seem like a woman who would be happy with a glass of fine wine."

Grace laughed. "How elegant. Give me a beer and I'm happy."

Nelson was silent, watching and listening to them.

"How did you find out about us, Mr. Dubose?" she asked, leaning forward in her chair. The soft timbre of her voice was soothing, inviting. He remembered how much he liked it when they were on the porch of the hotel and the sound of her caught him at once. "This isn't your typical story. A little offbeat."

Dean looked to Nelson to give the answer, but he had turned his attention to a board member.

"Way offbeat, which I like. Some people said I was crazy for pursuing it. But I read about it in a trade blog and knew I had to see it."

"Why?" Grace tilted her head to the side, waiting for his answer as he'd seen her do with Nelson at dinner. It made him feel special.

But Dean struggled to articulate exactly why he had been so struck when he learned of the Moringa tree, why it had inspired him so much more than any journalist or PR man. But the feeling had been immediate, unconscious, pure instinct. One day, he'd get someone to explain it all.

"Maybe I wanted to see Haiti," Dean said, finally.

"That's pretty offbeat. What do you think of it so far?" She smiled.

"It's real," Dean said, wanting to say more. "I can see why anyone would want to return."

Grace's demeanor changed and Dean was certain he'd said something wrong. How or why he didn't know. But Grace had become instantly somber.

"A toast!" Nelson was on his feet, holding a glass of rum high above him as if the tumbler was a chalice to be used for a benediction. "To everyone, each of us, for making the journey to this wonderful country and this special mission. Thank you!"

Dean saw Grace get up and leave the room. He considered following, but it was clear she wanted no company.

WISPS OF CHEMICAL SMOKE FROM THE MOSQUITO COILS DRIFTED THROUGH THE STACKS OF BUNK BEDS. The chemicals in the coils were toxic, intended for outdoor use, but they were the only defense against the army of mosquitoes. Dean listened to their faint whine, fearful of being pricked by a malarial bug. There had been no recent outbreaks, but the possibility of contracting malaria from mosquitoes was an ever-present danger in the tropical swelter.

"You're leaving next week?" the doctor at the clinic in Manhattan had asked, reading his answers from a form Dean had filled out. She wore a white lab coat over a business suit.

"Is that a problem?" Dean asked.

"Not for yellow fever and a tetanus booster, certainly," she said, moving to a glass cabinet filled with rows of medicine vials. She opened a drawer below and took out a long needle packaged in plastic.

"I would have you take doxycycline. But it takes at least three to seven days to work into your system. Even then, it's not foolproof. It might not be effective until you return."

"So, nothing for malaria?" Dean was incredulous. He'd known an uncle who nearly died from the disease he brought back from a vacation in China.

"You can take the pills. But you'll be back in the U.S. before it's truly beneficial. If you had come earlier to see us, different story."

She peered through frameless glasses that made her eyes as cool and clinical as her manner.

"Do you anticipate any sexual contact?"

"What?"

"Hepatitis B," she said. "It's endemic where you are going. It's transmitted through sexual contact. And it can be lethal."

The doctor betrayed no emotion as if she were reading directions off one of the medicine bottles.

"I'm going to see a client," Dean said.

She stared at him, waiting for a full answer.

"No, I don't anticipate any sexual contact," he said.

Dean was drenched in his own sweat and couldn't sleep. He listened to the chorus of breathing in the room, the scattered, sonorous snoring. He was acutely aware that Grace was sleeping two beds away. He'd seen her slip into the lower bunk in a body-hugging nightshirt. He'd seen her outside before, smoking a cigarette in solitude, staring at the sky. He guessed she had far more complicated reasons for returning to the mountains than home. In any case, he was disappointed that he'd somehow changed her mood for the night.

Outside, the cicadas chimed in from the moonlit darkness. He worried he would be awake all night and exhausted come daybreak. He had to get some sleep. It was vital that he be rested and alert. In a few hours, they would drive to the tree farm. He was excited beyond belief.

Dean propped himself up on his wet elbows then climbed out of his bunk. The cement floor was cool and slick under his feet. He pulled on his soiled khakis and damp T-shirt, got into his hiking boots, and hurriedly laced them.

Outside, he found a procession of lights moving up the narrow road. They stretched for miles, one after the other, flickering like an endless string of Christmas tree lights under the predawn sky. Dean thought it could be a line of migrants, marching to the city.

After a moment, people emerged from the darkness, some holding candle lanterns. A spirited old man led a donkey piled with stuffed burlap sacks. A broad-shouldered woman in an African print dress balanced a loose pile of green plantains on her head. A young boy followed behind his mother, carrying a satchel of fabric. All moved patiently, smiling or nodding as they passed.

"They are going to market."

Nelson was standing behind him, wearing only his boxer shorts.

"They are going to Leogane?" Dean asked.

"Latrueil. A few miles over those mountains from here. Every Saturday."

"Miles? Everyone just walks?"

"They leave their villages in the middle of the night so they can get to the market at dawn and set up."

Dean was impressed that so many would travel so far for a simple market. He saw a glimmer of the sunrise as it traced the distant, denuded summits. The warm air smelled of peat and dirt. He felt an earthiness, a stolid presence like nowhere else.

"Love this place," Nelson said. "They have nothing in the way of possessions, but it is a rich country."

Nelson strutted toward the road, his boxer shorts flapping comically in the breeze. He reached down and picked something up. It was a valuable mango, left by accident. He showed it to Dean as if it were a prize. With his curly white hair and scattered gold cavities, he seemed eccentric and daft, not the responsible chief of the governing board.

"Wonderful," he said.

"You think it was left on purpose?" Dean asked.

Nelson laughed heartily as if mocking himself.

"I wouldn't be surprised. That is how so many are here. Always, they want to give."

Dean thought of Father Charles and his immediate concern, his impulse to help a total stranger. He told Nelson about him.

"He told me his orphanage is here in Coluers."

"Father Charles?" Nelson looked at him with surprise. "Yes. Wonderful man."

"He was saying mass in an old, wood plank church in the slum of slums."

"Cite Soleil."

Dean nodded, remembering the gun shot. It had taken hours to fully recover his hearing. But, thanks to the priest, he'd been able to walk out.

"He invited me to see his orphanage."

"You should. We used to support it."

"Is it close to here?" Dean asked.

Nelson grinned and pointed at the distant trees. "Ten minutes or so through those rare trees."

Dean heard others stirring inside the barracks, the board members chatting in English. A short, deep laugh followed the slap of bare feet on the cement floors. Pots clanged unseen from the kitchen. Dean looked forward to breakfast and some coffee.

Nelson stopped, suddenly alarmed by the two Land Rovers parked under the tree. Both hoods were popped open slightly.

"Something wrong? Those open hoods?"

"I hope that's all," Nelson said, shaking his head, clearly disturbed. But he wasn't sharing what worried him.

THE SINGLE TREE SHADED THE LAND ROVERS FROM THE GLARE OF THE LATE MORNING SUN. But they didn't protect the car batteries. Both had been stolen sometime after the board of directors arrived. The car hoods were left carefully ajar so as not to alert anyone with a loud noise. The thieves had been quick and efficient. They knew what they wanted and how to get the heavy batteries out. One of the big SUV batteries, alone, could power lights, a computer, a television, and a radio for weeks.

"Right under our noses," Nelson said. He was dismayed, not angry, which Dean expected. Robbery is a personal assault.

Dean had heard something while tossing and turning in the bunk. He'd assumed the creak of metal was from the occasional breeze that blew off the dark mountains. As he reflected on it, the sound would have matched that of a hood being raised. But he hadn't been listening with the threat of a heist in mind and so dismissed it.

"We'll have to send to PAP to get batteries," Nelson said. "If the thieves didn't keep them, we might be buying our own batteries back."

"You've been through this?" Dean asked.

"More than once," Nelson admitted. "But we are a target. You get used to it. Some are desperate. They are not really to blame."

"Theft is a crime. Simple," Dean said. "I don't agree."

"You're entitled," Nelson said, showing a wan smile.

"How are we supposed to get to the Miracle Trees?"

"That's a problem," Nelson said. He looked over the aging board of directors who stood by the cars, waiting on a decision, hoping to be told what to do.

"Is there a hurry?" Grace asked. "The trees aren't walking away."

"There is a tight schedule," Dean said. "There isn't so much time to get this done."

"Get it done?" Grace asked, annoyed. "You make it sound like a chore."

"Not at all. I'm just anxious," Dean said. "Seems like I'm always getting delayed."

Dean took a breath, calming himself.

"We can drive later this afternoon if we get lucky finding batteries," Nelson said. "Or you could walk, Mr. Dubose."

"How far away?"

"Five or six miles."

Dean felt the attention of the board members. They were already hot. The nun was trying to cool herself with a personal fan. The battery-powered tool looked like a wand that she was waving over her perspiring neck and face.

"It's hot," Dean said.

"Maybe it's a good opportunity to visit Father Charles?" Nelson suggested.

"Father Charles?" Grace asked with surprise. "You know him?"

"Just met him yesterday."

Dean sensed her protectiveness of the priest. She was studying him with what seemed distrust, trying to decide if he was telling the truth.

"He helped me out of a jam," Dean explained.

"Yes, that's like him."

"Maybe you can guide him over there, Grace?" Nelson suggested. "The rest of us would benefit from a little shade."

"I have to get to work, I'm afraid," Grace said.

"I can walk myself over," Dean said. He was annoyed that Nelson was making this an issue.

Nelson and the board members moved away from the Land Rovers toward the community center. They seemed relieved and certainly uninterested in seeing the orphanage. He remembered Nelson's chance remark that they had once funded the orphanage but no longer. He hadn't thought to ask why in the moment, but he would. It was curious for an NGO.

Grace didn't leave. She hesitated, her face clouded in worry. Dean had the sense that she was changing her mind.

"See you later, I hope?" Dean asked.

"I'll go with you," Grace said. "You need someone to show you the way."

THEY FOUND A NARROW FOOTPATH THAT WOUND THROUGH YOUNG BANANA TREES. The wide, floppy leaves had to be brushed away to get through. Grace led the way, holding the leaves up like a curtain for Dean, who was just behind her. The sage at their feet released a sharp, herbaceous scent with each step.

"You know Father Charles well," Dean said.

"Since I was twelve," Grace said. She stopped. "He got me out of a bad situation."

Dean followed her deeper into the brush. There were unfamiliar chirps and bird calls around them. The humid air was cool without the sun beating down.

"I can relate," Dean said. "He broke up a gang that wasn't too happy to see me in their neighborhood."

"The Cite Soleil," she said. "You went by yourself?"

"I did."

The banana trees thinned, and the path widened until they stepped into the clearing. Two large, newly constructed cabins stood in the middle, still smelling of sawdust. The milled boards were smooth and yellow, not yet stained or weathered. A peaked, covered porch graced the entrances. A few kids sat chatting on a set of new wood stairs. They jumped up as soon as they spotted Grace.

"Bonjou!!!" Their cries shot through the compound. Dean stopped as they ran toward her, brimming with excitement.

"*Komen ou ye?*" Grace asked, bending on one knee so that she was at their height. "How are you?"

"*N'ap boule, n'ap boule,*" the children screamed in unison. Grace laughed, gathering all of them into her arms.

"Eske ou te we Father Charles?" Grace asked.

On cue, Father Charles strode out from behind a nearby hut. He found Grace and kissed her softly on both cheeks. The bald priest peered at Dean suspiciously. His arm lingered around Grace's bare shoulders. Suddenly, a look of recognition spread across his face.

"I did not expect to see you, Mr. Dubose."

Father Charles looked to Grace as if for an explanation of why she was with the journalist.

"We just met," Grace said. "He wanted to see you. Said you were in Cite Soleil together."

"Indeed, we were. Mr. Dubose witnessed more than he bargained for."

Dean nodded agreement. "I never thanked you. So, I jumped at the opportunity once I got here."

"The hand of God leads us to unexpected places. Come."

The priest turned and set off for the edge of the compound. The children fell in line behind him, skipping like they were following Peter Pan. Other kids stirred from the other cabins, spotlighted by the rising sunlight, quickly creating a crowd.

"You're not gonna say hey to me, baby?" a voice called. Dean turned to see a tall, imposing man standing back by the woods. He was dressed in designer slacks and a silk shirt as if he had just walked out of a chic club in the city.

"Herve," Grace said, dully.

Dean recognized him from Cite Soleil. He was the priest's partner, who had eyed him from the backseat of the white Mercedes. He was the person the gang had seemed to fear. Dean was shocked when Herve grabbed Grace roughly by her shoulders and then kissed her tenderly on her open lips. Grace neither avoided nor resisted him. She was passive, waiting for the greeting to end.

"Poppy tell you the news, baby?" Herve asked. He spoke with an intimate familiarity.

"About?"

"What do you think? Thirteen of these treasures gonna have a mommy and a daddy and their own roof over their heads."

Herve was beaming like a proud father.

"Thirteen? All at once?" Grace asked. She glanced at the distant children, worried.

"We are blessed!" Herve said. "But the lord will need your help, Lady Grace, now that you're back home."

Herve took her limp hand from his arm and held it with the casual possessiveness of a boyfriend. Dean was jealous although he knew he had no right to be.

"What kind of help?" Grace asked. Dean waited for her to move out of Herve's grasp and put him in his place. Instead, she relaxed into it like a lover.

"Help them prepare," Herve said. "Help them adjust."

"Where?" Grace asked.

"All over, baby," Herve said. "We've expanded our reach since you've been gone."

"Not surprised," Grace said.

Herve showed a charming, boyish grin as if she had made a joke.

"One day maybe they will come back like you. If we are lucky."

Come back? Dean was confused. Did Grace come back because she had once been an orphan here, too? It seemed remote. Maybe he had misunderstood, Dean thought.

The priest leaned his hand on the shoulder of a young girl, her hair braided and tied with a cheap silk ribbon. Her faded yellow nightgown was threadbare, sagging over gamine, dirt-smeared legs.

"There food at the center?" Herve asked. "I didn't get any breakfast."

"*Pan*," Grace said.

Herve motioned to the route they had just taken. "Come with me?"

"I'm showing Dean around," she said. "He's a reporter."

Grace spoke his occupation like it was a threat.

"We've met," Herve said. He made no effort to hide his dislike. Dean didn't know why, but Herve had been equally dismissive as he picked up Father Charles outside the slum. "But I need you right now. Okay, baby?"

Grace stared back at Herve, her gaze still as if under some kind of spell. She wasn't herself or at least how Dean had known her up until now.

"You'll be okay?" Grace asked. Her blue eyes were distant.

"I can find my way back," Dean said.

He watched in amazement as Grace followed behind Herve like a dutiful spouse. The bright, proud young woman had been replaced by a docile slave, moving as if in a zombie trance.

THE MERCEDES STOPPED OUTSIDE THE COMMUNITY CENTER. Grace went to open her door, but it had been locked and she couldn't open it. Herve looked amused. The air conditioning chilled her exposed neck.

"Been so long, missy, I wanted to talk," Herve said. "Wait with me."

"Wait for what?" Grace left her hand on the door.

Herve laughed without a trace of humor. Grace remembered where this had led before, and she was both afraid and excited. There was something in his raw, pure desire that she liked and was drawn to the way one is drawn to the thrill of danger.

Herve reached past her and pulled a sandwich bag out of the glove compartment. Grace flinched when his arm came near her. She remembered the green and black tattoo on his forearm just below the elbow. The fanciful mermaid looked more like a fish caught on a line.

"You be back for good, Lady Grace," Herve said. He pulled a tiny rectangular box of rolling papers out of the front pocket of his blue jeans.

"It's 'Lady' now?" Grace asked.

"I respect you, baby."

His eyes smiled at her, and she looked away quickly, unnerved.

The smell of sweet cannabis filled the car as soon as he opened the sandwich bag. The leaves and twigs looked like dried basil.

"You and me. We know how to make it nice here," Herve said. He pinched the leaves with his thumb and two fingers and dropped them delicately into a double wrapper.

"You and me make nice?" Grace said.

"I'm your man, baby. I know how to treat you and give you the things that you want." Herve expertly rolled the paper and cannabis into a tight, thin cigarette.

"What do I want?"

"Nice things. Like everyone. And you wanna be loved, baby. You wanna be taken care of. You want what I got."

"What is it you got? Money? I know you were born with a golden spoon, Herve. And for some reason you want more. Never enough."

"I got more than money," Herve said, glancing down at her crotch.

"Now I would like to get out. I have work to do. I've so enjoyed our little talk."

Herve slipped the hand-rolled cigarette into his mouth. A butane flame appeared out of his other hand, flickering just above his knuckles like a magic trick. The white paper tip ignited. He drew on it as soon as the flame fell. After a moment, he exhaled the sweet smoke.

"You and me." He held out the joint as an offering. Grace peered at the thin cigarette as if it were an insect. She remembered the sweet smell in the back seat of another of his trophy cars. Some European car. They were high, sweating in spite of the air conditioning. She liked the feel and smell of him, his surprising tenderness. She remembered, too, the sadness that gripped her afterwards, the feeling of falling back into the hole she thought she had dug herself out of.

"What do we have between us, Herve? Besides misery?"

Herve withdrew the joint.

"You come back for misery?"

"I came back to help, to make a difference."

Herve drew again on the joint and inhaled deeply. He held the smoke in his lungs for what seemed a long time. When he exhaled, there was only a bare wisp of smoke.

"Noble, Lady Grace. Noble," Herve said. He winked at her and looked down at the bulge that pressed through his tight crotch.

"I need help." He grinned.

"Is that supposed to turn me on, Herve?" She was disgusted. Herve took one more hit of the joint, then blew out the tip that glowed like embers.

"You got a *blan* sniffin' between your legs and now you acting like a kept woman."

"Dogs sniff. Men talk."

"Every man wants the same thing, Lady Grace."

Herve opened the ashtray and set what was left of the joint inside. There were scores of joint ends inside.

"You didn't say anything about the wheels, baby," Herve said. The mood had suddenly changed. Herve had lost his focus for a moment and was staring out the car window at the nearby tree.

"I don't care about cars," Grace said.

"Okay, baby. Okay. Just so you know. You need something, you just ask me. Anything. It's yours."

Grace pulled on the door handle again, but nothing happened.

"You can start by unlocking the door, Herve," Grace said.

The locking mechanism clicked open. Grace swung herself out into the hot sun.

"I met your boy in the Cite Soleil," Herve said to her back. "Charles said he'd come to see a slum. I mean, shit. Like a tourist."

"He does it for a living. He's a reporter."

"Doubt it," Herve said. "Can't be another one." But a look of uncertainty crossed his face for a moment. In less than a day, a second journalist had appeared with an interest in the orphanage.

"What do you mean another one?" Grace asked.

"Boy with a camera was poking around here, talking with Poppy."

"That's strange," Grace said. She wondered if Dean was actually who he said he was. "Dean looks to be on his own."

"Is that right?" He studied her face. It made him smile.

"Never saw you sweet on anyone," Herve said. "Didn't think it could happen. Not you."

"Why do you think you know me?" Grace was beside herself. He was so arrogant, so condescending, always had been. The rich, privileged BAMBA boy descendant—the acronym spelling out the five wealthy families that controlled Haiti—sneering at those with nothing.

"I know you, Lady Grace. I know you."

She closed the door quickly. But before she could walk away, the tinted window slithered down until it disappeared into the dark cavity of the door.

Grace felt Herve's gaze from inside the car burning into her backside and down her long legs. She hated that she liked it. He stirred something in her. It wasn't good, but she felt defenseless.

"I'll see you soon, baby," Herve called.

She felt a wave of relief as the Mercedes sedan finally drove off.

DEAN FOUND THE PRIEST ALONGSIDE THE MAKESHIFT ALTAR, STOOPED DOWN TO TALK TO THE GIRL IN THE WORN YELLOW DRESS. She was on the verge of tears, her dark eyes wide and thin, chiseled face taut. Dean stayed near the entrance, not wanting to invade their privacy.

The stucco walls around the chapel were studded with primitive art panels that depicted the stages of the cross. The paintings glowed in vibrant tropical colors, a far cry from the somber icons hanging in Dean's church in Charleston. He had spent his childhood moving past the reliefs every Sunday as he left the altar for communion, his hands folded piously out of habit. Now, he couldn't recall what each panel depicted.

Here in Father Charles' church, the depictions refused to be ignored. They pulsated with rich pigments, crudely applied, but the informality only made them more charming and accessible. Dean realized that all were black or brown, not a white man in sight. God in their image, of course.

The priest's voice dropped lower, the tones now soft and even soothing. The girl was sniffling, her face wet with tears, as she listened dutifully, her head bowed. But every time the priest spoke of the family—"*en famile*" and "*tu famile*"—the girl's small oval face would snap up in sudden, abject fear before collapsing, her face searching the warped floor beneath her.

"Sophie, Sophie," Father Charles said, shaking his head.

"*No kite, no kite*," the girl mumbled. *No leave!*

Father Charles was holding a vestment on one arm and stroking it nervously. Dean caught bits and pieces of the conversation that he worked to translate in his mind. All the words referred to houses or homes, food, wealth.

"*No kite*," the girl insisted. She was spirited and headstrong and had a way of standing that made her look ready to take on all comers. She spotted Dean and her eyes narrowed as though she had found the culprit. Dean could feel the fight in those brilliant eyes. Father Charles followed her look like a panning camera.

"Yes? Mr. Dubose?" Father Charles demanded.

"I came to talk with you," Dean said. "But later."

The little girl was past him in a matter of seconds. She had bolted from her spot, raced out the entrance, and vanished into the sunlight. Father Charles stared after her, looking drained.

"*Difficile*," Father Charles said.

"Upset."

Father Charles shook his head as if it were beside the point.

"She does not want to go, to leave us."

"To be adopted," Dean said.

The priest sighed wearily.

"Will she be leaving Haiti?"

"America," Father Charles said.

"That will be a big change."

"Come," Father Charles said. He led them out of the church.

"What do you like to talk about?"

At the end of the dirt clearing, some of the children had taken an old clothesline and had begun a spirited group jump rope. The kids shrieked as one of the girls missed with a shallow leap.

"So many children," Dean said, noticing not only those playing but scores of others hanging by the clearing or lazing around the steps scattered throughout.

"Many to love, too many to care for," the priest said.

"There's got to be thirty, forty kids in this small space." I don't know how you do it."

Father Charles tensed. An argument had broken out between a boy who had been sitting in the dirt next to the blue shack and the same girl who had bolted past him minutes ago. Holding one end of the jump rope, Sophia was shouting and egging on the boy. The game had long since halted. The other children surrounding them gaped hungrily like spectators at a fight.

"Always the fight," Father Charles said.

The kids were high-strung and agitated. All were barefoot, their T-shirts and jeans draped over thin frames like mannequins. The cheeks of an older, gangly boy, a teenager, suddenly erupted with hot tears. Sophia threw the end of the rope on the ground in disgust. She clenched her irregular teeth, a blazing white, and shook her head so that her braided hair snapped like whips.

"*Rete! Rete!*" Father Charles said. Enough! "*Sa k'genyen?*" he added. *What happened?*

"*Kisa pi nou fe?*" the boy demanded. *What must we do?*

He stopped crying and wiped his cheek with his thin hand, then wiped the other. His face was wide and strong, his flared nose held up arrogantly.

Father Charles brought his own hands together like he had inside the slum church, as if about to begin a homily. Dean realized it might be a nervous tic, a way of gathering himself in the midst of sudden stress.

"Li se yon bon tan," Father Charles said. *It's a good time.*

"There will be families. Food. A fine school. *Parans* to care for you. *Parans.*"

The priest was talking about adoption, which seemed to be imminent for these children. Dean was surprised that he had happened to arrive at such a turning point for the kids and the orphanage. They were going to have homes. It was rare and extraordinary.

The children, however, seemed frightened about leaving the orphanage, likely the only home they knew.

"Mwen pat vle ale," the boy pleaded, echoing the little girl in the yellow dress. *I do not want to go.*

His eyes welled again, glistening in the comforting, dappled light under the tree.

"I don't want you to leave." Father Charles pulled him closer and hugged him, burying his head in his chest. The priest held on a little too long, betraying that he, too, did not want to be separated.

"Pa gen moun renvoie," the boy said. *No one returns.*

"Change is difficult. To leave the home we know. But God has provided you with a future, a family."

"Se fanmi nou," the boy said, defiantly. This is my family.

The pretty young girl in braids stared at the boy until he met her gaze. She smiled at him sadly. They seemed like brother and sister.

"Ale jwe," the priest said. Go play.

The kids hesitated, looking from one to the other for guidance. Finally, they wandered back to the spot where they had been playing jump rope.

"We cannot take care of all these children. No one can," the priest said with resignation. He had the air of a penitent giving a confession.

"Doesn't seem to stop you from trying," Dean said.

"I must," he said, matter-of-factly.

"It must not be easy to find them homes, families?"

Father Charles turned back toward the chapel. Dean followed.

"God does."

"How does God do it?" Dean asked.

"The system is broken and corrupted. But we have help, thanks to God."

"Help?"

Father Charles nodded but didn't elaborate. Dean guessed he was alluding to receiving assistance from a charity or non-governmental organizations like most orphanages.

"These children will go to their new homes soon?"

"They will," Father Charles said.

The sound of the swimming rope and feet landing on the ground told them the kids were playing again. A few young voices broke through the silence.

"Grace told me you helped her," Dean said. He was thinking about the possibility of Grace being an orphan at one time.

"Did she?" The priest didn't sound surprised.

"How?"

Father Charles's lips showed a wan, sad smile in response.

"I invited her to live with us."

"Here?" Dean stared at him, confused. "At the orphanage?"

"It was different then. Difficult conditions. But not as bad as her home."

The kids were in a fight, again. They had stopped the game, and now two of the boys were pushing each other.

"If you'll excuse me," Father Charles said.

DEAN HIKED BACK TO THE ROAD. He heard the faint cries of the children in the distance as their voices mixed with the assorted calls of the tropical birds around him. It sounded almost like a school recess. He was reminded fondly of the loud playground near his and Cynthia's apartment in Manhattan. The cement play area was alongside 92nd Street, behind steel fencing topped with barbed wire. Dean liked the noise, the shrieks and laughter and whistles. It was the sound of life.

Cynthia went out of her way to avoid the playground. She told him repeatedly that children were better seen than heard. The noise grated on her. She'd had a happy childhood, but somewhere along the line she became convinced that she never wanted to raise children.

"It costs over a million dollars to raise one child," she said one evening as they sat eating takeout. Both were tired from work, not wanting to cook or go out. "That's a fact, Dean. I can show you the article. One million. That's before college. One million!"

"What's does it matter? You can't price kids."

"It's a numbers game," she said, her face dark with anger and resentment.

"You want to adopt?" the man demanded.

The voice knocked him out of his reverie. Dean glimpsed the silver Mercedes hood ornament spiked by the bright sun. He had neared the community center. Herve was leaning against the passenger side of the sedan, his eyes blocked stylishly with aviator sunglasses. He held a small twig in his mouth that he rolled like a lollypop.

"If I could," Dean said.

Herve smirked and pushed off the car and took a step away. They were about ten yards apart, seeming to face off against one another.

"Why do you come to the orphanage?" Herve asked, folding his muscled arms.

"Father Charles invited me. Why?"

"What else?"

"The food."

Herve toyed with the stick between his lips like it was a cigarette.

"They got people believing that shit. Miracle trees." He shook his head in pity.

"So, you already know what I'm doing here," Dean said.

Herve started, peering at him coldly. There was a blank indifference about him that chilled Dean.

"A photographer was here with us taking pictures," Herve said. "He says it was about the *sanguine*. Then you show up."

"Moroccan? Have a light beard?" Dean asked.

"You know him?"

"I met him in Port au Prince," Dean said.

Herve nodded, his dark eyes were tight and focused and cold. A faint smell of marijuana drifted off of him.

"You're a PR man," Herve said. "I checked up on you."

"I'm flattered."

Herve smiled. The pupils of his dark eyes were flat but shining. A red tongue shot out for a moment and licked his bottom lip where a tiny sliver of bark had remained from the stick.

"Don't be," Herve said.

"You sound like a man who doesn't want me finding out something."

"No, I just don't want you around here. Or Grace."

"So, you're threatening me."

"No. I'm telling you."

"We'll see," Dean said. He deliberately turned around and walked away. He wasn't going to be intimidated. Never had, never would.

20.

FATHER CHARLES SAT ON A FOLDING CHAIR IN THE MAKESHIFT CHURCH, LISTENING TO THE CHILDREN PLAY OUTSIDE. Kids can endure anything, he thought. They adapt to changing circumstances in ways that are impossible for adults. They are not weighed down with high expectations, sobering experience, or the bitterness of disappointment. They live in the present tense.

Yet he knew all too well the trials that awaited them beyond these hills. Later, they would learn and possibly despise him. He held their lives in his hands and it pained him. He didn't want that responsibility nor the guilt. The broker adoptions were necessary for the better of all, he reminded himself. Without the bargain they had struck, the orphanage would collapse under its own weight, and these children and the children to come would have nothing and go nowhere. There was nothing worse than to have no promise of a future.

One of the hand-painted stations of the cross on the wall across from him caught his eye. Christ was on one knee, the crude wooden cross pressed into his weak shoulder, holding him down. He had fallen but would stand up again and resume the agonizing journey to his crucifixion. Jesus Christ, the barefooted black man, seemed hopelessly cowed, unable and unwilling to resume. No matter what he did, the consequence was the same. He would suffer if he didn't move. He would suffer the moment he stood. There was no escape, no savior.

Father Charles turned to find his partner in the doorway of the church, silhouetted like a ghost by the bright light of the sun-drenched courtyard behind him where the cries of the children swept inside the clapboard building like a rushing stream.

"What did you tell the *blan*, Poppy?" Herve asked.

"Nothing."

Father Charles couldn't see his eyes or his features through the sun's glare, but he didn't need to see them. He knew Herve too well, understood what he was thinking, what he cared most about.

"He doesn't know anything."

"Why would you invite another reporter here? What are you thinking?"

"I hide nothing," the priest said. He liked and trusted the *blan*. He had integrity and felt something kindred in the man.

Herve shook his head at his friend. He'd heard this nonsense before. The priest always needed reassurance that he was not in a business. He was a religious leader, a lover of children, a pied piper.

Herve had to consider the effect of an exposé in the media. *Priest traffics children from orphanage*. He knew the media would frame their work as such. They would not understand or care to understand that his work was the work of adoption by other means. No official channels to invite certain graft and years of unnecessary delays affecting both the children and their would-be parents. No, the media hounds would sniff for the sensational, undeterred by complications. Money was being exchanged in the black market, and no government touched it. They would not let that be.

"You know how our client feels about publicity," Herve said.

"Our client?"

"Yes," Herve said tersely. He hated the way the priest relentlessly tried to suggest he was somehow not a part of the business end of the orphanage; the implication that he was above serving clients. He was the warm, pious priest. His partner was the cold businessman.

Herve stood up anxiously but remained in front of his chair. He gazed up at the stucco ceiling, his mind racing as he thought about all the messy things in life Charles disdained and thought beneath him. He considered telling Father Charles about the time he'd screwed Grace's scrawny ass in the back seat and left her wanting more. She loved it. But stripping his business partner of his beatific image of Grace could be a mistake in the middle of this upcoming transaction.

Father Charles seemed impatient now, too.

"He is not investigating our orphanage," the priest said. Herve was impressed that his friend almost always intuited what he was thinking. Always had.

"How do you know?" Herve asked.

"We did not talk about the orphanage at all. He was reporting on Cite Soleil."

Herve shook his head, certain any stories about that slum were a waste of time. No one cared.

"Is that the business you came to talk with me about?" Father Charles asked.

"We have a complication with transport," Herve said, letting his resentment at the priest slip away.

"Complication?"

"We will have to leave at night with the children," Herve said. In past dropoffs, they had made the trip in daytime with just two or three children and little fear of being stopped. But the larger group of children could arouse suspicion. Worse, they would be crossing the DR border as well, which would open them up to international crimes if they were caught.

"What's our solution?"

Herve smiled. He was the planner as always.

"We will need more drivers. And some kind of cover."

The priest laughed. "You talk like a gangster, Herve."

"We don't want to be stopped from doing what we must do, do we?"

"No. But I am sure you will figure something out."

Herve was already hatching a plan. He was excited about it, proud of his own cleverness.

"I will need your cooperation," Herve said.

GRACE WAS ALARMED TO FIND THE COMMUNITY CENTER EMPTY. In the back of her mind, she feared Herve had not driven away but had parked his luxury sedan and would soon be walking in behind her. She hated that some part of her was drawn to his erotic promise—the smell of his skin and hair; his hard, tough, overwhelming desire for her—as if she were under a Vodou spell. Herve's unshakeable confidence confused and frightened her. Most of all, his natural arrogance, the sense of entitlement common to the island elite, made her feel helpless.

Grace stopped next to the dining table, piled with dishes and silverware from dinner the night before. She remembered that the Moisson board members had been scheduled to visit the bakery earlier. Nelson, dear adoring Nelson, would likely have got everyone going even sooner. The short, white-haired lawyer, as huggable as a stuffed teddy bear, radiated enthusiasm. His love for being alive touched everyone, but especially her. He made her feel good about herself, about her choices, whatever they were or would be. He was the doting father she never had.

Grace loved watching his ebullience at the breakfast table, exhorting the others to hurry, reminding them that there was much yet to be done. He inspired and led like a happy pied piper.

But the group had left a mess behind. Dirty plates, caked with dried beans and rice, soiled silverware and coffee cups spread across the table, on the metal folding chairs, and even on the cement floor. As she strolled past the littered table to the bathroom, she picked a few banana peels out of her path.

The bathroom smelled of overuse. It reeked of urine, the new toilet bowl stained and streaked with flushed excrement. The once-gleaming sink was also soiled with a layer of scum, dirt and used soap. Grace sat on the porcelain and relieved herself, glancing at the freshly painted white walls that still smelled sweetly of acrylic.

The potpourri of bathroom scents suddenly transported her to the villa's bathroom in Pétion-Ville. Every morning she was made to scrub the tile floor and the designer toilets after the boys had finally gone to school—the same small academy to which she had once been promised admission. But that had been a lie, a lure to her parents who wouldn't check up on it anyway. How could they? A poor villager could not just walk into an elite school in a wealthy enclave. *Restaveks* were expected to endure. Her fate was to live with another family who could at least feed her.

So, instead of sitting in a classroom, she knelt on the hard floor and anxiously strived to clean the surfaces to a near polish. If she didn't, Grace knew she could expect Madame to grab one of her boys' leather belts and slap her hard on her back like a slave. The belt stung horribly and left swelling that took days to simmer down.

Grace screamed and cried, but the house was empty and her pleas to stop would echo through the large empty rooms of the villa. Madame would pull her hair back like it was a rope and tell her to stop the yelling or she would hit her harder. Sometimes, Madame didn't even need an excuse to beat her. She came to take a kind of pleasure in it.

But it was the boys Grace didn't dare remember. They liked to stick things inside her like she was a doll. She pushed them away, but one would hold her down while the other pushed and pulled and came. Grace had not yet had her first period. She hated the indelible memory of their grins and cackling laughter. They never really left her.

Grace stood up reflexively, flushed the toilet without turning around and stepped over to observe herself closely in the mirror. She didn't know what she hoped to see in the reflection or what difference she might find in herself. But there was no denying she did feel different. It wasn't only her return home that was changing her.

Dean had stirred a feeling in her she didn't think was still possible after all the disappointment in Brooklyn. Men had used her as a plaything, and she rarely protested or resisted. Most were married men or hooked on something and otherwise unavailable. Nothing lasted, which she came to believe was the way of relationships and love. In the end, she felt undeserving of any care and kindness.

Where Dean seemed to see a beautiful confident woman, Grace didn't. Her eyes were set a little too wide apart to be pretty, despite the pleasing shade of blue. Yes, her lush brows were flattering. But her nose was like a white woman's, not the bold, flared nostrils of island beauties. She had never developed the voluptuousness they carried, either. She was boyish in comparison, with small breasts.

She could never forget the ugly scars on her backside, the host family tattooed in her psyche as well. Fortunately, few men she was intimate with asked about it. When they did, she lied and talked about surgery. She came to invent a tale about an accident at the sharp corner of the gunite pool that graced the villa where she had lived as a *restavek*, a pool she had never so much as set a foot in. Only the host family had been allowed.

Grace knew that Dean didn't know or see that twelve-year-old. She guessed that in his soft, adoring eyes, she was regal, witty, a joy to be around. She was no former servant, no meek and subservient worker whose entire life was under the thumb of the wealthy Port au Prince family. She was her own, proud self. Grace herself feared that she would never stop being that household slave, another *restavek* in a country teeming with them.

On good days, she knew she could dress herself to look like a New Yorker, a savvy career girl ready to take on the world. But it was a costume. She knew what Herve did—that she would do as she was told, as all *restaveks* did. She could try to resist, of course. There was free will and the desire to rise up. She could be a female Toussaint, who had led the slave rebellion to liberate Haiti from the French. But she could not fight her own past, the beliefs and habits that had made her.

Grace turned and walked back to the kitchen closet to gather the cleaning supplies. She picked up the plastic bucket, the dime-store mop, the spray bottles of cleaner, the used sponge. As if in a trance, she marched back to the bathroom and began to clean. First the sink. She sprayed it with the white bubbles that swelled like beach foam at the edge of the shore. The smell of ammonia nearly gagged her the moment she rubbed the sponge against the dirty sink. She studied her wet, calloused hand.

Dean had an educated white man's fingers, pale and elegant and somehow earthy and strong. She wanted to hold that hand in hers, feel his warmth and adoration radiate. She could picture it, feel it. She giggled the way a young girl does when she surprises herself. Her laugh was young and full of happy self-mockery. Grace really had gone sweet on him—quickly, as it always happened, at least with her.

She let go of the sponge and rinsed her hands of the detergent. She shook both hands to air dry them as she walked out of the bathroom, through the dining area and out the door. She was walking faster, afraid. Of what, she didn't know. She hardly knew Dean, in fact had just met him. Yet she felt she knew him, and he knew her. Time was relative, both for good and ill.

When she reached the lone tree, Grace shielded her eyes from the sun so she could see further down the road. It was utterly empty. She checked the adjoining hills, and there was no sign of Dean hiking back to the community center. She was impatient for him to return.

Grace liked the flattering light he framed her in, the clean image of a privileged and educated woman. She wanted to see herself that way. Despite her past, she never stopped trying. A Polish soldier and her handsome mother had given birth to a girl with refined, upper-class looks. She had learned to speak well and clearly. Whenever she was charged with picking up the boys at their private school, people were impressed with her diction and the way she carried herself as if she were the mother. But Grace did not share their wealth and privilege. She was a *restavek* always and never seen as anything more.

Grace folded her hands together, almost in prayer, and turned to look in the direction of the bakery. The leashed chicken poked the ground near her feet, chortling dumbly along. She considered setting the animal free and letting it roam. But she knew that chicken was food, and the animal would be scooped up by someone within the hour and rushed to the chopping block for a meal.

Grace decided to walk back to the bakery. There was more work to be done. She didn't want to stay alone at the center and do nothing and certainly no more cleaning.

DEAN ARRIVED OUTSIDE THE COMMUNITY CENTER LOOKING FOR GRACE. Instead, he found the aging, portly lawyer along the road, riding bareback on a grey mule. Nelson wore the usual broad-brimmed straw hat and pilot-style sunglasses that made him look less like a lawyer and more like a party guy on vacation in the tropics. He was a character, a wandering soul as much as a professional. Dean could see the radical student in him, the kid that had marched in protests and been there when racism showed its ugly face in Alabama.

As Nelson ambled closer, Dean noticed the bruised mountains reflected in his mirrored frames. His face was blotched and ruddy from heat. He seemed much older. The mule, too, ambled forward in tired plodding steps. It would have been much faster to walk.

"Where did you find the cab?" Dean asked.

"A loyal friend, once you get the knack," he said. The mule halted alongside Dean. Nelson swung his chubby legs over the sloped back of the animal and slid off. He stood uncertainly, taking a moment to straighten his short legs, traced with delicate maps of varicose veins. He clutched the old rope, preparing to lead his steed to the community center.

"How was Father Charles?"

"He cares for many, many kids," Dean said.

"He does, yes. Very dedicated."

"But Moisson doesn't support it anymore. Why?"

Nelson looked away at his steed whose head hung lower to the ground.

"I need to get my friend some water," he said.

Dean followed Nelson, who now carried an old steel bucket that he dipped into the catch basin. The mule plunged his nose and mouth into the warm, cloudy water.

"Something going on there?" Dean asked.

Nelson pulled off his straw hat and wiped his red forehead with his bare arm. He exhaled loudly.

"You sound more and more like that reporter you say you're not."

"I'm curious."

"Curious. That's all? Well, it's successful," Nelson said. "It's made Charles much loved here."

"No doubt," Dean said.

"Did you see something over there that worried you?" Nelson asked.

"There were the grounds, the children. But nothing else you would expect."

"Like?"

"No visitors, no parents to be, no agencies, no paperwork," Dean said. "No record of the children at all."

Nelson stepped away to lead the mule to a sapling on the side of the cinder block center and tie him up with a fraying hemp rope. He reeked of body odor.

"The orphanage often goes outside the usual channels of adoption," Nelson said. "We weren't comfortable with that after a time."

Nelson took off his straw hat revealing the thinning, silver hair matted to his head. He looked tired, beaten down by the heavy heat.

"You like some water?" Nelson asked. Dean followed him inside the community center. He thought of a staffer at the PR firm and her husband, who had adopted a child from Ethiopia. But it had taken two years, including repeated flights to Africa for visits to an orphanage in the poor countryside. There were sizable fees involved. There was a saga of paperwork and legal agreements. Paper upon paper.

Nelson grabbed two bottles of water from an open carton on the floor of the community center and presented one to Dean. His hands were thick and spotted with brown moles. Tattoos of aging.

"The usual adoption channels are like the roads here; they'll get you there, but it could be longer than you ever dreamed," Nelson said. "Worse, the government expects a bribe, as does the recipient. But even then, no guarantee. When it does happen, it can take years."

"So, this orphanage speeds it up somehow."

"They manage to get around all that corruption, all those delays on both sides of the sea."

"How?" Dean asked.

Nelson smiled wanly.

"Better sometimes not to know everything. Don't you think?"

"No. I don't."

"As I recall, you're here to help with the trees. Do we have the time to worry about how an orphanage works?"

Nelson disappeared inside the barracks. Dean stared after him, acknowledging to himself that the miracle trees needed to be the focus. Time was limited and he wasn't a reporter anymore. He wasn't on the clock to investigate suspect operations. There wasn't likely anything there, anyway.

Dean squinted into the haze that veiled the bare hill. He spotted the shimmering outlines of the bakery. Grace must have gone there to work. He set off toward it, wiping away a new stream of sweat that dripped from his chin. The air made him feel as if someone was holding his throat.

THE BAKERY WAS UNDER CONSTRUCTION. Dean followed the sound of a DJ on the radio chattering from inside the cinderblock walls that formed the core. He walked through a doorless frame, past cutouts for interior windows. A collection of plastic cafe tables was wrapped in packing material and covered in construction dust.

Dean heard movement in the kitchen and prep area. He stooped below the low, stucco ceiling. The sudden coolness made it feel like a basement. Two bare light bulbs dangled from a wire over a stainless-steel table.

"Oh, it's you," Grace said. She wore a new, red scarf that neatly framed her face. It somehow made her look even prettier.

"You and Father Charles seemed to get along famously."

"He's like a father as much as a priest."

Grace smiled at him for the compliment.

"I thought I'd help you with your power problem," he said, laying his hand on the new industrial oven. It was cool to the touch.

"You did say you could fix it," she said, smiling. "Can you?"

"Let me have a look," Dean said. The oven had few obvious moving parts. The controls were behind and below it. He studied the knobs and pipes and connections. He tried to identify each part. When he felt Grace studying him, he stooped down and peered closer so she wouldn't detect his uncertainty.

"You know these things?" she asked, doubtfully.

Dean understood she was teasing him, but it only made him want to impress her more.

"Tell me again when the power went off?"

"When?" Grace looked at him oddly. "I was putting in a new tray of dough and the oven had gone cold. I hit the igniter and it clicked. But no flame. Did it a few times, then more. Nothing."

Dean checked the two propane tanks. One gauge was empty, the other full. He felt her eyes studying him, which he liked.

He got down on one knee and turned off the valve for the empty propane tank. Then he opened the full one. He waited a moment for the gas to enter and then flipped the ignition switch. The gas oven rumbled to life.

"*Gras a dye*," She said, excited. She grabbed both of his arms without thinking.

"You did it."

"Well," Dean said. "The switch was off."

Grace bolted to the long, rectangular oven door. She grabbed the handle and opened to the interior metal shelf. The smell of yeast spilled out. Inside there was a rainbow of ceramic bowls covered with old, worn cloth.

"These are ready."

"Ready?"

"To make bread."

Grace grabbed two of the bowls in each hand and carried them over to the prep table. She scooped a handful of flour from under the table and flung it on the steel table. In the next motion, she spread the chalk white powder to prevent the dough from sticking.

"You're going to make bread right now?" Dean asked.

"No. We are."

Grace had mixed the yeast, water, and flour in each bowl hours earlier and given the dough time to rise. She slipped off the frayed cloth from an egg blue bowl, then used a metal spoon to carefully scrape out a smooth mound of the bread dough. She plopped it on the powdered table.

"Follow what I'm doing?" she asked.

"I'm not a baker," Dean said.

"You will be," Grace said.

The radio was playing an Afro pop tune. The tempo was upbeat and driving, perfect work music. Dean attacked the first bowl and plunged the spoon into the dough. The goo stuck to his spoon.

"You have to flour the spoon and work the edges of the dough in the bowl. Like so."

Her strong hand guided the lip of the spoon around the mound, teasing the dough off the bowl. At the last moment, she used the bowl and spoon to slip the dough effortlessly onto the table.

"Nice trick," Dean said. He followed her instructions and was pleased with himself as the sticky flour came off the bowl.

Next, Grace sprinkled flour on top of the mound and pressed into the flesh-like dough to knead it. She massaged it with ease, her practiced hand tossing more flour on it as it took shape. Dean mimicked her, but his dough fell onto the table like a dead fish.

"Gentle," Grace said. She shaped her dough expertly into a smooth triangle and moved it aside.

"These will end up baguettes?" Dean asked. Grace's square mounds were already lined up in the middle of the table.

"The best *pan* in the district. Actually, the only *pan*."

Together, they emptied the dough out of all the bowls. Grace took a flat, square knife and chopped four even pieces. They were to take each piece and roll it into a longer, log shape, the nucleus of what would become a classic baguette.

"We need to let this rise again," she said.

The rolling went slowly for him. He kept adding too much or too little flour to keep the dough from sticking. They worked silently, and he felt the ease of companionship alongside her. He liked the smell of the yeast and sweat and the dirt floor and Grace, especially Grace.

"Almost," Grace said. She had found a long shallow baking pan and put each rolled log on it, sprinkling all of them again with flour. Dean understood why there were so many bags of flour stacked from the floor to the ceiling along one of the cinderblock walls.

"Time for the oven," she said. Dean opened one of the doors, turning away from the blast of heat. Grace inserted the pans and he closed the oven, liking the teamwork. She turned away and walked toward a sliver of sunlight breaking through a corner gap.

Outside, the humid air was as hot as the oven. The cement shade had shielded them from the white sun. But Grace was relieved and turned her face to the late afternoon sky like a sunbather. Her dark, black hair sprouted from the edges of the cloth that fit tightly around her face like a nun's habit.

"I need to show you the future," Grace said.

Dean followed her up the slight incline, before stopping at a new white slab of cement. A matching cement bench looked out at the brown hills rolling into the distance. Anywhere else, it would be a prized overlook for hordes of tourists anxious for a tour break.

"This is the outdoor cafe," Grace said, excitedly. "There will be trees one day and umbrellas. We will be a destination."

"I can see it," Dean said. He was doubtful, given the poverty, but he wanted to be hopeful for her sake.

The light was waning with the late afternoon sun even as the heat remained dense and relentlessly hot.

"You will have to come back and see," she said, grinning.

The hint of a future intrigued Dean. He was neither looking nor expecting one in the midst of a temporary job in the middle of the Haitian countryside. It seemed, like the possibility of a crowded café in the middle of nowhere, highly unlikely. But the affection lifted his spirits. They shared an interest in each other, and the recognition of it fueled his own.

HERVE LEFT FOR LEOGANE IN A HURRY. He'd almost forgotten what a beauty the skinny bitch had become, those brilliant eyes that missed nothing and those tight, muscular thighs. He wanted Grace again. Maybe something more. He'd been giving thought to some fulltime snatch. But the *blan* was a problem. She was sweet on him. He confused her, making Grace not understand what she wanted, what she needed.

He worried she didn't get white people. They ruled or acted like they did. He remembered those mansions on the canal in Ft. Lauderdale, the way the *blan* saw him and his father when they rented there. They didn't pretend to act as equals. In their eyes, a Haitian who shared the same wealth and education was suspect, even a fraud.

A country of slaves remained slaves no matter how they were dressed up. Herve and his family were assumed to be inferior.

Even when he acted alone in business, with no connections to family or friends, Herve was reluctant to befriend any *blans* at all. His father encouraged him to cultivate at least strategic relationships with white men. But Herve refused to even try. The few *blan* he met were bluebloods, an elite to which he was never granted entry.

Herve liked to think of himself as self-made. He had enjoyed family advantages, yes. But he'd found some success on his own initiative. He was proud of it and he wasn't going to let any *blan* play with it.

Herve kept his car window open to let in the nighttime air. He loved nights like this. Not too hot or cold, the air like a woman's breath on your neck. He kept an apartment in Leogane with a revolving door of available local women. A few colored *gourdes* bought some fine pussy. But he was most looking forward to a dish of Anita's peppery chicken Creole. The sauce was like no other. A double of Kentucky bourbon after, savoring the sweet, syrupy burn down his throat.

There was still work. Herve had a few problems to solve with this deal. But scheming was his strength. He could solve them, the way he did most obstacles. But as he considered his options, he kept seeing that bitch, that beautiful bitch, Grace, racing to get out of his best car. She was just afraid. She wanted him; he was sure. She wanted money, too, for herself and her bakery. What kind of fool moved back to the mountains to bake bread?

Grace, he decided, could be as starry-eyed as those earnest Moisson do-gooders. She could be as foolish and naive as Poppy with his devotion to his religious mission and saving souls. Herve thought it a waste of time and energy. In the end of things, God didn't matter. No one was going to be saved unless they saved themselves.

Herve noticed it was darker than usual on the road. There were no stars. His headlights illuminated the empty road. He heard the sonorous rumble of distant Vodou drumming and wondered if anyone he knew was having a service. No one came to mind. But he was grateful to hear the beat, as familiar as the road to Leogane in the darkness.

He laughed, suddenly, thinking of the *blan* chasing a mulatto from Casales. The whole village teemed with the runts of Polish mercenaries, white Europeans who came to fight against the slave rebellion but ended up joining instead. Their progeny were the whites mutts in the country, for better or worse, mostly worse. The *blan* knew none of this. He followed Grace's pretty, sweet ass like a hound following a bitch in heat. He didn't care that it was obvious to everybody.

A man doesn't do that. You don't go lapping after pussy. The pussy comes to you. It doesn't matter if it's a smart, pretty bitch like Grace. They come. Especially a *restavek*. They are the bottom, the untouchables, if there were a caste here. They know how to serve, to do whatever they are told. She wasn't the first *restavek* he'd had.

Still, something about her made him anxious. He paid her more than he had other women, too. When they had done it in the car, however, he felt different, something he couldn't describe even to himself. There was no denying it. She wasn't like some of the others. But it had floored him when she had walked away like nothing happened. It was special and she knew it. The bitch just wouldn't admit it.

It suddenly occurred to him that Grace could help him with his logistic challenge in getting the kids to the DR. Herve hadn't thought about it before, not really. He clapped his hands together above the steering wheel like a trick. He let the Mercedes swerve, grabbing the wheel a moment before it would have spun out of control. He was good, really good.

Grace and her *blan*. He pictured the loving couple driving beautiful children across the DR border. No one would suspect. It was so simple.

Herve pressed on the accelerator. The Mercedes engine roared, bouncing on the rutted road as it picked up even more speed. He could get Grace on board. Her maternal instincts, always strong, would power her through. The *blan* would follow.

The road smoothed under the truck's wheels, and the dust stopped its angry whipping. He was on a paved road, and a few of the lights in Leogane were visible ahead like fallen stars in the velvet night. He remembered the drink he'd had with that photographer. Herve liked those old cameras. The Moroccan lush loved the aged rum. He drank it like clean water, his speech slurring as the night wore on. Herve stayed sober and alert.

"I find that a girl can be bought for one hundred dollars American," Ali had said.

"Yeah?" Herve said. "I'd say that is pricey here."

"Not a prostitute. A person. A human being."

The photographer took another drink. He didn't even know he was already drunk.

"People say you know what goes on around here," Ali said. "That is why I am here."

"What people?" Herve asked.

"Word on the street is that nothing happens without you knowing about it."

It was true. But there was no way the foreigner could have known. He was using flattery to get something from him.

"Whoever your people are, they give me too much credit."

"So, you do not deny kids are bought and sold here?"

"Most things are for sale," Herve said.

"Even children from an orphanage?" The journalist's voice was clear and resonant.

"What are you saying?"

Herve studied the foreigner, remembering Poppy's story about the man taking pictures, hundreds of pictures. The Moroccan claimed he was creating a portfolio of the *sanguine* and the other young children at the orphanage.

"There is a black market. The product is children, especially teen girls."

"How do you know this?" Herve was genuinely worried.

The photographer ignored the question.

"You must know about it," he said.

"I don't," Herve lied. "But I am not surprised."

He pretended to be indifferent, but he was thinking already about what might need to be done about this whistleblower. He couldn't be allowed to threaten the business. Journalists were too much like mosquitoes. They just needed to be eliminated before they hurt anyone.

"Why do you think I would know about this?" Herve asked.

"I think you do," Ali said.

Herve was impressed by the man's fearlessness. But it was not a good sign.

"I am sorry to disappoint you," Herve said.

The foreigner didn't look satisfied. He nodded curtly.

"I must be going," he announced and stood up, a little unsteadily.

"You are leaving?"

"I must get back to Port au Prince. Thank you."

They shook hands.

"Are you going back to PAP in the night? The roads are not good."

"I have a driver," he said, waving as he disappeared out the door.

Herve felt a tremor of panic. The journalist might have pictures, irrefutable proof if the evidence got in the wrong hands. No court, no law enforcement would see it as anything but trafficking. They wouldn't recognize the greater truth, how the market in homeless kids was not ruthless at all but a means to a better end for all.

Herve was on the verge of making more in one exchange than ever before. He wasn't going to endanger that progress and the future it promised. Like any businessman, he would have to protect his investment. Still, he hesitated. Violence was a last resort.

But he made the cell phone call. He described the photojournalist, the make of the car on the only route back to Port au Prince. It was a dark road. Accidents happened.

Herve hung up and ambled down the wood steps before turning onto the night street. He heard music spilling out of the restaurant as if accompanying the light shining out of the glass window. Herve was hungry and ready to eat. He had a taste for soup and French bread.

But he also had appetite for a woman. He needed one tonight. It would feel good. He wanted Grace. But he knew he would have to wait. Tonight, he would have to make do. He had cell numbers and plenty of cash.

DEAN COULDN'T SLEEP YET AGAIN. He tossed and turned in the humid night, nauseated by the sweet smoke from the mosquito coils. But it was the faint rumble of the drums, beating in the darkness, that got under his skin. He sat up, listening pensively, his anxiety growing. The Vodou percussion was brooding and melancholy. He felt a menace in the persistent pounding as though the drum was portending a terrible force.

He was being superstitious and paranoid, he knew. Yet, he could not escape the sight of Herve standing on the road by the orphanage. He didn't recall the face so much as the fierce focus of his dark eyes. They made Dean feel as if he were seen through a bullseye.

Dean stood up quickly. He was still sweating. The others slept soundly in their bunks. He looked across the room at the bunk where

Grace slept. Her slender foot and ankle were barely visible. She was utterly still, asleep like the others. She was snoring lightly like a sloppy teen.

He walked to the closed door, shut to reduce the mosquitoes, and recalled baking bread with Grace. He revisited the warm intimacy as they worked in silence together, kneading the dough, cutting, and rolling in the flour. The smell of the yeast, of the baking loaves was intoxicating. But mostly he thought of the look and smell of her. Her growing interest in him was clear, a vulnerability that both aroused and frightened him.

Dean opened the door as quietly as he could and stepped out into the heavy darkness. A slight breeze rose up to greet him. The drums beat louder out in the yard, unchecked by the brick walls. Somehow, they felt less threatening in the open. They inspired him to imagine what might be taking place in the distant hills. There could be a ceremony, a vigil dedicated to the unseen spirits. He found he liked the rhythm of the sound, the steady, hypnotic repetition. So many religions offered a similar worship, a technique to break one out of the thinking mind and into the unthinking spirit where all belief dwelled. The Buddhists had their stoic chants, the Christians their vespers, all often sung in the cave-like darkness, lit only by candles. He liked them all because he had always been attracted to the mystery of forces and powers unseen.

Dean remembered being an altar boy. He had worn the vestments over his street clothes, the formal attire he would have worn were he attending Sunday mass. He had learned when and how to ring the brass bells during the liturgy. When and how to kneel, what prayer response was expected. He liked the cloying stink of incense.

Dean hadn't been to church in years. But the ethics of the church stayed with him. The idea that one should love everyone, even one's enemies, like oneself. It was a core belief, as radical now as the day Jesus proclaimed it. So, the priest had been accurate about never leaving the religion of birth. Maybe he had never really stopped being a Catholic.

In the midst of his reverie, the drums suddenly stopped. The roar of night insects rushed in to fill the void.

"Couldn't sleep?" Grace asked from behind him. Surprised, he spun around to face her. Her eyes gleamed in the starlight. Grace had her hand on her slim hip, draped in an oversized shirt, studying him with something more than concern. He looked at her long, dark legs. A faint scent of moringa blossoms wafted off of her like a freshly peeled orange.

"Overtired," Dean managed to say. He felt a rush of excitement, but didn't betray it. Grace sauntered closer until she was just behind him. Out of the corner of his eyes, he caught her studying the night sky. A blanket of sugar granules. He thought he could feel her warmth even though their bodies weren't close to touching.

"No light pollution," he said. "Nothing to hide those stars."

She smiled nervously with her full lips. He stared at them despite himself, wanting to feel them. The crickets played; cicadas buzzed. The brush was still and dark and seemed to breathe in the soft night air.

"I feel at home here," Dean said. He looked up again at the sky, which seemed to vibrate.

"Do you really have one?"

"You know the old song. Home is where the heart is."

Dean turned. Grace was not studying him with curiosity. She wanted what he did. Dean was startled by the sudden change in her and his own quickening desire. He watched her in wonder. Grace was beckoning, opening herself to him. Dean leaned his head toward her, feeling he was crossing much more than the intimate space that separated them. He was flush and eager and wholly absorbed in the moment. He felt the moist shock of her lips on his. He breathed in the orange scent, the faint sour sweat from her damp neck. It was rich and powerful and felt as substantial as her shoulders. They kissed more deeply. Dean felt the heavy night air slip over and around them like a soft blanket.

THE OBSCURE, UNGAINLY TREE BORN IN SOUTHEAST ASIA WAS DISAPPOINTING IN PHOTOS, RESEMBLING AN OVERGROWN WEED MORE THAN A VENERABLE OAK OR MAPLE. The moringa was a runt in this pack of towering trees. But the moringa was a true miracle. The leaves contained as much protein as steak, as many vitamins as any number of green vegetables. The hanging pods, which dangled from the heavy branches like drumsticks, held green beans. The leathery bark from the trunk was a medicine cabinet. Ground to a powder, it was used to treat everything from a sore or infection to epilepsy.

The story of the moringa also had many angles and uses for Dean. The tree was ripe for journalism. It was the country's silver bullet that could heal the environment and stem the massive hunger and poverty in one, perfect shot. Yet no one knew about it. No news organization or even website had reported on the revolutionary tree. He was anxious to change that.

Dean crowded against Grace and Nelson in the back seat of the Range Rover. It was a late model car with leather seats and limo-like legroom.

"Finally," Nelson said.

He made it sound like they were on their way to Oz. Dean thought about the woman sitting alongside him, about the surprising kiss. It was a quiet bond. He could smell the lemon lip balm stick as she was tracing her lips, and he wanted to feel those lips again.

"Do you know this photojournalist wandering around?" Nelson asked.

Dean was startled by the question. He assumed it was Ali after all the descriptions of the stranger.

"He's not with you then?" Nelson asked.

"No. Said he was with Reuters."

"You know he did something extraordinary at the orphanage."

"Extraordinary?"

"He took a portrait of every single child."

"Really. Well, it is his job," Dean said.

"That's the thing. People here don't like to be photographed," said Nelson. "You have to ask permission and, usually, you don't get it."

"Father Charles said he was very persuasive," Grace said.

So he knew about Coluers when Dean had asked him at the hotel. He was likely headed there or back when their paths crossed at the market. Ali had been gruff and evasive. Why would he be so interested in photographing children? He must know or suspect another kind of exchange might be going on at that compound.

The road to the moringa farm was a rolling course of barren hills, one steeper than the next. The rollercoaster ride went on for miles.

Finally, as they descended a low hill, Dean spotted the farm. At first, he dismissed the small plot of six-foot saplings as nothing more than tall, thick weeds. But as they came closer, he spotted the strings staking the fledgling trees to the ground. They grew in planned, even rows. It reminded him of the early, green corn plants that sprouted along the backroads of South Carolina.

"Moringa!" Nelson called. He was grinning as if pointing out a massive forest of mature trees. Dean had imagined miles of majestic thirty-foot miracles. A few hundred weren't going to rescue the vast, denuded country.

Dean pulled himself out of the back seat and waded with the others through the swamp-like heat. The sun was spiteful, its rays pricking their faces like sharp pins. Dean held up one hand to shield his eyes from the glare.

He gravitated to the group until he was part of the semi-circle surrounding a newly-constructed shack. Just inside the open wood door, there were thirty-gallon plastic bags piled high with pale green drumsticks that had been harvested the day before. They looked like piles of overgrown squash.

Dean was distracted by a tall man in dirty trousers. He strutted toward them, sporting the tan, Australian bush hat worn by soldiers.

"*Bonjou, bonjou,*" he called out. "I am Dennis. *Bienvenue.*"

He had an intelligent face and the diffident demeanor of a professor. He pointed to the far end of the dirt plot where men and women in baseball hats and scarves struggled to stake a small tree into the ground.

"That is number 521," Dennis said proudly. There was a murmur of approval among the group. "The family will be one thousand strong before the rainy season."

In just two years, he informed them, the saplings would grow into fifteen-foot moringa, ready to be harvested. The branches would be pruned on some and spur thicker growth. Others would be chopped down entirely to make room for more. It was an agroforest, trees grown speedily like ears of corn.

"Fifteen feet!" Dennis said. "Two years. That's a lot of nutrition per square inch."

Dennis pointed to the small, unremarkable hill in the distance. The base of the hill was dirt brown, then it filled in with green leaves as its canopy rose higher into the white-hot sky. Dean recognized with a start that it was one tree in a small forest, come to life.

"There," Dennis proclaimed. "Just two years."

He let the fact sink in as if it were needed. There was something of a preacher about him.

"You can also begin to *harvest* at two. Cut it down and use it!"

Dennis turned and ducked inside the shack. Dean liked his theatricality. The guide had the unbridled enthusiasm of a young teacher. He reemerged with a small plant in one hand, its tiny leaves just sprouting. In his other large, dark hand was a fistful of lime green pods, spiking in all directions.

"We begin with the leaves. Within a month, this will have many."

Dennis held up the tiny plant with reverence. He described a list of the plant's nutritional value, from high protein through the cornucopia of vitamins. Intelligence and vigor shined through the man's face, the opposite of his mangy appearance.

"The pods are next," Dennis explained. He set the tiny tree on the ground and picked up one of the drumsticks, which was double the size of his hand. He split the coarse skin to reveal round green beans inside.

"You have to be careful when to pick. Too old, they are mush. But when you cook them young, they taste like they look."

Dean remembered them tasting mealy like lima beans. It helped to know they were good for you.

"Some get old and brown," Dennis continued. "That's on purpose."

He explained there was a small, ivory core inside the brown beans. Those tiny cores would be ground up into a powder then dropped in foul water. Like some new age alchemy, they transformed silted river water into clear, potable water.

"The powder acts as a flocculent," Dennis said. "Like aluminum sulfate. It causes a chemical reaction that makes impurities clump together and fall to the bottom of a container."

"And you can drink it safely?" Dean remained incredulous. If true, he could only imagine the gift it would be to so many poor communities who had little or no access to clean drinking water.

"If you boil it," Dennis said. "Clean is relative. The seeds can't rid the water of E. coli and other bacteria. So, it would be better to purify as all drinking water is."

Dean considered that drinking water in New York, piped down from pristine reservoirs in the Catskill Mountains, was still treated with chlorine at the final stages to kill any bacteria that might have hitched a ride.

"Then there is the bark," Dennis announced. He spoke with growing intensity. "It has been a source of natural medicine for three thousand years. Treats everything from infections to wicked sunburns."

Everyone watched, disinterested as if they had heard the sermon before. Dean understood he would have to be selective about what got reported about this project because too much did sound like a boring lecture as it likely would to readers and media consumers, especially online.

Dennis carried one of the small trees in a green plastic pot. He held it out in front of him as the dirt and dust leaked out the bottom. The ground was also chalk dry. It had been days since the rain had fallen and already the sun had sucked up every drop.

As they moved further away from the shack and into the field, Dean discovered far more baby trees than he had expected. There were hundreds. As they approached, he was pleased by a familiar citrus scent, the smell of Grace. Yet it was coming from the miracle trees.

At the end, two boys waited for them, holding a small collection of shovels. They would ceremoniously dig a hole and plant. Nelson was the first to accept a gleaming, new shovel from one of the boys, then he abruptly handed it to Dean.

"I thought you'd want to be first," he said.

Dean took the shovel in his hand and searched for a spot to plunge the curved steel. He smelled the dry dirt. He tried to sink the shovel, but it bounced off the hard-packed ground. He repeated the motion and was able to loosen a few inches.

"What is that smell?" Dean asked.

"Moringa blossoms." Dennis motioned to small, white flowers sprouting on a few thin branches. "The oil from the moringa is used as a base for perfumes in Paris," Dennis continued. "You may know it as ben oil."

They were drenched in their own sweat when the digging and planting were finished. Dennis and one of the workers had brought bottled water and umbrellas for protection from the sun. The group accepted the warm bottles before choosing spots on the ground to sit. The buzz of cicadas floated across the open field, filling the silence. Nothing stirred in the oily heat.

Dean considered the harvesting of these trees. He glanced at the hot landscape, looking for something industrial, a place or facility where the trees were chopped, skinned, and powdered into food and medicine. But there were only more trees, cooking in the sun.

"How do you harvest these trees?" Dean asked.

Dennis took a swig of water. "We cut them down every four months," he said. "The bounty is picked up and taken to Jacmel, a town by the coast."

Jacmel. The jewel city of his friend on the tap-tap.

"It's close?"

"Close by truck. A few hours on the trail," Dennis said.

"You mean walking?"

Dennis laughed. "In Jacmel, the trees are made into food and medicine."

"Processing is by hand," Nelson said. "In a small warehouse."

"Could we drive there?"

"Not today, I'm afraid. We have work at the center."

Dean watched Nelson walk back to his planting area. He was thinking about time, about how little he had if he was going to gather all these facts and return to New York to get the media excited about these trees.

"How long walking?" Dean asked. He decided hiking the footpaths as most locals did would allow him to see the country through their eyes.

"A few hours. Bring plenty of water," Nelson said. A few in the group took a new sip from their water bottles, their white faces blotched with heat.

Dean turned to Dennis, who was watching him with amusement.

"It's a single path?" Dean asked. "Won't easily get lost?"

"More or less. Just head west on that trail." Dennis pointed to a dirt footpath barely visible at the edge of the plantation.

"You're really walking there now? Alone?" Grace asked. She held one hand over her eyebrows as a shield from the white sun.

"I'll see the country," Dean said.

Grace stood up and brushed the dirt off her clothes.

"You're coming?" Dean asked.

"I love Jacmel, and I haven't been for too long."

THE FOOT PATH LED TO THE BASE OF A SHORT, STEEP RISE. A rusted brown shanty perched on its summit, the corrugated tin walls leaning against each other like playing cards. A short, four-foot tree squatted near the worn front door, its thin, oddly delicate branches blossoming with the now familiar moringa blossoms. These gave off a slight lemon odor, more like dish detergent than fresh fruit. Dean wondered why. He still couldn't accept that the miracle tree didn't have some toxic flaw.

"*Alo! Alo*! Francine!" Grace called as they approached.

A petite woman in a soiled nightgown emerged, shuffling on flat brown sandals. Her face was as deeply wrinkled as old bark. Small, chestnut eyes lit up, struggling to focus on Grace's smiling face. She acted as though she didn't even notice the *blan* alongside.

The two women hugged, clinging to one other, their faces inches apart, speaking in Kreyol too rapidly for Dean to fully understand. Women always seemed to seek connection with the same impulse that men kept reserve and distance. He envied that easy, instinctive intimacy.

"*Li te ale nan Port au Prince,"* the old woman said. Someone had gone to Port au Prince.

"*Retounen*?" Grace asked. When does he return?

Francine's thick lips turned downward, and she looked at Dean, acknowledging him for the first time. There was the cloud of cataracts in her eyes, dimming her vision.

"*Ou beau blan*?" she asked coldly. The wrinkles at the corners of her dry lips quivered. She said boys always followed Grace.

"*Zanme*," Grace corrected her with a playful sternness. "He is a friend."

"*Zanmi? Coute au ale?"* Francine asked, her lips spreading into a wide, gap-toothed smile of relief. She looked at Dean differently, with vague curiosity and not concern for Grace.

"We are on our way to Jacmel, Francine." Grace put her arm affectionately around Dean's shoulders. Francine seemed to see them differently.

"*Mange*," Francine said. The old woman reached out and grabbed Grace's free hand. The threesome stood awkwardly for a moment, Grace with her arm slung on Dean, Francine holding her hand as though competing with Dean for Grace's touch.

"*No, merci,* Francine," Grace protested. "We have enough."

"She is like a mom to me," Grace said to Dean.

Francine let go of Grace's hand, and the two women regarded each other—one impossibly old, one near mid-age—and the generations hugged again. The old woman regarded Dean for a moment as though conferring her blessing. Grace smiled in appreciation.

"Laurent is very well," Grace said in parting. "He is happy."

Francine brightened at the information. She acted as if the news of Laurent was what she had been waiting to hear. Suddenly, her eyes clouded further with bright tears. She reached out and found Grace again, holding her differently. The heavy burden of loneliness reflected in her old face.

Grace impulsively took the old woman's wrinkled hand. She looked into her brown, unfocused eyes, offering comfort, empathy. He saw her squeeze the weak, thin hand in goodbye.

The well-trodden trail wound across the hill like a living thing, then slipped through the grass down the side. Dean squinted up at the blanched disc hanging in the cloudless blue sky. There was no escape from it, no reprieve. He touched his cheek. It was like testing a flat griddle.

"Laurent is her son?" Dean asked. He was thinking about the woman's last glance, which seemed to grudgingly accept him. He hadn't thought about how a white man would be received in a small village.

"Her grandson," Grace said.

Dean glanced at her profile. There was something irregular about how her chin hooked down toward her throat. He'd seen it before in an acquaintance who had been in a car accident and busted his chin. He wondered if she had had a similar fate. Or was it from something darker, like a fight. He wanted to know more and more about Grace.

"Laurent lives in Port au Prince?"

"No," Grace said. "Laurent lives at the orphanage."

"The orphanage?" Dean was confused. A boy with a grandparent is not an orphan.

"She could not afford to feed or take care of him," Grace said. "Father Charles can."

Dean knew the poverty was extreme. He understood, intellectually at least, that some were so poor they often went for days without eating. Children starve quickly, and the depravation harms them or even hurries them to a young death. But he didn't understand how some could give up trying, to just push a loved one away and hope for the best, praying someone else would provide.

On the horizon, the bruised, black and blue clouds drifted listlessly over the scowls of the bald peaks. Dean spotted a few dwarf trees sprouting across them like sprigs of hair. He felt as though he were looking at a country of old, weary men.

"You know *restaveks*?" Grace asked, suddenly. "They are children that must be given away, too," she continued.

"Because they are too poor?"

"A young girl becomes a *restavek* when she is given to a wealthy family as a domestic servant," Grace said. Her diction was terse like someone reading from a legal paper. "An exchange. The wealthy family gives this little girl her food, schooling, and shelter in return."

"So, she's a servant. Is that what a *restavek* is?"

"Maybe more than that."

Dean was reminded of the Old Slave Market in the historic area of Charleston. Africans had once been made to stand on tables, naked but for chains, as wealthy buyers evaluated them like livestock, checking for health and bone structure and sometimes checking reproductive parts with gloved hands.

Dean learned about the Old Slave Market on a school trip in elementary school. He'd walked past it many times since, picturing men, women, and even kids his age, standing there waiting to be purchased. He was relieved by the fact that it was early history, no longer allowed in the United States since the late 1800s.

"Parents just hand over kids?"

"Hundreds of thousands."

Dean didn't believe her. If the government allowed it, the international community would not. No donor would tolerate the practice. It was barbarian.

"You don't believe me?" She pinned him with her look of resentment.

"So many? All of Haiti is a million, two million people. One out of five would be servants for the wealthy?"

Grace wiped the sweat from her forehead and squinted at the sun. She swallowed like someone thirsty. Dean watched her closely, suddenly understanding why she was telling him about the child slaves.

"You were a *restavek*."

"Smart boy."

Dean was stunned. He pictured a little girl holding her mother's hand as she walked her to live in a new home. A daughter become slave. Had she even known what was happening?

"I'm sorry," he said after a long pause.

"Me too."

They walked along the dry dirt, clouds from their own footsteps drifting over the grasses.

"How long?"

"You never stop being one."

Dean could only imagine what Grace had been through, a scar that never healed. He was suddenly angry for her, furious at her mother, at the rich family, at the country that would allow it. He had no words.

A century ago, the dogs of poverty had been set loose on this new republic and had been biting and gnawing on that meager bone ever since. The children of slaves coped as best they could, he thought, but nothing breeds nothing. It was the opposite of the rich man's creed that you need money to make it. Here, starting with nothing, you lost more.

FATHER CHARLES DID NOT WANT ANOTHER GRACE. So, he chose the thirteen children for transport based on their ages and genders, not their personalities or looks or anything endearing. He did not want to feel the pain and guilt he'd experienced when once having to choose Grace. But God, Almighty God in his wisdom and compassion, had found a way to forgive his devoted servant and deliver the little girl back, a grown woman full of life and love. It was a miracle.

At dinner, he studied the chosen carefully, wanting to see how each child was responding to their imminent departure. He didn't want them to be upset. They were on their way to a better life, one where a fine meal wasn't measured by the ratio between rice and brown sauce. Real sustenance. Each and every child would, hopefully, soon be with a loving, stable family in New York or Florida, going to school, learning English, inventing themselves and a future that was unimaginable in little Coluers.

"Poppa," Tamara called and put her tiny, bird-thin fingers on his thick arm. He winced in surprise. The priest had not seen or heard her approach.

"Why are you so sad?" she asked, her big eyes round and adoring. Even at her age, Jeanne had an instinctive empathy, the soul of a helper.

"I am not sad, Tamara. I am tired," he said, proving it with a tired smile.

"You're lying."

Father Charles wasn't pleased. He was reminded of her arrogant willfulness and, at that moment, he didn't much like her. He regretted he had not chosen Tamara above the others. But then he couldn't bear the thought. She was special.

"Why do you think I do not tell you the truth?"

"You are sad and tired, Poppa," she said, certain of her analysis.

Father Charles laughed in spite of himself.

"Because, Poppa," she continued. "You worry too much. *Pa enkyete w!*"

"Go along and *manje*," Father Charles said, shooing her away with his hands. He stood up as she skipped away. He needed a walk. He was also hungry, but he couldn't face the beans tonight after the fine meal in Pétion-Ville. He strolled out of the eating room, deciding he should head over to the community center. He could eat and talk with Grace if he were lucky.

Herve marched along the path in the woods like a man on a mission. His long, familiar face and furrowed brows were set with the seriousness of purpose. Father Charles knew the look too well. He'd seen it when Herve lost a soccer game, when he was ignored, when things didn't go the way he wanted them to go.

"You remember I told you we need two drivers for our journey to the DR. Best if they are foreigners."

"Why is that?"

"Cover."

"Cover from whom? It is a difficult journey, Herve. And dangerous."

"Dangerous?" Herve shook his head. "No. We must have drivers that pose no threat at the border."

"You have already a solution, it seems," the priest said.

Herve smiled at his partner, naming the prospective drivers simply with his expression.

"You are kidding," Father Charles said, but he also grasped the shrewdness of Herve's choice. They would be trusted far sooner than any Haitian crossing the Dominican border. Most of the guards looked down at those wanting to cross over for low-paying jobs. Some hated them. They were no better than chattel.

"Grace won't do it," Father Charles said.

"I wouldn't be so sure."

Father Charles didn't like even the possibility that Grace would be placed in harm's way.

"What if I won't allow it?" Father Charles said, issuing his own threat.

"Then you raise the money for all this," Herve said. He pointed to the orphanage. There were half-finished frames of new housing, the machinery being used to build a septic tank, the first of its kind in Coluers.

"You want to watch this all die?"

"There are thirteen children who would not mourn," the priest said.

Father Charles wanted to be done with the exchange. He wished he could call this the end. He was bothered by the business of the children, of what it had become. It was escalating, getting too big, going out of control. The pending deal involved more of his children than ever. He should never have agreed.

Yet, he regretted that this business was the most likely route to realize his mission, however flawed. The good end blesses the means. God is reached sometimes through thorny paths.

"Grace might agree if I ask," Father Charles said. She was indebted to him.

"Yessir, and the *blan* will follow her ass anywhere."

"But he has no passport, Herve. It was stolen in PAP."

"How do you know?"

"He told me."

Herve nodded, looking off at the rolling mountains.

"No passport," his partner repeated, smiling. He seemed very pleased.

"He can't travel across the border," Father Charles added.

"We'll see," Herve said.

DEAN STOPPED AT THE EDGE OF THE PRECIPICE, SPELLBOUND BY THE SIGHT OF THE GREEN AND BLUE SEA IN FRONT OF HIM. The calm water shimmered like colored glass under an equally still, cloudless sky. His eyes were inevitably drawn to the blue horizon and the sprawling reach of the ocean. He took a short breath of the thick, briny air that smelled faintly sour.

There was a field of trash strewn along the water's edge which immediately disappointed him. Somehow, he had expected the seaside town to be pristine. But it had as much beach litter as the Rockaways in Queens.

"We made it," Grace said, coming alongside him. They stood close to one another, clothed in heavy perspiration from the long hike. An ease and comfort settled over them. Dean could not remember feeling so content in the company of anyone.

"Where is the processing place?" he asked. Gentle waves rolled in close to the sandy shore and bubbled up into a frothy white foam.

Grace pointed to another cliff, this one sprouting palm trees and a jumble of brightly painted bungalows with commanding ocean views. They wouldn't have been out of place on St. Bart's, he thought. It was easier to ignore the pollution than he thought.

Together, they scrambled down the steep path that began just below the ledge. A lizard darted past his foot and ducked into the nearest rock. There were small clumps of sage dug into the dry soil. It was desert-like.

Plastic containers and shards of trash were strewn like gravel along the shore. They kept walking until they were through the dense field of trash and stood on clean, white sand. Dean took off his shoes and kicked them to the side. He pulled off his wet socks and tossed them further along the sand so they might dry in the hot sun. Then he stepped into the warm water, one eye peeled for glass or anything that might cut his foot.

Grace watched him with amusement. He hadn't bothered to roll up his chinos, so the cuffs were already soaked.

"Feel good?" she asked.

Dean didn't answer. He peeled off his shirt and unhooked his brown leather belt and slid it out of the wide loops. He slid out of his pants, shook them and set these, his only pair of pants, next to some plastic cartons.

"Don't mind me," Grace said and laughed.

"I won't."

Dean walked further into the water and turned to face her.

"Join me?"

"You just jump right into everything, don't you?"

Dean laughed and dove into the water. He let out a small grunt of joy as he surfaced, the long, hot trail they had hiked momentarily swept from his sore legs.

He was surprised to see Grace hesitant, wary about entering the water as if it might somehow bring harm.

Dean flipped onto his back like a seal, floating on the gentle water. He wondered if the water was clean. It didn't look polluted. He started a backstroke, his eyes still on Grace.

Dean was pleased to see her finally slip off her shirt, then shorts, and she tossed the clothing behind her in the sand and trash. Grace splashed into the sea behind him and disappeared.

He was treading water when she surfaced. Her eyes were closed; her wet, jet black hair plastered next to her cheeks in a way that made her seem much younger, an awkward teen, the angular tomboy she claimed she had been. His attention lingered on the mature curve of her wet lips. When her eyes opened, as if from sleep, she was looking at him, reflecting the shimmering hue that surrounded them.

They moved closer, drawn effortlessly like a current. He was aware of her wet lashes, her fine nose that trembled almost imperceptibly, the last streaks of water rolling over her high cheekbones and, finally, the sweet anticipation. He felt her attention on his lips followed by a look that somehow communicated he should act.

Dean pressed his lips to hers and felt the thrill rush through him, wanting more. He kissed her more fully, feeling the easy fit of both her lips and her small breasts, which had drifted just below his, coaxed gently together by the sea. He pulled her closer, kissing more aggressively. They paused.

"I think that has been on my mind since we met." Dean studied her, unable to suppress a smile.

"We think alike, I suppose."

They kissed again, longer this time, finding an easy intimacy. It was rare and precious.

When they returned to shore, Dean spotted the white blouse discarded in the trash and sand. He bent down to pick it up.

"Let me get it," she said with an odd urgency.

"I can't look at how gorgeous you are?" he teased.

"I'm an old-fashioned girl."

It was a transparent lie. But he walked past the blouse and faced away, toward the rugged cliffs, to grant her privacy. He heard her light steps on the sand.

When she stooped to pick up her shirt, Dean stole a sidelong glance. He was hungry for a glimpse of her bare, exposed body. He was shocked to see long, mottled scars that protruded from her shoulder to the middle of her back. They were molded like squid tentacles.

Grace quickly slipped on her blouse to cover the scars. Dean decided to act as though he hadn't seen them. It was clear she had not wanted him to see.

"I could stay here all day," Dean said, breezily.

Grace drew her wet hair behind her long neck. She glanced down demurely at the sand as she seemed to conjure a small hair band out of thin air and expertly cinch her black hair. Seawater slipped down her regal, brown shoulders, sliding to the small of her back. Framed by the Caribbean sky and sea, she looked both glamorous and vulnerable.

His mind drifted back to the thick, dark scar like a passing cloud. He was very curious as to what he had really seen on her back. Did he see a birth defect? The wound from an accident? Or was it, he feared, the mark of a *restavek*? A slave.

"Off to town?" Grace asked. She stepped forward, her composure intact.

THE BOULEVARD WAS LINED WITH OLD FRENCH COLONIAL BUILDINGS AND CEMENT STOREFRONTS, MOST WORN AND CHIPPED LIKE OLD POTTERY. Scooters and motorbikes buzzed past as Dean and Grace walked by parked cars on their way to a group of palm trees near the top of the hill. Humid, briny air rose up from the harbor below. Dean was dripping sweat from his chin. He stopped for a moment and stared at the blue and green sea in the distance, sparkling with white sunlight.

"*Mwen renmen li.*" Grace smiled, stopping alongside him.

Dean didn't love it. Not yet. The heat had become oppressive, bearing down like a bully.

"Is the warehouse very far?" Dean asked. He tried to wipe away the sweat spilling over his eyebrows. But his forearm and hand were dripping with perspiration, too, and he only managed to sting his eyes with the salty sweat. Only minutes ago, he'd been in the cool water of the sea. Now, even in the shade, it must have been ninety degrees.

"We can get a taxi," Grace suggested, studying his pale, wet face.

"I'm fine," he said, managing a faint, insincere smile.

"I can see," Grace said, laughing gently with affection. He admired her eyes, as deep and hypnotic as the sea down below. Her sleek nose and chin gleamed with promise. She seemed younger, and he thought he glimpsed the young girl in her, slyly observing the world unfolding around her.

The warehouse, as everyone called it, was about the size of the community center back in Coluers. The walls were cinderblock as well. But the roof was a plastic tarp, tied at the ends with worn rope. Dean followed Grace further inside the open door. Some of the workers glanced up from their work, dark eyes peering over white cloth face masks like they were in a hospital.

A huge tub of moringa leaves commanded the middle of the floor. Hundreds, maybe thousands, of green moringa leaves soaked inside. A long table against the wall was fitted with mesh nets, the sun finding them like a spotlight, where a woman in a cotton white doctor's gown was dumping handfuls of the wet leaves and spreading them out to dry. A gap in the tarp allowed the sun to virtually cook them dry.

Grace appeared, her arm entwined with a teen boy in a new, crisp Baltimore Orioles baseball cap. He looked smart and serious beyond his years.

"Andre," Grace said with an easy affection. "This is his place. He's happy to show you around."

There wasn't much space to cover. In addition to the tub and drying tables, there was a metal sink in the corner and an assortment of plastic cafe tables where more people in white masks pounded the dried green leaves with mortars and pestles into something resembling pesto.

“You see how clean we must keep it here?” Andre said. He looked at the spotless cement floor with pride. “Very important that no mold grows or bacteria. It would ruin all the moringa leaves and seeds. We would have to dispose of them.”

“You could probably do surgery in here,” Dean said. He considered what element of the production might be the most difficult to get in Haiti. He thought of those water bottles sold as clean on the street.

“Where does your water come from? Is it shipped in?”

Andre shook his head and led them to the corner sink. There were dry brown pods from the tree. Some had split like chestnuts to reveal a white core. He took an empty stone mortar and pestle and handed them to Dean.

“If you would be so kind,” Andre said. Grace laughed at Dean’s stoic reaction.

Andre cracked open a few of the nuts and dropped white seeds into Dean’s mortar. The seeds broke instantly under the press of his heavy pestle. Dean pressed them harder into the stone as he’d seen the workers do. Before long, the moringa seeds became a chalky powder.

Andre took a plastic water bottle filled with clear water and spooned the powder inside.

“This is clean water,” he said, shaking the powder until it dissolved into tiny dots and flakes in the water. Then he knelt down next to a ten-gallon water cooler, worn and nicked from heavy use.

“This is water from a stream where some wash their clothes.”

The water was brown and cloudy with silt and pollutants. He emptied the bottle into the cooler and covered it with a coarse piece of canvas.

“Now the magic happens,” Andre said with a grin. “Next time you take a look it will be as clear as the water at the waterfalls.”

Dean was skeptical. He followed Andre out into the heavy, hot air outside. Andre led him across an alley to another warehouse, this one all brick and locked as securely as a bank. Inside were the moringa products ready to ship. Andre unlocked the metal door and flicked on the bare ceiling bulb that illuminated stacks of plastic bottles. There was moringa powder, ben oil, dried leaves.

"Some will go to Whole Foods," Andre said. "We have a new contract."

The upscale supermarket, catering to urban sophisticates, hardly seemed like a good showplace for moringa. But it meant money to pour back into the business.

"How about here?" Dean asked. "Do people here get anything?"

"Of course,"Andre said. "I heard you enjoyed the food yourself."

Dean believed the lure of profit corrupted even the best intentions. A business created to feed the people and better their lives could be threatened by the quest to profit from it. Money gleamed like the most prized gold, luring the best for its own sake.

"Speaking of food," Grace said. "Maybe a little meal is possible–if you are finished here."

An old woman, her skin pocked like charcoal, arrived at the table. She regarded them with affection like she was thrilled to serve a happy couple. She handed out the menus like precious documents.

As she walked away, Dean remembered he had no cash or card, no way to pay for their lunch, the sumptuous one of wine and seafood Grace had described.

"Something wrong?" Grace asked. She easily read the anxiety in his face and manner.

Dean had never been without money. Carrying cash and credit cards was as habitual to Dean as clothes. He wasn't wealthy, but he also had never been in serious need. He always had means. The fact that he didn't at this moment bewildered him.

"Thinking about the miracle business," Dean said.

"You're lying," she teased.

Dean smiled with his lips. He considered suggesting they leave. But he decided to buy time, let the meal progress until he came up with a solution. What did people do in a situation where they had nothing? They looked to trees for miracles.

"I am reminded of that boy in the orphanage," Dean said.

"The boy?"

"The grandson who was sent there to have something to eat."

"They had no choice. But it was a gift that the orphanage and Father Charles welcomed him. Yes?"

Dean nodded without enthusiasm. All the suspicious details at the orphanage roared back into his mind—the lack of paperwork, the secrecy, the absence of clear foster parents. There was something more going on than the care of children. A business maybe. He thought of his meeting with Herve.

"Your friend funds the orphanage?" Dean asked coolly.

"My friend? You are speaking of Herve?"

"Yes. Herve."

"I've known my friend since Brooklyn. As much as anyone knows him."

Grace said she had met Herve in Brooklyn at a fundraiser in Park Slope, an event that doubled as a recruiting party for Harvest. She was a bank teller longing to find direction.

"You and he?" Dean asked. His envy of Herve was like a wound he couldn't help poking, checking to see the depth of the injury.

"Jealous?" Grace asked. She seemed pleased.

"You needn't be. Herve doesn't love women, he collects them."

Dean was startled by her bitterness. But he thought there was more than a hint of attraction embedded in the anger, as though Herve had spurned her, dumped her for another woman.

"Women likely come easy to him," Dean said.

"He buys them, Dean."

"Prostitutes?"

"No, *mennaj*. Girlfriends."

Grace nodded, looking down at the wooden table. She seemed agitated and angry.

The old woman came to the table with two settings bundled in paper napkins. She set them down without a word or even a glance. Then she left, her eyes downcast as if she sensed the tension in the air.

"Where does Herve get his money?" Dean asked.

"He's a boy from the Bambam," Grace said.

"Bambam?"

"One of the elite families. Six control most of the country. We call them Bambam after the letters of their last names."

"His last name is Frenoy, right?"

"He changed it. Came from the name of one of the family's servants. He didn't want people to know he was from one of the elite families."

"Why would that matter?" Dean asked.

"You mean who cares? Herve does. He wants to be a self-made success. He's spent a lifetime trying to impress his old man who doesn't care. Herve doesn't really think a lot of himself. He's insecure."

"Fooled me."

The old woman reappeared with a flourish. She carried two thick white plates piled with red hot lobsters split in half with browned plantains piled alongside, smelling strongly of vegetable oil and spice. Steam rose faintly off the hard shells.

"Did we order this?" Dean asked, surprised.

The old woman stepped back, admiring both her two plates of food as well as Grace's pleased reaction. Grace thanked the woman before she wished them *bon appetite* and left. Dean watched the lady walk away, wishing he had just told the truth about not having money. This meal was not going to be cheap.

Dean picked up the fork and knife, the smudged utensils wrapped in a single paper napkin. He tried a piece of plantain, grateful to taste the warm, filling food. They ate in silence for a short time, breaking off the spindly legs of the lobsters and cutting chunks of the firm flesh from each small tail.

Dean watched Grace eat for a moment. She sawed away a bite-sized morsel of lobster meat with deep concentration before setting the knife neatly on the side of her plate. She picked up her fork, stabbed the meat, and brought it to her smooth lips, opening them just wide enough to slip the lobster inside her mouth. She remained careful, even dainty, like women in Manhattan accustomed to fine dining and manners.

At the last moment, she glanced up at him.

"Her husband catches the lobster," Grace said after she had swallowed.

Of course, they would have come from local waters. Dean pictured the trashed beach, the casual pollution. Grace was watching him.

"It won't get you sick."

Dean noticed the old woman was standing just behind them. She took a lull in their conversation as an opportunity. She slipped in front, shyly, to ask about the meal.

Grace answered for them, glancing at Dean for affirmation and agreement in a way that couples did. Her appreciation and words made him feel closer to her, as if they really were a couple. The old woman suddenly grabbed his arm and hand in a gesture of thanks and connection. Dean was still not used to this directness. He felt a measure of guilt rise up in him, too. He was going to have to tell her that he would return later with money and a little extra for her waiting for it.

After the woman left, Dean folded his hands together and faced Grace. He was surprised how nervous he felt.

"You know I got robbed on the way from the airport," Dean said.

"You have no money?" Grace seemed amused.

"Broke," Dean said, pretending he wasn't embarrassed. He pulled on his dirty shirt, still damp from the ocean and sprinkled with sand. He made a show of smelling it. "These are the same clothes I've had on since I landed."

"I believe it. I can smell them." Grace stood up, ready to leave.

"You're leaving?"

"I'll be back. I want to have a word."

Grace seemed to be gone for a long time. Dean leaned back in his chair and took a sip of the warm white wine. The Chablis tasted slightly sour. He looked down the steep hill at the sea and cement wharf below. There were a few tourists strolling around makeshift booths where artists sold their wares. He'd noticed the candy-colored paintings, wood carvings, and tin sculptures on the way up. "Naive" art was big in New York. There were articles and posters about homegrown artists without formal training taking on High Art. The simplicity had become a virtue, the rough technique a sign of authenticity. Poverty and lack of training had become virtues for the painters.

He felt Grace's hands resting on his shoulders. She was facing the sea as well. He closed his eyes. Her touch was light and easy. A brine-scented breeze brushed his hair and cheeks.

"What are you staring at?" she asked.

"I was thinking about the art on the wharf. It's worth a lot in the city these days."

"I know. Hollywood moguls and Wall Street are snapping them up."

"Ironic," Dean said.

"Maybe. But it's a great thing. Haitian art deserves to be collected."

"Are we getting arrested?"

"Not yet. We can get the money for lunch to her later."

"Later when?"

Dean was planning to leave Haiti in a day or two.

"Right," Grace said, coolly. "You're on a deadline. Let's go see the art."

Their arms bumped into one another as Dean moved toward the street. Neither of them uttered another word. Dean took Grace's hand. It was light but muscular and fit together well with his. Her skin and warmth felt like an embrace. They started down the long hill toward the harbor.

SMALL, PLYWOOD STUDIOS WERE SCATTERED ON THE CEMENT WHARF LIKE A CAMPGROUND. The bright-colored folk paintings were everywhere. Grace adored them, more so since she had left the country. She had always kept a few prints tacked to her wall in New York as mementos from home. As they wandered past the huts, she noticed a barefoot artist lounging on a director's chair. New oil paintings hung from a line behind him as they dried like caught fish, dangling in the fierce sun.

"Jerome?" Dean asked.

"My friend!" Jerome jumped out of his chair and came over to Dean, taking his hand and arm, then hugging him like a long-lost brother.

"You have come to the jewel. I am so happy."

"You know one another?" Grace asked.

"We met on the tap-tap," Dean said. "Without him. I would never have gotten a seat."

Jerome smiled. "I see now there is a jewel with you."

Grace smiled wanly and looked away from Jerome at the portrait behind him. It was an elderly couple holding hands. In the background were an old wooden house, a few palm trees, the suggestion of a long-shared past. The figures were cartoon-like but also moving. The weight of age fell on their sagging shoulders just as a tired happiness showed on their long chestnut faces and wise, if tired, eyes.

"That is Old Love," Jerome said.

"Yours?" Dean asked.

"Is there such a thing?" Grace asked. "Old love."

Grace studied the shimmering painting, her eyes squinting at the details. There was no child or grandchild in the picture. Only landscape. Why no children? No daughter? Had she been given away, too?

"Love never gets old, yes?" Jerome said, smiling as if he had made a joke.

"This couple you painted is known to you?" Grace asked.

"Very good. Yes. My aunt and uncle. You are observant."

The old woman in the picture stirred the faint memory of her own mother. She was thicker, her features rounder.

"You are from Casale, yes?" Jerome asked, noting her green eyes, common only in that village.

Grace grimaced as if he had mentioned a place she would rather forget. The morning her father had taken her to the capital, her mother was crying, but wouldn't hug her or say goodbye. It was to be a brief trip.

"Not everyone there is a descendent," Grace said. "I've always wanted brown eyes."

"What on earth for?"

"To look like my mother."

Colors denoted class on the island for many. The darker the color, the more authentic. A lighter color was mixed, mulatto, half-breed, a mongrel. She longed to be dark, black, and proud. Grace felt always apart through no fault of her own but of breeding, then poverty. You are what you are born.

There was an awkward silence as the pleasantries stopped.

"It was good running into you, Jerome," Dean said. "Didn't think I'd see you again."

"I am not surprised," Jerome said somberly, like a mystic suggesting it was in the stars. "And at an opportune moment."

But Jerome needed a favor. He had an errand to run in another part of town. A hotel owner who had purchased art in the past wanted to meet with him about a new commission. Money. But he could not leave his work unattended, and he did not have the time to pack everything away in his hut to lock up. He had been pining for a solution when they had appeared like a heavenly gift.

The house was the size of a large shed. Grace saw rolled-up canvases through the single, stationary window as well as art material in one corner, a foam mattress in the other. Although there was no plumbing or cooking stove, Grace guessed that this simple, plywood shed might also be his home.

"Would you mind?" Jerome insisted, looking at Dean, not her. "I trust you. I won't be long, and you can enjoy a break here, yes? There is water inside. And ganga if you like."

"How long is long?" Dean asked.

"Thank you, thank you," Jerome said and hugged Dean. He bowed like a southern gentleman at Grace. "Less than an hour."

Inside the hut it was warm, the sunlight blasting through the single window, really just a pane of glass fitted into a cutout in the wall. The room smelled of oil paint and ripe oranges. There was a small tray of fruit next to the bed in a homemade ceramic bowl. There were yellow-green mangoes and ripe bananas, in addition to the oranges. Grace stooped down and picked up a small, plump mandarin orange. She brought the mottled skin to her nose and smelled the fruit, closing her eyes for a moment to focus all attention on the sweet scent. It had been her favorite fruit as a young girl, and she still treasured it. They were plentiful when she was growing up, and she remembered the roughhewn wood bowl where they were left out for all to enjoy.

Grace tore the skin off the mandarin, filling the humid air with the citrus sweetness. She smiled and handed Dean a tender wedge and took another for herself. She slipped it whole into her mouth, bit into the soft flesh, and felt the syrupy burst of flavor.

"I've never seen anyone enjoy an orange that much," Dean said.

"Mandarin," she corrected him. "For a long time, Haitian mandarins were used to make Cointreau."

"The French aperitif," Dean said. She felt his eyes linger on her wet lips. She wanted to feel his lips on hers again. It had thrilled her to feel his desire and how it awakened her own.

"He is a very good artist," Grace said.

"They call it Naïve art in some places," Dean said. "No training. Self-taught."

"Naïve? Funny. Art is art, no?" The label sounded condescending to her.

"There's an entire museum devoted to unschooled artists now."

"A segregated museum."

"Not by race," Dean said.

"By what then?"

"Formal skill, not talent. No one taught them, but they managed to make something special. It's raw."

They moved together toward the canvases alongside the wall until they were alongside the mattress on the floor. She noticed the foam mattress was clean, a white sheet stretched tight across it like a taut sail. She caught Dean's eye, who also studied the foam mattress.

"You like art?" she asked.

"I love it," Dean said.

Grace nodded, then slowly extended her arm to him. Dean met her eyes and took her hand into his. She felt a charge go through her and let him pull her toward him. Her lips found his, and they slid down to the mattress.

The sultry air was sweet with the sea and fruit. She liked the feel of his hand, gentle but strong like he was. She felt comfortable and safe. She was anticipating his hands on her, unbuttoning her shirt, sliding off her clothes. She longed to be held and loved by him. He made her feel special.

The mattress was just big enough for the two of them. She had liked kissing him and the warm tingle that traveled up her thigh.

She let him pull her into his arms. Her lips were waiting when he found them. The kiss was fuller, more sensual than any before. She found his tongue and teased it with the tip of her own. He squeezed her body tighter against his. He savored her body as something precious and rare. She had little experience being treated so gently. The surprise of it pushed her outside of herself and the moment. She waited, fully expecting it to turn into the harsh groping of the men she knew, men who treated her as she feared she might deserve. She never stopped remembering what she had been, forever was. But Dean's gentleness calmed her, slowly peeling away her doubt and fear. Grace opened to him. She was stirred with wonder and desire.

But her old self weighed on her. She feared exposing herself to him. The scar was as recognizable as a brand. She was always so careful to keep it a secret. But as she emerged fully naked, she felt a twinge of another, old teen fear. She had always been disappointed in her smallish breasts, feminine but not quite as ample or womanly as those she had grown up around. She was too thin, too bony, without the soft, fleshy hips and stomachs of the beautiful lush women in the countryside.

As his warm, supple hands slid from the small of her back toward her shoulders, Grace froze. He was about to feel the mark, what she had been so careful to conceal on the beach and in the sea. It was too late. She wanted him.

"Is it still painful?" Dean whispered, his fingers light as silk on her scars. She didn't want to talk about or acknowledge it. Better to forget.

"It's a scar," Grace said.

"Someone did this to you," Dean said. "Why?"

"Because I forgot. Because I was late."

"Late?"

Dean stopped in surprise, leaning back to look at her.

"The Madame. I was late to chore. I was hungry and ate what the boys left behind."

"So she whipped you like an animal?" Dean asked.

"The end of an extension cord."

Grace trembled, suddenly, and was angry with herself. The days of a *restavek* should be behind her. But the Madame's hate-filled eyes glowered anew at her, the hot, violent, ugly temper. So many times, Grace had watched the disgust fill the woman's face before the violence came.

"Many times," Dean said, feeling the length and breadth of the scar on her back. "To a child, a young girl."

Grace made a noise somewhere between a laugh and a snort.

"I'm sorry," Dean said, watching her eyes well up. Grace bit the side of her lip and nodded. Dean pulled her against his bare chest and wrapped his arm around her. She felt safe. Valued.

Grace was shocked that his tenderness coaxed her to recall Herve. She remembered Herve's strong thick hands on her, his burly arms yanking her to him like she was as light and pliable as a doll. His hunger for her was wild and powerful, and she felt intoxicated. When he thrust himself inside her, she winced from the pain but squeezed his taut torso with a pleasure that made her feel like a whore. The harder he thrust himself, focused only on his own pleasure, the more she wanted it and, oddly, felt she deserved it. She was just another bitch. She had always given whatever was ordered.

"I am sorry," Dean said snapping her out of her reverie. "No one should have to go through that, to be treated like someone's slave."

Her quiet excitement for him had vanished like a passing breeze. She stared at his kind brown eyes, which only made her push away.

She rolled out of his arms and to the side of the mattress. She wanted to be alone. She closed her eyes, willing herself not to cry. She believed she was being foolish. There was no reason to be angry or resentful of Dean. She turned back to him, still confused, and touched his intelligent face with her fingers, and was relieved to feel her tenderness and attraction to him return.

HERVE WAS WAITING IMPATIENTLY FOR THEIR RETURN. He slouched alongside an empty table in the late afternoon darkness of the dining room. He wasn't accustomed to waiting for anyone. But he was desperate. The shipment had to go through if he was going to grow the business the way he wanted. He brightened when he spotted Grace, ignoring the *blan* standing beside her. Herve guessed he'd had her. It was evident in his calm air of possessiveness. Grace pulled her hair back with both hands.

"I was told you'd gone to Jacmel," Herve said. A sly, sardonic smile creased his dark face for an instant as if he were mocking them both.

"You were well informed," Grace said and smiled back at him.

"I want to talk to you, baby," Herve said.

Grace raised her dark, delicate eyebrows.

"Talk."

Herve started as if he'd been slapped. He recovered quickly and smiled wanly, pretending calm. He felt the *blan* watching him intently, but he ignored that displeasure as well. He told himself it didn't matter that the American had gotten Grace. What mattered was the business.

"The orphanage needs your help," he said. Herve explained that there had been a delay in transporting the children to the Dominican Republic because the original drivers had backed out.

"Why the Dominican Republic?" Dean asked, suspicious.

He made a face Herve hated because it assumed Herve had to defend or justify himself. But Herve ignored his irritation.

"Flights out of the DR are cheaper," Herve said.

"But you have to cross a border. Isn't that a problem when transporting children?"

"I don't drive," Grace said, which was true.

"He drives," Herve said, indicating Dean.

"Maybe you should ask him?" Grace said.

Herve met the *blan*'s narrowed eyes for the first time. There was no love lost between them.

"We need your help. Without drivers, the kids go by boat."

"You're not going to do that," Grace said.

The daily supply boat was dangerous for passengers. The old skiff was routinely overloaded with nonpaying passengers, and drownings at sea were routine, if they were even reported at all. It was travel at your own risk.

"If I have no choice," Herve said. "I go by water. The children must go."

"You are serious." Grace said.

"Gotta get those darlings to their new homes and families," he said. "That means the airport at Pedernales. Tomorrow."

"Father Charles will not allow it," Grace said.

"Poppy has no choice, either," Herve said. "They must get over the border if they want to have their new families."

"You don't have the right," Grace said. "These are children's lives, not cargo to move. They aren't currency either, as much as you worship that."

Herve pursed his lips into almost a kiss, staring at her. He turned away and shuffled toward his waiting Mercedes.

"I know how to drive," Grace called after him. "Just no license."

Herve smirked, but his plan was unfolding better than he hoped.

"Since when do you know how to drive?" Herve asked.

"In Brooklyn," she said and folded her arms. "What do you care?"

"The children," Herve said. "Their safety, baby."

"I'll drive," Dean said. He and Grace looked at one another with a kind of understanding that many old couples did.

Herve slipped inside the Mercedes. He started the engine, and a puff of black diesel smoke blew out of the tailpipe. The sour smell was sickening in the dense heat.

"Wheels up at five," Herve said and closed the door.

Grace came alongside Dean as the Mercedes pulled away. They watched the dust cloud spew behind as the sedan rolled along the dirt road toward the lone strip of blacktop.

"Thank you," Grace said softly. She took his hand and led him back toward the community center. "I know you hate him."

"We could be accomplices, you realize," Dean said.

"To what crime? Helping children?" Grace said. "I'm fine with that."

"I hope that's what we are doing," Dean said. "I hope."

DEAN STRUGGLED TO KEEP THE OLD VAN UNDER CONTROL, CHASING THE MERCEDES' TAILLIGHTS IN THE DEEP DARKNESS. They bounced along the dirt road, kicking up dust that looked like dirty snow in his high beams. Dean squinted through the swirling cloud of dirt and white light, now frightened for himself for volunteering. Seven of the thirteen children were crammed into his van.

Dean understood he was knowingly digging himself deeper into a hole with no easy escape. There was nothing to prevent others from seeing him as a trafficker—if that was what the orphanage was doing, and he was nearly certain it was. Now, for better or worse, he was part of the operation.

The girls were sound asleep in the rows behind him. Kids adapted to anything. The prospect of change, of difficulty, didn't terrify them the way it did many adults. Grace's head rested against his shoulder, riding even the jarring twists and turns of the road. Somehow, she too appeared to have fallen peacefully asleep.

Dean had rarely felt this comfortable and relaxed with a woman. As much as he'd been attracted to Cynthia's beauty in the beginning, there was often a slight but persistent distance. They wanted a connection, a fire to join them together, but it never came. Their lives were dedicated to their careers. The more he tried to forge a deeper intimacy, something like love, the more he felt alone together.

New York was never this dark. Dean watched the Mercedes' red lights make a long, wide sweep. He could see the pinpoints of uncountable stars far above them. But, otherwise, it was complete darkness like an impenetrable curtain. He was getting tired staring into the monotony. There was no other traffic, so he decided to close his eyes for just a moment.

Suddenly, the van was bouncing out of control, scraping through a field of brush. Dean hit the brakes in a panic. He couldn't believe he'd fallen asleep. The van came to a stop, but his breathing raced on. The chalky dirt swirled in the beams of light.

"What?" Grace was awake, drawn to the headlights. She watched like someone hypnotized by the flames of a campfire, then checked the children in the back. They remained asleep.

"A pothole, "Dean lied not wanting to admit he'd fallen asleep at the wheel and put their lives at risk.

"Did we lose Herve? I don't see the car."

"Up the road." Dean was disappointed that her first thought waking up was the rich boy. "We'll catch them."

Dean made a wide turn through the low brush to get back to the road. He was lucky they hadn't crashed. But it wouldn't happen again. His adrenaline would make sure of it.

Dean used the rearview mirror to check the two rows of young girls dozing in the back. They leaned against one another's small, dark shoulders like dominoes, their mouths open, breathing loudly.

Four in the back, three in the way back. He hoped they were on their way to adoption, to a better life than they knew.

When they had first climbed in the van, Dean had been impressed with their beauty. He had recognized the girl in the yellow dress. She had pleaded with Father Charles to remain at the orphanage and not go to America. She wore a blue checkered sundress now, her face scrubbed to a beatific shine.

"The girls are striking," Dean said.

Grace stared out the window as if she hadn't heard.

"Like a van full of hand-picked models. Should we take anything from that?" Dean asked.

"If they were ugly, you'd feel better about it?" Grace asked.

Dean wanted to think the girls just happened to be the most attractive of the orphanage. It could be a matter of chance. But Dean believed there was design in the selection, choosing children who were most valuable and desired on the open market.

"You're still looking," Grace said with an air of disappointment. "You just won't accept or understand how orphanages work in my country."

"Not true. I'm not looking for a scandal to report on. I'm past that anyway."

"Are you?"

Dean shook his head. Of course, he needed a good story to keep his job. But it didn't have to be an exposé. He loved the miracle trees. It was media-worthy without being at anyone's expense. He wasn't interested in revealing the dark side of humanity. He wanted to do something positive, to make a difference, to make lives better.

The glassy sea appeared off to the side under an awakening sky. The surface was the color of pewter in the faint light, gleaming like a polished tray. The brine air wafting through the window was tinged with the smell of fish and decay.

"We must be getting close," Dean said. The lights of the Mercedes were nowhere ahead of them. But there was only the single road, no exits or turns to be worried about.

"This will be so difficult for them," Grace said. She watched the young passengers with concern. A few girls were awake, following the sea with wide eyes.

"You know the stories of the prisoners who are freed?" Grace said, suddenly. It was clear she had been thinking about it for some time.

"They don't want to leave their cell. They are afraid of their own freedom. The cell is all they have known."

"The kids are prisoners? Now who's looking at the dark side?"

"Prisoners of poverty is what I'm saying. You can't process it when you're twelve. What you think is that you've done something wrong and are being punished for it."

Dean understood she was talking about herself, her own imprisonment as a *restavek*. It must have been a nightmare.

The girls were all awake. There were languid stretches and yawns. The kids seemed as unconcerned as when they had left Coluers. But Grace was beside herself, as if she was the one being sent away and not the orphans.

"But it's different at the orphanage," Grace said. She spoke dreamily as though in a trance. "They are loved and valued."

"Valued," Dean agreed. The orphanage could turn out to be little more than a holding pen, caging the children before they were sold. But Grace didn't understand his meaning. She heard it as agreement, as affirmation of her own view. Dean wasn't about to correct her.

The dirty, white Mercedes appeared in the shadows at the side of the road. Herve stood motionless outside the door, edged in the metallic light of the sunrise. He and the priest had waited for them to catch up after Dean had gone off the road. He wondered if they had seen his mistake. As Dean's van came closer, Herve nodded and climbed back inside the car and sped off onto the empty road that led into town.

"Why was he waiting?" Grace asked. "Are we going that slow?"

"No. He's driving that fast."

THE OUTSKIRTS OF THE BORDER TOWN WERE BARREN. A few tired palm trees slouched among patches of dry shrub. Dean struggled to keep up with the Mercedes as it barreled into the border town, whipping red dust and road trash against the crumbling cinderblock houses. The wind flapped the hanging clothes on rope lines.

Dean saw a new cement bridge in the distance—the border that led into the Dominican Republic. The riverbed on either side of the fenced bridge was bone dry, white as the cement of the bridge. Dean groaned.

"What's wrong?" Grace asked.

"I don't have a passport," he said.

They were passing crumbling, cinderblock houses that seemed closer to being in ruin than inhabitable. Chickens were leashed to boards alongside. A one-pump gas station was set away from the road, surrounded by stacks of bald tires. But there were no people anywhere, no one walking or busy outside their homes.

"You won't need it," Grace said.

"How do you know?" Dean was surprised and suspicious.

"It's not office hours," Grace said.

Just before the bridge, they passed a blue shipping container, its midsection converted into a cutout doorway. There was a sleek "Customs" sign painted on the side, sporting both English and French. The blue and red stripes of the Haitian flag drooped from a wooden flagpole. There were no customs officers in sight.

"You're saying customs is closed?"

"Just not open. It's a business."

"I thought it was a service."

"If you have the money."

As he drove onto the bridge over the dry riverbed, the landscape changed instantly. High, leafy palm trees rose on the other side, crowded together with old, mature green deciduous trees. The road underneath the van eased onto smooth blacktop.

The girls in the back were chatting again and all at once, as though school had just let out and they were free in the schoolyard. They were smiling, their eyes bright with anticipation and the approaching lush border.

Dean was concerned when he saw the chain-linked gate ahead, flanked by a guardhouse. There were no border guards for the DR either. There was only dark shade in the low-slung booths. A double-gated fence, however, blocked the road into the country. A metal lock and chain dangled from its midsection.

"This the official crossing?" Dean asked.

A sign posted working hours as 9-4. The Mercedes had parked next to it. Herve stepped out with the engine still running and strolled to the back trunk. He pulled out a black chain cutter and carried it toward the locked gate like it was a large key.

"He's going to cut the lock?" Dean asked.

"It looks that way," Grace said.

Herve snapped the chain in one motion, and it collapsed to the ground like a dead snake. He slid one of the gates to the side, just enough for a car to pass through.

"That how you cross the border after hours?" Dean called out the window.

"No time to wait for them to open."

Herve got back inside the Mercedes. Dean watched dully as the sedan pulled away and disappeared into the green splendor of the Dominican Republic.

"Are you waiting for something?" Grace asked.

"We can't do this," Dean said. "They stop us across the border, we're screwed."

"If we stay here, it will be worse," she said.

The authorities might want to know why he was transporting young girls across national borders without documentation. Outside, music and radio chatter rose unseen.

Grace pointed to a long line of immigrants walking across the dry creek bed below the bridge. They carried plastic jugs of water, gym bags, or nothing at all. Day workers.

"There is not always money to pay to run them. So, people cross. Back and forth. Every day."

The workers climbed through the bushes on the Dominican side and turned in the direction of the road. They were neither looking for guards nor making any pretense to hide. They were simply following a well-worn route that happened to take them into another sovereign country.

"We're sneaking in," Dean said.

Herve knew the border crossing would be closed. No wonder Herve insisted they leave long before dawn, even though it was more dangerous to drive at night. Of course, they would arrive without having to worry about guards or paperwork. There would not be a soul to question where or why they were transporting children.

"Everyone does it," Grace said. "Who can pay the tariff?"

The children behind them were alert and wary like kids listening to their parents argue, waiting to see if it would resolve.

"Dean," Grace said. "Can we go? Please?"

"You knew about all this?" he asked.

"It's not a secret," she said, dismissively.

They spotted the white Mercedes a mile ahead of them, winding through the new, single-lane road that cut through swaths of open marsh and mangrove. Dean checked the rearview mirror, certain he would spot a police car in hot pursuit. *Objects are closer than they appear* was stenciled on the mirror. But there was only the empty road receding behind.

There was no turning back anyway.

Within a few miles, a chain-link fence appeared at the near horizon, at the edge of a small, private airfield. There was no control tower directing air traffic, just what looked like a large cement garage. A single airstrip stretched from one end of the grass field to the other.

"*Nou rive!*" Grace said to the girls. They looked at the empty tarmac with wide-eyed wonder. Dean followed the Mercedes through the open gate and out onto the tarmac. An orange windsock fluttered near the landing strip. Nothing else stirred.

THEY WATCHED HERVE THROUGH THE DUSTY WINDSHIELD AS HE STEPPED OUT OF THE WHITE MERCEDES. He pursed his lips disdainfully and searched the blue, empty horizon. He looked tense and impatient. On the side of the runway, the lone windsock hung limply from a skinny pole like the morning's catch. The air was still and overly heavy.

"*Mwen pe,*" the pretty girl in the yellow dress whispered from the car. "I am afraid."

Grace grabbed the girl's small hand, wrapping it firmly in hers like a blanket.

Soon, dark, bobbing circles appeared high in the distant sky. Herve nodded as the distant nose and wing of the airplane sharpened into view like a focus ring from a camera. The sleek, white jet was on approach, the only plane anywhere.

The silence was suddenly broken. Herve spun around as if he had heard a rifle shot. Dean heard the engine, too. A patrol car, its electric blue and white light flashing, was speeding past the perimeter fence. A trail of dust swirled behind it as the car made a reeling turn and shot through the open gate. Dean feared the worst. They were about to be caught. He, too, would be handcuffed and charged with trafficking.

"Are they coming for us?" Grace asked. She held the hand of the girl even tighter.

But the police car stopped before it reached them. Two customs police bounded out and hurried to the glass doors of the terminal. Neither cop even so much as glanced at them, or their cars. Dean had a vague notion to take this opportunity to escape. He could drive Grace and the children out of here and back across the border into Haiti. They would all be saved. Dean hesitated. If he drove off, and what he believed was true, there was little doubt he and Grace and the children would be hunted down.

The high-pitched whine of the approaching aircraft echoed over the airport. The wheels were down and locked, its sculpted nose raised like it was sniffing the air, the blade-like wings lined up perfectly with the landing lane. Dean watched the wheels hit the blacktop with a brief screech and a puff of smoke before the tail of the plane flew past him. He could read the call letters on its tail, the aviation equivalent of a license plate.

The white jet rolled within a few yards of where they were parked before it stopped. The plane's windows shimmered like shark gills along the sleek fuselage. It turned its tail to face them at the last moment. Dean read the call letters: NEB1929. N marked it as U.S. registered. EB meant it was New York-based. Of course, anyone from anywhere could have rented it for the trip through a private broker. But he would check it out later.

Dean turned off the van engine which had begun to overheat. A hot breeze fluttered the grasses along the clean, new runway. There was a loud pneumatic pop, and a panel near the cockpit opened. Red stairs on a pedestal emerged, drifting to the ground as the rest of the panel raised upwards. The motor of the stairs stopped.

A tall, middle-aged man in khakis and boat shoes lowered his head as he came out. He stood tall on the first step, surveying the scene like a general appraising the battlefield. He wore a pressed button-down shirt and tortoise shell sunglasses like a yachtsman.

Behind them, the two uniformed police officers emerged from the terminal, the glass doors flashing behind them. They were coming to the plane. Herve intercepted them, greeting them in fluid Spanish, shaking their hands in turn. He gestured back toward the closed doors of the terminal like a nightclub owner urging special guests to accompany him into the secret back room. The officers followed him.

Father Charles came out of the passenger side of the Mercedes. The priest ambled toward the plane as if he were walking on eggshells. He was afraid. Of what or who, Dean didn't know.

"Father Charles!" The greeting echoed over the quiet airfield. "Polizia?"

"A surprise to us," Father Charles answered.

"Wheels up," the man ordered to the pilots inside. The blades in the jet engines started to rotate and whined back to life.

"You are not leaving?" Father Charles asked.

"A business precaution," the man answered, showing a nervous smile. "In the event we must leave quickly."

The girls pushed open the van doors behind Dean and scrambled out of the back seat. They stopped and stood in place, gawking at the gleaming plane, the promise of adventure and a better life. The high roller, in turn, was alarmed at the young girls being displayed along the runway in plain sight. He backed toward the stairs, checking the terminal entrance door where the police had disappeared with Herve.

Dean took a breath. He didn't need any more clues. Everyone was afraid of the police just as any thief or criminal would be.

"Please," the high roller said. "If the children could wait in the van."

Father Charles called to them in a calm, reassuring voice. They were confused, not sure what he was asking. Instead of returning to Dean's car, they watched the other girls escape their pen in the back seat. A trio of toddlers and one lanky, teen girl ran happily onto the hot tarmac as if it were a playground.

"All of them?"

"The cars are hot," Father Charles said.

The high roller stopped to consider. He studied the young, pretty girls.

"Inside then," he said. "They are too pretty to be out in the sun."

The girls hurried toward the plane's red carpeted stairs. Dean glimpsed the teen girl in the yellow dress. She was more curious than afraid. Maybe she wanted to leave now, like the other children, excited about a new and comfortable future, the one they had been promised, he was certain. The priest followed behind his young flock.

Dean stared with growing fear and revulsion. He felt he knew where they were headed. Slavery. The sex trade. God knows. He needed to act, to stop this trade. Even if he were somehow wrong. But he knew he wasn't. They were being sold, just like those back in Charleston a century ago.

The banker directed the girls inside the private jet.

"There is pop and cookies," he said. He sounded like a scoutmaster. Dean could make out the calf and high heels of a woman just beyond the door. The flight attendant was greeting the children. He felt a pang of doubt.

Human traffickers, as far as Dean knew, didn't use flight attendants for contraband pickups. Charter flights, however, often did. Maybe what Herve claimed was true. The children were being flown out in the most effective way possible, from a country without a functioning government, even if no one seemed to know where they were going.

Dean felt as if he were sinking into the soft, warm tarmac. The sun was already breaking down the hard surface. He then saw Herve. The BAMBAM son, a boy with all the wealth and advantages of the elite of Haiti, strolled toward the jet as if he had all the time in the world. Behind him, the police car was turning away, its blue lights no longer flashing. They drove off to the exit. Dean was astounded. They were no longer in danger of arrest or anything else.

The high roller was waiting. He held a thick manila office envelope at his side. Herve and the banker shook hands with an easy familiarity.

"A new partner, Herve?" Dean heard the high roller say.

"A driver."

"A white American?"

"You think 'cause he's white he must be in charge."

"No. But more than a driver."

"Don't worry how we do our job," Herve said.

"I never worry, Herve." He smiled breezily. Then he gave a half-salute, a gesture that made Dean think of some old-fashioned yachtsman, before trudging up the shaking stairs and into the gut of the plane. A moment later, the red stairs followed him.

Every boss has a boss, Dean thought, as he watched Herve turn away and walk back toward the car. He looked chastened, subdued from his interaction with the high roller.

As the jet taxied to the end of the runway, Dean thought about all the business he had just witnessed. The police had left because they'd been bribed. Herve held a fat envelope likely full of U.S. currency, not gourdes. Everyone was profiting. Dean had just watched. He had done nothing to intervene. It's what reporters were supposed to do, he reminded himself. They were witnesses. But Dean had long yearned to do more. He'd just missed his chance.

THEY STOPPED FOR BREAKFAST AT AN OUTDOOR RESTAURANT ON THE OUTSKIRTS OF PEDERNALES. They had the old porch to themselves. Herve was in a celebratory mood and ordered his usual bourbon on ice to sip with eggs and brown beans. Dean was surprised to hear Father Charles ask for a steak, cooked very rare.

"Red meat. My one vice," Father Charles said sheepishly.

"Who was the American?" Dean asked with a barely concealed edge. He was angry at them and himself.

"Our business partner, *blan*," Herve answered.

"What business would that be, Herve?"

The middle-aged Dominican waiter, his round, pug-like eyes glazed with sleep, slouched forward, waiting for all to offer their meal orders.

"You don't like black people," Herve said, peering at Dean. "I can see it in your eyes."

"This isn't about blacks and you know it."

"You don't like us when we are in charge, when we are calling the shots. I see it." Herve rolled his neck stiffly as if his collar was bothering him. His thick neck muscles pressed through his skin.

"Do you?" Dean said. "I see you've got a nice envelope full of cash. Am I right?"

"The families pay us," Herve said. "What do you think?"

"The families?" Dean asked with deadpan sarcasm.

"*Blans* like you."

A young Dominican woman with the same round, sleepy eyes as the waiter arrived carrying a tin tray with the coffee and drinks. Herve grabbed his tumbler of bourbon before she could even set it down on the table.

"I saw the police didn't get a chance to chat with your partner on the plane. The *blan*, I mean," Dean said. Herve studied the amber syrup of the whiskey in his tumbler.

"They look for *picadors*," Father Charles interrupted.

Dean was surprised the priest had rushed to Herve's defense. Somehow, he had relegated Father Charles to a support position, someone who aided Herve but was not a partner in crime. But, of course, he was, and the thought disappointed Dean. He wanted to think better of the priest.

"*Picadors* are forced to work on the sugar plantations of the wealthy. They are Haitian and Dominican. But mostly Haitian."

Dean listened, thinking about how many more times he was going to hear about some form of slavery. It hardly seemed to matter where it happened, by what color or creed of people. Dean worried that slavery—the use and abuse of the defenseless—was as natural to human behavior as war. People used one another because they could. He wished it wasn't the case, but maybe he was just tired and feeling cynical after what he had witnessed.

The food arrived on thick, handmade, ceramic plates. A faint steam rose from Father Charles's steak as it sat in a pool of blood and brown grease. The priest cut into it greedily, separating the flesh from the streaks of pale fat. Dean turned his attention to his two eggs, cooked over easy and bathed in vegetable oil.

"Missy," Herve said, addressing Grace. "Your reporter thinks we are up to no good."

Grace took a careful bite of her eggs, her eyes downcast at the chipped plate. She was falling back into whatever catatonic state Herve induced in her.

"Your reporter thinks we are trafficking," Herve said, facing Dean directly.

"Are you?" Dean asked.

Herve pursed his lips, the edges stained with the grease from the eggs. Then he leaned back and laughed. The deep, throaty laughter sounded menacing.

"You insult us," Herve said. "You think you are better than us because you are white and a foreigner and can do and talk like we don't matter. Like your partner from Spain."

Ali? Dean was startled at the mention of him. It also put him on edge even more, like a sixth sense recognizing a threat.

"He is not my partner if we are talking about the same person."

"Well, doesn't matter," Herve said. "Not anymore."

"Why not anymore?" Dean asked. He felt the dark eyes on him, shining with reptilian indifference.

THE ROAD BACK TO THE BORDER WOUND THROUGH FLAT, EMPTY LAND. Blue distant mountains marked the horizon and leading up to them were swaths of bright green stalks that reminded Dean of bamboo. Sugar plantations had once been part of the Carolina economy, too, a vestige of colonial times, like the slave trade. He imagined the *picadors* baking in the afternoon sun as they whipped through the ripe sugar cane with machetes. It was brutal, exhausting work and painful. Swinging the heavy blade across the skinny stalks often made paper-like cuts on bare forearms.

Dean drove in moody silence. What was behind this compulsion to use others for profit or simply power? He wished he knew. There were other paths to wealth and power that weren't necessarily gained on the backs of others and certainly not on those of children. He felt a duty to expose what he had found in the hills of Coluers. He would report on the miracle trees as well, but he knew which investigation would command attention. He had come to file a positive story, one that spotlighted the best in people, what he believed was an innate desire to do good, to help others. But he worried he had been holding out the whole time, hoping he would find a different story.

Father Charles slouched in the passenger seat. The bald priest had switched cars with Grace. Herve claimed he needed to discuss the continued operation of the bakery with Grace, in private. She had acquiesced, following him to the Mercedes as though he had hypnotized her. He had some kind of hold on her that Dean didn't understand. She didn't like him. She even seemed at times to despise him. Yet, she was drawn to him against her own interests, even against her own survival, like the proverbial moth to the mortal flame.

"I am worried about Grace." The priest broke the silence between them as if reading Dean's thoughts. Charles watched the long line of sugar trees as he spoke. "When you are gone back to New York, will she leave as well?"

"Back to Brooklyn?" Dean asked with surprise. The priest seemed to be implying Grace would follow him.

"She wants a home. I believe she came back to Haiti to find it."

"So why would she leave now?" Dean asked, even though he understood the priest was indeed thinking of him and Grace being together. But it was absurd. He barely knew Grace. They were lovers, yes, and he liked her far more than a friend or a travel companion. But he was getting ahead of things and he was certain she wasn't. Besides, from that moment on the hotel porch, it was clear her relationship was with the country she had once left.

"She is my blessing," Father Charles said.

Dean wanted to roll his eyes. "She told me about it," he said.

"You know about her past."

"She was a rescue outside one of your churches. If rescuing is what you really do."

The priest hesitated as if waiting for the accusation to settle to the floor like dust.

"Grace had the heart to escape. She could have been caught and beaten by her owners. Maybe worse."

"She was beaten and worse," Dean said.

"Yes," Father Charles said quietly. "She found a servant of God and the holy spirit gave her courage as to all men."

The fierce, tropical light blasting through the windshield had begun making Dean's head throb. He wiped away the grimy sweat dripping like candle wax down his cheeks. It was always so hot, unbearably hot. The steering wheel trembled from the rough road.

"There are no *coincidences*," the priest said, pronouncing it with a French accent. "*Coincidence* is the hand of God working out his plan."

Father Charles glanced upward at the worn roof of the van as though it were the gateway to the celestial heavens.

"And you have your plan, Father," Dean said.

"Mr. Dubose, you are mistaken about our program," Father Charles said. His voice tried to be soothing like a Catholic holy father in the confessional. Dean could even picture the screen and the pious sign of the cross made with one hand that had been a weekly occurrence at his church in South Carolina.

"How am I mistaken?" Dean felt more perspiration running down the back of his neck.

"Without funds, there is no orphanage," Father Charles said. "You understand? All the children would be turned away without funds. They would have no home."

"No, I don't understand." Of course, Dean understood all too well. The question was why the priest thought he could persuade him otherwise.

"The orphanage is not the evil doings you suspect," the priest said. "Poverty is the evil. And the greed that creates it."

The tall trees at the border came mercifully into view. A line was even forming at the checkpoint. Yet, the border guards seemed to be waving everyone through. Dean wondered, absently, if it had anything to do with the children. But, of course, the guards couldn't know. There had been no one at the checkpoint earlier.

"It's all greed, Father. Yours. You give the girls to your partner and he hands over money. How much do you get a head?"

"You are an arrogant man, Mr. Dubose," the priest said. "Like so many *blans*."

"This is not about race," Dean said.

"It is about privilege. You are accustomed to being listened to and valued. For no reason other than the color of your skin."

"You're not privileged? I know about the private school, the elite familes."

"You see, we are given a list." Father Charles reached into his pocket and took out the envelope that Herve had slipped out of the fat manila envelope and given him after breakfast.

"A list of what?" Dean asked.

Father Charles explained that the list was handed over at the close of each transaction. It contained the names, addresses, and contact numbers of each family awarded a child. The list was more valuable to Father Charles than anything, except the children themselves. He held it lightly but carefully as though the plain paper was fragile.

Dean couldn't tell if he was lying. But the paper did contain names and addresses. New York, Indiana, Florida.

Dean was late in bringing the van to a stop in line.

"Why are you telling me this now?" Dean glanced at the guards, who were peering into the vehicles ahead. Dean felt something wasn't right.

"I want you to know. We are not bad people. We are on a mission."

"Who follows up and checks that the children go to those addresses?" Dean asked.

"You saw him. At the plane, yes?"

The yachtsman. He hardly looked like a man of charity, out to see homeless children in happy homes. Dean clung to the plastic wheel, worried that he might be mistaken about the priest and the orphanage. Their operation was illegal and suspect at the least, but maybe it wasn't a case of child trafficking so much as it was a way to circumvent the legal system to benefit the children.

"How much does it all cost?" Dean asked. He thought the sum of money might give him a clue. He blinked away the new beads of sweat that had slipped into the corner of his eyes.

"I am not sure. But all is given to the orphanage, to other children now and in the future. We do not profit."

"You don't know how much is charged? How is that, Father?"

Father Charles sighed. He wiped his own, wet forehead.

"You're going to tell me Herve handles all that."

"There are others who must be paid. The government, the handlers. I do not have the skills that Herve has."

Dean watched men and women moving in loose groups, some with suitcases on their heads. Dirt bikes screamed in and around the crowd as they left the DR. Dominican soldiers in desert tan uniforms and soft hats ignored the passing crowd as if the exodus had little to do with their job.

"At one time, the families pay us only," Father Charles said, shaking his head at times gone by.

"Back when?

The priest launched into a memory of a time when he used to read the letters from couples, desperate to have children of their own, begging to have a child from the orphanage. But the governments decided they were too old or too poor or too something and had rejected their official applications. So he and Herve wanted to change the system.

"We work around the rules now as then," Father Charles said, proudly.

"So do criminals," Dean said. He was angry at himself for not remembering his lost passport. The consequences were approaching, and they were in uniform and armed.

Father Charles was facing away from him, his gaze fixed sorrowfully on the river churning in the distance. The water was a muddied teal that seemed artificial like the pools of chemicals outside a factory.

The car ahead inched up a length and Dean followed. One guard ahead had his rifle at his side, casually pointed at the car. Dean felt a cold trickle of fear.

"Do you keep up with the families?" Dean asked. There seemed to be an omission in the priest's story, and he wanted to find out.

"No longer," Father Charles said, sadly.

"Why no longer?"

"There are too many children, too many families now."

"Too many?" Dean asked with alarm. "Hundreds? Thousands?"

"Many," Father Charles said.

"Can I see the list?" Dean reached for the envelope.

Father Charles let him take it. Dean opened it and scanned the list. There were thirteen addresses, each in a different city. One was in Queens.

"Why a different city for every child?" Dean asked.

Father Charles shrugged as if he didn't know and the answer didn't concern him.

Dean wondered if the list was merely a gambit, a fake document to satisfy some mid-level authority. Maybe the priest checked it. But he didn't scrutinize anything. Maybe it was a cover for his own conscience. He could no more admit what he was doing to himself than he could to authorities.

Two more cars moved forward. They were close to the border guards. Dean wasn't sure what he would say if they asked for his passport. Maybe they would not.

Dean thought of Ali. The priest had allowed the photojournalist to take pictures of the children. He asked Father Charles if the photographer who had visited him had taken many pictures at the orphanage. Were any on the list?

"I don't know," the priest said. "He wanted to take more."

"But he didn't. Why?"

"He went back to PAP."

Dean remembered the look in Herve's eyes earlier at breakfast. The photographer didn't matter anymore, Herve said. As if he were long gone.

"He was a liar," Father Charles said.

"What?" Dean was surprised.

"He said he was telling a big story about the street children, the *sanguine*. Many come to us. But he lied. He lied," the priest said.

"Lied?"

"It was about our orphanage! Like you."

"How did you find that out?"

"Herve."

Father Charles ripped the list from his hand, angry, as he had likely been when Ali had fibbed his way to access. Dean felt a dread sink into him and fill his head and throat like nausea. He saw Herve's dark eyes again. They were coldly satisfied. Suddenly, Dean was frightened for his own safety.

The last car ahead drove off. Both guards regarded them through the dirty windshield. One waved them to approach.

"Where are they?" Father Charles asked, searching for the Mercedes.

HERVE PULLED UP TO THE LONE GAS PUMP IN TOWN TO FILL UP HIS TANK FOR THE LONG HAUL BACK TO COLUERS. He gave the boy attendant a small tip and winked when his dark eyes lit up, amazed at the thickness of the folded American money in the man's outstretched hand.

"*Mèsi, mesye*," the boy said and hurried to pump the gas.

Herve and Grace waited in silence. Her hair fluttered from the air conditioning that continued blasting from the dashboard. She sat uncomfortably straight in her seat, brooding. Herve's decision to speed ahead onto a side road that allowed them to pass Dean and Father Charles in the van had been premeditated. He was scheming, only Grace could not figure out what he was after.

"Never thanked you, baby. For helping me out."

"I came for the children."

Herve smiled as though she had made a witty reply. He glanced at her smooth chin, held high like a regal beauty. He liked her willfulness, her apparent lack of fear of him. It turned him on.

The boy removed the rusted pump and tapped on the roof to signal that the tank was full. Herve let his hand drop out of the window in thanks, then started the engine. A few cars and pickups rumbled by in the direction of Port au Prince.

"Where are they?" Grace asked. She turned and searched behind them in the direction of the border.

"They'll get here," Herve said. He waited for the traffic to pass, then pulled slowly onto the road and accelerated quickly to highway speed. The weatherbeaten cinder block storefronts of the town blurred in the rearview mirror, dissolving into the gleam of the shimmering midday sun.

"Aren't we going to wait for them?" Grace said. She had turned to look for the van behind them. But there was only a squat supply truck, choking on puffs of diesel smoke.

"Your boy will catch up," Herve said. "Trust me, baby."

Grace continued to search behind her. They should be in clear sight by now.

"Sweet on the *blan*," Herve said in a mocking tone. He still couldn't accept that his own *restavek* bitch was seriously interested in the American reporter. Not that it mattered. Soon, the *blan* would be gone, one way or the other. Yet her affection for the lanky, out of shape white boy got under his skin.

"He give it that fine?" Herve teased.

Grace slapped him hard across the face.

He was stunned. He stared out at the road ahead, his chiseled face harsh and drawn. Somehow, he was keeping his easy temper in check.

"Watch it, bitch," Herve said without looking at her.

"Why aren't we waiting?" Grace demanded.

Herve held the leather steering wheel loosely. The car bounced unpredictably as it roared over the divots and dried mud ridges that littered the road. Herve put his hand on the dashboard in appreciation of his luxury car's performance. It was the hushed sound of money. Music.

Grace spotted a pale-green tree further up the road. The mesquite was tall with a thick, gnarly trunk and stood alone, surrounded by a mix of dry grass and scrub. Somehow the desert-green bark had been spared in the endless harvest for charcoal.

"Pull over by that tree," Grace said. Her voice had changed. It was no longer strident or angry. She was asking in the fetching way she had learned to do long ago with men who wanted her.

Herve raised his eyebrows in response. But he obeyed her and stopped the car under the shady canopy. Grace opened the door and jumped out into dappled shade. The clusters of leaves just above her head hid long, slender thorns which she was careful to avoid. The sweet resin smell of the mesquite, heated by the sun, was refreshing. It had been decades since she had last smelled mesquite, and it reminded her immediately of late mornings in Port au Prince when the boys had left for school and the Mama had gone to market or wherever she went in the early part of the day. Grace was left alone, then, chores ahead of her. But, for one brief moment, she savored the smell and the quiet of the wealthy neighborhood. She felt alive.

A delivery truck sped by, then a dented white pickup spewing a thin cloud of dust. She waved away the chalky cloud, tasting it on her dry lips. She peered back in the direction of the town. When the dust finally settled, there was only an empty road as still and silent as the hot blue sky.

"Baby," Herve called. The door shut cleanly and he walked around the car until he was facing her near the bumper. "Baby. It's a long trip."

"Something happened."

Herve studied her with a bored air. He considered most women to be fundamentally simple and focused on the moment where they found themselves. Reasoning and its cousin, deduction, weren't in their make-up. Well, except for Grace.

"You worried about the Pedernales border? No one gonna stop them from coming into the country. Everybody wants out where the money is."

Grace considered this, her eyes narrowing as if the possibilities were sprawling into the distance in front of her. It was true her own people crossed into the DR every day, if they could, in search of food or work. There was nothing over here but poverty. The DR was a rich country by comparison.

"They'll be along," Herve reassured her. "Come."

Grace remembered the money Herve had slipped to the border guard. He had been sly, disguising it with his hand. She had been intrigued with his skill but hadn't considered how unusual it was to bribe on the way back into Haiti. Of course, many paid to have the opportunity to enter the Dominican Republic illegally. There were jobs, food. But returning to Haiti was another matter. No one paid to return to poverty.

"You gave money at the border?" Grace asked.

"Tourist fee," Herve said. "Don't worry. Your boy carries dollars."

"He's broke," she said, feeling a tinge of fear.

"What?" Herve laughed.

"He was robbed in PAP, by children."

Herve grunted. "Serves him right. Poppy has cash. Can we go? There ain't no breeze out here."

Grace studied him, thinking about the bribe. Or was it a payoff?

"What's going on?" Grace asked.

Herve shook his head with impatience and made as though he were going to get back in the air-conditioned car.

"What did you do?" Grace asked.

"Fine," Herve said. He stopped by the side of the car. "We'll wait."

"What did you do?" Grace repeated, fearful he had paid for something involving Dean. He was known to hire goons regularly. She had seen it herself.

"It's hot," Herve said, making sure to meet her eyes. The green glittered like jewels against her dark skin, as beautiful as he had ever seen them.

"You're afraid of him," Grace said, taking a step toward Herve. "Afraid of what? You have something to be afraid of, Herve?"

"The *blan* is looking to score big for his career. Wants to make a name for himself. Be a superstar. Don't matter what or who it is. He kicked away a mound of the dirt at his feet as if it were dog feces smelling up the road. "That's what reporters do. Use people to make their name burn brighter."

"You're wrong about that," Grace said, pleading. She wasn't so sure.

Herve leaned back and laughed with genuine humor. A line of a few cars whipped past, the hot wind throwing granules of dirt in their faces.

"He's got you, baby," Herve said. He spit out the dirt that landed on his lips. "Can we go?"

"How much?" Grace asked suddenly.

"How much what?" Herve's annoyance was sharpening into anger. But he recognized her suspicions.

"The adoptions," Grace said. "If that's what they are."

Herve shrugged as if the question were inconsequential. Screw it. He would tell her. She was a slave. She didn't matter except to him. She was just another bitch with a nice ass.

"Three thousand a head."

Grace understood that adoptions cost money. Parents paid fees to governments and agencies and others. In this country, many others have their hands open. The system had long been corrupt, and she knew Father Charles sometimes went around the system. But Herve talked about the children like they were products, things to be sold.

"It's hot out here," Herve said.

He turned and got back into the Mercedes this time. Grace hesitated. She wondered if they had talked about her in the same language years ago when she was sent, alone, to the United States. Grace dismissed the thought, knowing Father Charles treasured his children. Herve was a different matter.

Grace followed Herve's lead and stepped back into the air-conditioned sedan. She closed the door after her and stared straight ahead. A desert rolled past them. There were glimpses of the teal sea in the far distance. Bare and beautiful.

"Why you come back?" Herve asked. "The truth, baby."

He believed it could be him. She was a little sweet on him, his skills, and he was rich. Herve could give her what she wanted.

"I told you. For Coluers."

"Give back? What did you ever get?"

Grace had no answer. But she was thinking of Father Charles, of his love and willingness to rescue her. She thought of Nelson and Moisson who embraced her and made her feel normal and treasured.

"Don't matter. I'll take care of you, baby," Herve said. His strong hand was on her thigh, warm and firm. She felt a tingle run through her that was so disarming that there was a brief, almost dizzy lightheadedness. She liked being touched by Herve, in spite of her opinion of him. Her body didn't care about his principles.

She felt his fingers slide down to her wet underwear. She hated how her body was reacting. It was wrong.

Herve was kissing her neck, whispering. He wanted her. She leaned away and felt him only press her harder. She didn't want this. She tried to push him away, but he was too strong and too heavy. Before she knew it, he had her pinned against the seat and the door.

"What are you doing?" Grace said, angry. She squirmed, wanting to get away. Herve ignored her. He was pushing back her underwear.

"No," she said. She thought he didn't hear her. "No."

His pants were down to his knees. She felt his legs against her own. She couldn't believe what was happening.

"No," she said, more loudly this time. Herve was excited and charging along in his own heat. She tried the door handle. It was locked. He was going to rape her. She relaxed for a moment and let him go, enough to free her arm. She swung with all her might and banged his ear sharply.

Herve started. She had stunned him. Grace raised her elbow and slammed the tempered glass as hard she could. But it only bounced off and she screamed in pain.

"Shut up, bitch."

Herve tried to spread her legs wider. But Grace kicked wildly, and her flailing knee hit him hard in his groin. He slapped her across the face. She punched his ear yet again and landed it squarely. His dark eyes went vacant for a moment, dazed by the hit. Grace managed to push his legs off of her. Then she dug her nails into his neck and felt the warm blood on her fingers.

Herve stopped. He felt the deep scratch on his neck and looked at the red stain on his fingers and palm. He pulled up his pants and hooked his leather belt. He rubbed his ear, shaking his head at the same time. He was furiously calm.

"I should fuck you," he said as he got back behind the wheel. Grace stared at his bloodied neck, shaking and terrified. It sounded to her as if he had said I should kill you.

"We'll have all the time in the world, baby," Herve said and adjusted the rearview mirror. There was no traffic at all behind them. Grace turned and glimpsed the emptiness. Dean and Father Charles were still nowhere in sight. She was alone and unprotected.

"Give me a napkin out of there."

Herve motioned to the glove box in front of her. Grace pulled out a white paper towel and pressed it against his neck until his blood spread across it like an ink blot. She grabbed another napkin and repeated it. This time there was less bleeding.

"What did you pay for?" Grace asked. She dropped the soiled towels at her feet.

Herve pulled onto the road and accelerated. The Mercedes rumbled over the pock-marked lane. The sunlight pouring in the window sickened Grace.

"What did you pay for?" Grace repeated, her voice even more shrill.

"They will be along," Herve answered finally.

Grace knew he was lying. She saw the details of the journey through a new, harsh lens. The cutting of the chain at the Dominican border. The American broker picking up his merchandise. She was furious at herself. It was as plain as day. Dean was right. The orphanage was trafficking in its own children. Herve would make sure none of it reached the ears of the public.

A GROUP OF SOLDIERS IN SMART, TAN FATIGUES, MATCHING HATS AND BLACK ASSAULT RIFLES WAITED ON THE HAITIAN SIDE OF THE BRIDGE. They peered through the fine mist of chalky dust that drifted over the anxious crowd. Most were on foot and trudged past the border patrol without regard to a line or protocol. Many carried valuables on their heads—a battered suitcase, cloth sacks of rice, dark green plantains. A dirt bike and an old man on a pony tried to work around the streaming refugees.

"This is customs?" Dean asked. Below a skinny pole flying a red and blue Haitian flag, a pair of guards stopped a Japanese pickup truck, its flatbed overloaded with cargo and workers perched on the pile. Meanwhile, other passengers hurried past and onto Haitian soil.

The old man on horseback, his head shaded by a broad-brimmed straw hat, clopped past as well. Dean was reassured. Maybe they would not be stopped and questioned either. But he had to warn Father Charles.

"I don't have a passport," Dean said.

"Yes, you told me. When you were robbed. You have money, yes?"

Dean squinted through the dirty windshield as if he hadn't heard the question. They would need cash if they were stopped. There were fees.

"There is a tip expected," Father Charles said. "Or they can make things difficult for us."

"Right," Dean said, realizing things were about to get difficult.

"Do you have your passport?" Dean asked.

"*Souri ou se paspò ou*," the priest said and smiled.

"A smile is your passport," Dean said, recognizing the words of the passport official back in Port au Prince when he had explained there was a wait to get his document and, in the meantime, there was his smile to get him around. Not here, though.

Dean steered the car closer to the bridge, making room for the soldiers. He pretended to be looking into the town ahead as if he expected not to be stopped. But the guards' collective attention perked up as he approached. A group of soldiers, all in wraparound sunglasses, faced him. The dark, unreflecting lenses made him think of the obsidian eyes of insects.

Dean started when a new soldier seemed to appear out of nowhere, raising his uniformed arm in an order to stop. A black assault rifle strap dangled from his burly shoulder. The uniforms were freshly laundered, the collars crisp and neat. It wasn't the border patrol he expected from the poorest country in the western hemisphere.

The dark face of the soldier was in the window. He regarded Dean and the priest slowly, one to the other. He wore a light beard of dust on his long cheeks and smelled of sweat and sweet ganga.

"Passports," he barked.

"We visit Pedernales," Father Charles piped in, smiling as though he were greeting one of his faithful congregants. It was absurd.

"Visit?" The soldier was not impressed. He motioned to two soldiers who slouched against the open gate. Both pushed off and marched toward the van, taking the assault rifles off their shoulders in the same moment.

"From our village in Haiti," Father Charles continued, his rich voice smooth and confident.

"Passports."

"I left mine at the hotel by mistake," Dean lied. He didn't think the truth would get him very far. This explanation was at least more plausible than having to explain he had been robbed days ago. Naturally, they would want to know how he came into the DR without one.

"In Pedernales?" The soldier was amused. "There is the hotel?"

"No, in Punta Cana," Dean said, remembering the name of the prime resort area in the DR.

The soldier seemed ever more amused by his answer.

"*Vacanze? Junto con padre*?" You and the priest together?

"No," Dean said. "I am giving him a ride to his orphanage."

"No children along?" the soldier asked.

"Of course not," Dean said, shaking his head as if insulted.

"There." The soldier pointed to the blue-painted shipping container that was the Haitian customs office. "Your van."

Dean took a breath, realizing only then that he had been holding it, fearful of what was coming to pass.

"There?" Father Charles asked.

"He wants us to pull the van over there so they can search it."

Dean took his foot off the brake pedal. As the van coasted forward, he considered not stopping at all. He hadn't seen a military vehicle that could chase them. They could be through the town and out on that deserted highway to Coluers in a matter of minutes.

Father Charles was studying his face. "This is a misunderstanding. You would make a problem out of a trivial thing."

Dean checked the soldier in the rearview mirror. He had taken the assault rifle off his shoulder. He merely had to lift it to fire. Reluctantly,

Dean steered the van to a patch of dirt next to the shipping container. He turned off the ignition and readied himself for whatever was coming next.

"*Merci*," Father Charles said, quietly.

FATHER CHARLES AND DEAN WERE SEPARATED BY TWO CUSTOMS OFFICERS. Dean was led to the shipping container and the priest escorted beyond the makeshift customs office. They were informed that they were being questioned about their missing passports.

Dean stood alone inside the dim customs office. The door was locked behind him, muffling the sound of the busy street. The dank, earthen floor smelled as musty as a basement. The high roof of the sheet metal container was flat and dark. There was a cheap metal desk nearby and two plain folding chairs. It seemed more like an interrogation space than an office.

Dean sensed movement on the floor nearby. He squinted into the corner where sunlight leaked through like smoke. A snake was stretched out in the dirt. It must have squeezed through the opening, sliding unseen from the dry riverbed. Dean watched and waited. He cast about for a weapon to protect himself if need be. The folding chair was the only possible object. Dean decided he would use sound and vibration to turn the snake away and get it to retreat.

Dean jumped, rising as high as he could before landing flat on his feet, sending a tremor along the ground. He repeated it again and again in rapid succession. But the snake was still, undisturbed. He searched for its flickering tongue. The more he looked, the more he began to see a different shape, a dull and round head. Then he noticed the knot in the middle, the breakage at each end. It wasn't a snake at all. He had conjured one out of the stick from a tree branch.

Dean laughed at his childish terror. No poisonous fangs were looking to sink into his arms and legs. His own fear had created this vision, a fact that told him just how on edge he had become. But he sensed something more lurking in this stop to check passports. He felt the undercurrents of a setup. It made sense. If he was out of the picture, there would be no exposé about a sordid business run from an orphanage. He assumed Herve was behind this border stop, not legal papers.

He heard the voice of Father Charles just outside. He was chatting. The door opened and the clerk and the priest came inside. Their ongoing conversation didn't end until the officer shook hands warmly with Father Charles. Dean hoped it was a good sign.

"This is the journalist?" the officer asked in English. The officer's face was as dark as licorice with flecks of grey in the buzz cut that flanked his wide ears. Father Charles gave a slight, curt nod.

"Come with me," the officer said. There was no trace of an accent in his perfect English. He was educated. Dean was relieved these were not thugs.

"Wait. Am I to remain here?" Father Charles asked as they started back out the door.

"We will not be long," the clerk said.

Dean's eye stung from the harsh light outside. Only a few stragglers wandered by from the border. It was getting later.

Dean was led to another metal door cut out of the side of the long shipping container. The shell of metal, he realized, had been subdivided into separate chambers. He thought the building a novel use of junk that otherwise would have ended up as scrap metal. A commercial light hung from the ceiling and illuminated another metal desk and two bare chairs.

"*Tanpri*," the officer said, motioning for Dean to sit opposite him.

"You are a *journalist*," he said.

"No, I'm not. Are you charging us with something?"

"Should I be?" The officer leaned forward. His face was long and sharp like a pencil. "*Ka mwen* I dee?" the officer asked, pleased with the fear he had instilled.

"I don't have an ID," Dean said.

"No *carte du journalist*?" The officer rubbed his smooth chin. His thin knuckles were sharp.

"Maybe you don't want anyone to know your identity?" he asked suddenly in English.

"I am not a journalist," Dean said. "Did the priest tell you that?"

The officer leaned back in his chair and folded his skinny arms.

"Father Charles told me about the young girls," he said. "He tells us he has an orphanage in Coluers. He is dedicated to helping children."

Dean dreaded what he knew was coming next.

"He tells me you were driving his children to the border."

"No. We were driving children from the orphanage. Both of us," Dean said.

"You would like to share with us why you were driving them?" He flashed his tall, yellowing teeth like a growling dog.

"Father Charles shared that with you, I'm sure," Dean said.

"In your words, please," the clerk ordered.

Of course, the customs clerk was looking for an inconsistency, a mistake that confirm his suspicion of Dean. He tried to choose his words carefully so as not to contradict what he imagined the priest had stated.

"We were delivering them," Dean said, immediately worried that he had used the word delivery—like a package. "To their foster homes."

"Where are these foster homes?"

Dean had a sense he was being mocked, led along a path the clerk already knew well.

"The United States."

"America?" The clerk feigned surprise. The priest had told him.

"Yes, the orphanage had arranged for them to be transported from the airport."

"Why not flown from our country?"

"Father Charles told you."

The clerk gave a wan smile with his thick lips, which told Dean he had guessed correctly. The priest had told the literal truth.

"In your own words, please."

"I don't know why the orphanage chose not to use Haiti."

Dean took a short breath, which he had been unconsciously holding.

"Why were you helping?" the clerk asked. There were puffy bags of charcoal skin under his eyes, and his manner was firm and direct.

There was no escaping the irony that he was being probed about the very crime he sought to expose. He had come to bear witness to the operation, to write about and publish the truth about the orphanage. The actual perpetrators were gone, except the priest. He wondered what had happened to Grace. Their car had been behind them for most of the trip.

"Tell me about the woman," the clerk asked. There was a faint spark of amusement in his dark eyes.

"I was helping her."

The man chuckled as if Dean had told a joke.

"The priest says her name is Grace. Like the prayer."

"She was behind us in line," Dean said. "He must have told you that."

"I don't see her. Or the man with her."

"Herve," Dean said. As soon as he heard himself say the name out loud, he understood Herve had set them up to take the fall. He must have known about Dean's lost passport and told the border guards who was driving the car with the priest.

FATHER CHARLES CLUNG TO THE STEERING WHEEL AS THE VAN RUMBLED OVER THE ROUGH LANE LEADING OUT OF TOWN. He wanted to stop and fill up at the lone gas station on the route to Coluers, but he didn't dare. He felt lucky to escape. Someone had tipped security about the transport of children across the Haitian-Dominican Republic border.

The van shook as it crossed over a series of divots. He felt the loose skin hanging from his aging body. His stomach was queasy, and he could taste bile in his drying mouth. He was getting too old. He wanted to get home, back to the orphanage and the children. He had never liked being involved with the details of the business—the travel, the money, the bribes.

A tap-tap appeared far ahead, dust swirling into the blue sky behind it. When the bus came into full view, Father Charles was surprised to see almost no one on board. Petrale was isolated. Few people had reason to travel there. Suddenly, the old van slowed, and the steering wheel shook in his hands. The speedometer dropped steadily. Father Charles pressed hard on the gas pedal, but it went all the way to the floor. The engine shut off and the wheel locked.

Father Charles struggled against the locked wheel. He glanced at the tap-tap fast approaching. The van was right in its path. There wasn't much time. He could chance jumping out and warning the driver. But if he was too late, he and the van would be hit head on. Father Charles closed his eyes for a moment and prayed. A strong, heavy wind spewed through the window in answer. The tap-tap swerved around the van, kicking up dirt and a hail of small stones which rattled the doors like bullets.

Father Charles waved the dust away from his eyes, his heart pounding. He was finally able to see the tap-tap disappear in the rearview mirror. He let himself fall back against the headrest. That had been close, he thought, relieved. He looked down at the gauges in front of him. The speedometer needle had fallen beyond zero. In fact, all the needles had collapsed, including the fuel measurement. The car had run out of gas.

Father Charles groaned. He should have stopped at the gas station. It wouldn't have taken long. He berated himself for not thinking clearly and rationally.

The road was empty, the countryside utterly quiet. Father Charles stepped out of the van and slammed the door closed. The sound was lost to the vast space. He gazed up into the white-hot sky and closed his eyes. The sun bore into his eyelids. He put his hand on the roof. He screamed. The roof was a hot plate of steel. Father Charles shook his hand to cool the burn and stepped further into the road. He looked in the direction of Coluers, then back behind him to the border. No cars. No buses. No trucks. He was marooned in the middle of nowhere.

Father Charles took a deep breath. Patience was a virtue, as he always preached. He would wait for a sign.

COLUERS WAS QUIET BUT FOR THE CHORTLE OF THE CHICKEN TETHERED TO THE TREE. Grace looked for Nelson's white SUVs, but they were gone. She ached from the rugged drive. When she stepped out of the chilled car, her legs were momentarily numb, and she had to wait for the circulation to return. She felt Herve's hungry eyes on her as she moved toward the open doorway of the community center.

Grace's anger at Herve had lost its edge during the long, punishing car ride. He had insisted that the orphan "exchange," as he called it, was designed to help the children. It kept the orphanage open and paid for the new rooms being constructed. He didn't understand why he couldn't profit as well. Nothing came for free.

Grace hurried to the indoor bathroom, still sparkling clean from her work earlier. She relieved herself gratefully on the toilet. Before she flushed, she noticed the utter quiet that had settled over the compound. Sound carried far here. But there was no rattle or whine of a car engine or even a tap-tap rumbling in the distance. Nothing but the warm afternoon breeze.

Grace studied Herve as he peered at the distant hills. He strutted to his car. The Kreyol word *bok-batay* came to her mind. The fighting cock. Before climbing inside the Mercedes, he turned to her.

"I'll be back, Missy," he said. She knew what he meant, and it sickened her. She would have no protection.

Grace stared dumbly at the German sedan as it sped across the barren hills. He would have raped her on the side of the road, she thought. She had fought him, but that isn't why he stopped. A scrape, a punch, meant little to him. He wanted her the way he liked his whores. He would get her to come to him, to open herself up freely. He wanted to own her.

The sun was continuing its steady retreat into a crimson sunset in the direction of Jacmel. She bolstered herself with a thought of Dean, the way his attention and respect made her feel better than she had any right to feel. It wasn't right somehow. They were from different worlds, headed to separate futures.

The growing feeling for him was undeniable. Yet there was no future. Dean would leave and return to the woman in New York. Maybe, she thought, it was good. No complications. When you knew something good was temporary, sometimes you focused on the moment with gratitude and gave up worry about the future.

Grace turned and walked back to the community center. She glanced at the road to her bakery. One day she dreamed it would be filled with people from villages all over, like those who marched all night to market. Except they would be heading to the best *boulangerie* in the country. She smiled at the hope. This would come to pass, she was certain.

When she reached the open doorway of the community center, she heard the engines behind her. For an instant, she was struck with terror. Herve. But when Grace turned around, there were Land Rovers, one behind the other, driving toward Coluers. She smiled, happy to be able to see and hug Nelson, someone who could help and protect her.

THE MOSQUITOES BEGAN BITING AT DUSK. Some emerged, whining, from the damp floor of the shipping container. Others slipped through the gaps in the doorframe of the custom office's only entrance. Dean slouched in the same metal chair where the officer had questioned him earlier. He was alone, left to fend for himself. He knew now what he had not realized earlier: he was a prisoner who would have to buy his way out or risk disappearing altogether.

The last time the door had opened, the priest had walked in, looking nervous and agitated. He had announced he was leaving but would return. But his sincerity was strained. Neither of them believed it. Dean understood the priest had every reason to abandon him. Dean had made it abundantly clear that he would report the orphanage's trafficking of children. An exposé would shut down his orphanage and land Father Charles in prison.

When the door locked behind the priest, Dean took comfort in the vain belief that Grace would somehow return. They would drive back to Coluers, together. He pictured her hopeful expression, a romantic readiness that made him feel like a teenager. Those bright, soulful eyes radiated an infectious enthusiasm for life—despite or because of what she had been through.

The mosquitoes pricked both sides of his neck like pins. He felt the blood on the bumps, which were larger than he expected. Malaria, he thought. Please don't let me get malaria, too.

Dean jumped out of his chair, suddenly vigilant, and went to check the door again. The metal handle was immoveable. He held onto it and pushed against the door with his shoulder. When there was still no movement, he stepped back and rammed it. But he bounced off, his slight shoulder smarting from the harsh contact.

Next, he stooped down to examine the bolt that held the door in place. Mosquitoes whined around his ear. He couldn't bust through the bolt, but he reasoned he might be able to pry it away from the door frame. But the frame, too, was metal. Dean turned from the door, finally, and walked away.

Time crawled along even more slowly after he returned to his chair. He drifted in and out of a stupor like he had the flu. The mosquitoes continued biting, but he slapped them away mechanically without thought of malaria anymore. He wiped his lips, tasting some of his own briny sweat. He was thirsty, very thirsty. He hadn't drunk anything since the restaurant.

He was angry with himself for trying to reprise his professional role as a journalist. He had no business trying to go back and resurrect what he might have been in his youth. It was vain and childish. He had no business wanting to expose corruption in a struggling, poor country. He had come to help, to use his knowledge and experience to make a difference. It wasn't about him, at least he hadn't thought it was.

Worse, Dean thought, he'd gotten into this mess over his need for a woman. Maybe for love. It was foolhardy, romantic to a fault, racing to save the day like a starry-eyed idiot.

Dean stood up suddenly, thinking there might be water somewhere inside the shipping container. He walked the perimeter, but there was only dirt and no bottles of water. He wiped his lips again and swallowed. His throat was coarse and dry. He returned to his seat and closed his eyes.

After a time, the sound outside the door seemed to have dimmed with the light. There were no car engines idling. He could hear a few, indistinct voices calling out in the distance. The light at the bottom of the door was tinged with the rust color of late sunset. Dean jumped out of his chair. The working day was done. The guards were off duty.

He was locked up for the night. He was a prisoner.

Dean screamed and banged the metal sides with his clenched fists. The hollow space echoed with the sound. Anyone could hear it, including the border guards. But when he stopped and waited for a reaction, there was nothing. The giant tin can that surrounded him creaked from an unexpected gust of wind. They had no legal right to detain him like this. It was against the law.

But money made the rules. He thought of Herve suddenly. He and Grace would have seen the van parked next to the customs shipping container. But they had not stopped. Herve had not stopped. Dean understood why he wouldn't.

There were no coincidences. Father Charles was right about that. Dean was alone, unprotected. It was a plan. He was being set up to disappear. Why had he not understood until now? He had foolishly assumed that the border security guards upheld laws, as they would in the U.S. But money talked louder here. It made the law. Dean was certain that somehow Herve had arranged this with a few well-placed American dollars.

Dean tried the door handle again. He had to get out. He rammed the metal with his shoulders, much harder than before. He tried again and again, crazed with punching through. But nothing so much as budged.

THE ANGEL APPEARED AT THE END OF THE DARKENING ROAD. Father Charles had faith his angel would arrive sooner or later. But tonight, he hoped an angel might be driving in the direction of Coluers, not back to the border from where he had just come. Still, the priest felt blessed. He expected last-minute rescues, although not with a sense of entitlement or blind hope. In fact, he didn't believe he deserved the help. But it would arrive, unbidden. Every time. He could only thank God, humbled by His mercy.

The stars had begun to fade and disappear into the blackness. The high beams first flashed into it like floodlights. As the vehicle sped closer, Father Charles listened to the guttural rumble of the engine and the animal-like whining of the gears as the car or truck bounced over the many small potholes. The priest stood calmly outside his broken-down car, recognizing the cab of the small pickup truck as it emerged more fully out of the darkness.

Hours earlier, Father Charles had sat pensively on the front hood in contemplation. The dark land and sky that sprawled in all directions had awed him with its quiet majesty. He had embraced the peace of the solitude, accepting that few traveled this remote road. He recalled a spiritual exercise when he was in the seminary that called for him to imagine his own significance in ten thousand years. The obvious answer terrified him. It was a reminder of more than mortality. It was a reflection on vain, earthly strivings.

But God, endless God, with no end or beginning, would always be significant. Jesus Christ, unlike the man who died on the cross, would live forever. He who followed him would also live forever. But to follow Jesus meant to follow his teachings. He was a man who placed others first, not himself. He was no more significant than the dry weeds that rustled around him in the night breeze. But, in serving Jesus, serving others, he would live always. This was significance.

The truck slowed as it approached. Father Charles waited, grinning toward the driver who he could not yet see. It was a defense more than a greeting.

"*Allo. Tout bagay anfom?*" came a voice. Is everything okay?

The broad-faced man smelled faintly of whiskey. Father Charles knew the scent well because of Herve's penchant for bourbon. There was another, smaller person in the front seat, but the priest couldn't make out any details.

"My van, no petrol," the priest explained. "I did not think to fill up before leaving."

"Where do you go?"

When Father Charles mentioned the destination, the man's placid eyes widened comically in surprise.

"Coluers is a very long way. We are driving to Petrale. This direction."

Father Charles hesitated but knew he had little choice. He could take this ride back to Petrale or remain alone in the darkness, possibly for the entire night.

The young boy in the passenger seat made room for him. He looked about ten or eleven, sharp and observant, but he became meek trapped between the two adults. Father Charles smiled at the boy and thanked the driver.

"My nephew, Phillipe," the driver said as they bounced along the miserable road.

Father Charles couldn't see any family resemblance. The boy was thin with sharp, bird-like features and narrow-set eyes. The father was big and broad-shouldered with a middle-aged, watermelon stomach. His round, lazy eyes looked over a wide, flared nose. He was drunk.

"It is easier to drive in the day, yes?" Father Charles asked. He was curious why the man and his son would be driving so late at night.

"No. The sun, the heat is bad," the man said.

"Your home is in Petrale?" the priest asked.

The driver shook his wide head. He and the boy lived in a small town much further up the coast, one whose name Father Charles didn't recognize.

"The boy is visiting," the driver said.

"Family?"

The man didn't answer. He was struggling to watch the dirt road, strewn with shallow holes that alternately popped up and disappeared with the headlight beams like buoys on a dark sea. Father Charles didn't press for more information. Instead, he turned his attention to Phillipe, who stared dully ahead.

"You have been to Petrale before?"

The boy nodded sharply without looking at the priest.

"I am Father Charles," he announced. "Thank you for helping me."

The big driver seemed to instantly sober when he learned he had picked up a priest. It was very unusual. The boy, too, stole a glance at him.

"We go for work," the man said.

Father Charles understood without any more being said. There was no work in the impoverished border town. The only possible job was across the border in the Dominican Republic at one of the sprawling sugar plantations.

"You have been before?"

The man shook his head. He knew enough to cross the border while there was no one guarding transit. Every worker knew. A tired silence fell as the truck rumbled over a series of potholes, shaking them and the car. Father Charles clung to the shoulder strap and relaxed.

God works in mysterious ways, he thought. He was returning to the border town. There was a reason.

DEAN WAS SITTING IN THE SOUR-SMELLING DIRT WHEN HE HEARD THE TRUCK RUMBLE TO A STOP OUTSIDE. He jumped up, forgetting the ache of his arms and shoulders. His hands were swollen from battering the door with the metal chair.

The truck doors opened, followed by men's voices exchanging greetings. Dean froze. The moment he feared was here. There was nowhere to run, to hide, to escape. The truck rumbled off, followed by the sound of footsteps approaching. Dean braced himself. He might be able to lunge at them. No, that was senseless. It worked only in the movies.

The footsteps stopped on the other side of the metal door, and a key was inserted. Dean took a deep breath, his pulse beating so hard he could almost hear it. The door opened slowly out into early morning darkness.

In the doorway stood Father Charles.

"It is time to go, yes?"

"What?" Dean asked. He searched the priest's placid face, feeling relief but also confusion.

"We don't have much time," Father Charles warned. "We must leave."

"Where are we going?" Dean asked.

"Please. We must go." He held the door open to the warm, heavy air. "Before they come."

Dean followed the priest out the door into the blue darkness. He felt awkward and out of his element in the open air. The dirt street was empty. A dog barked unseen in the still silence as they hurried away from the shipping container.

"Where's the van?" Dean asked.

"It is of no use," Father Charles said.

"They took the van? They can't do that."

Dean stopped as if it might help him think with more clarity. The priest's words came back in his mind. They were running from someone, but who? Herve's thugs? The border police?

"Wait," Dean said, walking after him. "Where are you going?"

"The harbor," Father Charles said. "Please keep your voice low."

A few minutes later, they came to a small, impromptu fire on the beach. It was crackling and sputtering from chunks of plywood and assorted trash. Dark faces huddled around the glow of the flames. Some people waded into the black water beyond. There was a moored boat bobbing a few yards from the shore. The vessel sat in the dark water like an oversized bathtub, the bow and stern both round and just barely above the surface. There was luggage and cargo stacked on one end, and some passengers had already begun lifting themselves over the edge and climbing inside.

"Where does it go?" Dean asked.

"Jacmel," Father Charles said. Dean glimpsed the fear in the priest's slack face, his wide eyes shimmering from the uncertain light of the bonfire.

"Is it safe?" Dean asked, even though the answer was obvious. The weathered boat looked like a disaster waiting to happen.

"I don't know," Father Charles said.

Dean wondered why the priest was risking his own safety to help both of them return to Coluers. Father Charles had every reason to want to see Dean disappear. Yet here he was not only rescuing him from the jail but facilitating his escape.

"Did Herve set me up?" Dean asked.

"Yes."

"Who are we running from?"

Charles didn't answer. He watched as more and more passengers splashed and clambered onto the boat, causing it to rock. The priest had a strange, unfocused expression on his face. There were women with children, small groups of men, teenagers. A pregnant woman held another infant tightly against her swollen breasts.

"First come, first served," Dean said.

"The trip is made every day," Father Charles said. "Do not worry."

"Let's grab a seat while we can," Dean said. He took off immediately, headed to the dark water whose crests flashed bone-white under the stars. There were yet more passengers in the water, wading to the boat. Dean stopped at the water's edge when he realized the priest had not followed. Father Charles was standing still in the loose sand behind him, gazing out at the vast sea like a navigator searching for rogue currents.

"What?" Dean asked.

"I cannot swim," Father Charles said. He smiled with embarrassment.

"You don't have to. It's no deeper than your waist. They are walking right up to the boat."

"Yes?" He squinted into the darkness and the outline of the crowd splashing through the water.

"Follow me," Dean said.

The water was bathtub warm. There were rocks and shards of broken coral underneath, slowing their progress. Dean fought for balance on each rock below, felt the sharp edges of the coral push into his waterlogged shoes. A brine-scented breeze, thick with the stink of seaweed and dead fish, blew across them. Clumps of wet sea grass clung to his waist. Father Charles followed him, checking the sea parting around him as if he expected something to suddenly rise from its depths.

At the edge of the boat, Dean pulled himself up the side and climbed in first. Everyone was talking excitedly at once. There were smiles and sudden laughs, as if the passengers were about to embark on a holiday cruise. Dean turned back to the priest, who had stopped.

Father Charles rested his hands on the side of the boat. He watched the others. Dean offered his hands. The priest smiled and grabbed them both, locking his grip. Dean braced his knees against the hull and heaved the heavy priest up the side and onto the boat in one swift movement like he was flipping a hooked fish on deck.

Father Charles grinned at him, then laughed with the familiar warmth that Dean remembered from first meeting him at the entrance to the Cite Soleil. He was a good man, Dean thought. At heart, he was a good and caring man.

They found a spot closer to the wide bow and claimed it, as more and more passengers squeezed around them, seeking their own place to sit. The bodies crammed in the boat smelled dank and unwashed, enough to make Dean want to hold his breath. He looked to the shore and saw that there was no longer anyone around the fire, which was quickly shrinking.

The idling engine suddenly rumbled to life, sending a sheet of oily diesel smoke wafting over all of them. There was coughing and scattered cheers as the boat lumbered forward. Dean checked the thin, brightening line at the horizon, fearful of what the day might bring. He knew there was a long journey ahead.

"We go home," Father Charles said.

They watched the passing shoreline together as the border town slowly slipped away. The boat turned into the onshore breeze as they headed further out to sea and the yellow horizon, where swaths of brilliant salmon streaked under the dark clouds like sunset and not the beginning of a new day.

GRACE WOKE WITH A START. She was drenched in sweat and feeling feverish. Her stomach cramped sharply. She was moments from throwing up, so she ran past the other bunks and fell to her knees in the bathroom. She arched over the toilet, her body convulsing. A brown stream splashed into the basin. She vomited again and a third time before collapsing against the open seat of the toilet, utterly spent.

But she felt better, her breathing recovering as if she had just made a sprint. She thought of the old, brown grease that coated the eggs she had eaten at the cafe in the DR. They had made her queasy even then, but she dismissed it, thinking it was the tension among the men that was making her stomach feel uneasy.

"Food poisoning?"

Grace turned to find Nelson studying her with concern. With anyone else, she would have been deeply embarrassed to be seen sick and dressed only in thin underwear. But Nelson felt like a father to her, and his blue eyes did not even seem to register how little she wore. He was only worried about her.

Grace pulled herself up and stumbled to the sink. She threw water into her face, careful not to swallow what fell on her lips. She stood, propped up by the sink, staring into the porcelain surrounding the drain. It would need cleaning again.

"Let me get you some water," Nelson said. "And for God's sake, sit down a moment."

Grace glanced over at the toilet, concentrating on her stomach, worried she might get sick again. But the nausea had passed. She hobbled over to one of the folding chairs and sat down.

"No word still?" Nelson asked, returning with a warm water bottle. After Herve had left, Grace had sought out Nelson to tell him about their trip to the DR. She didn't mention a word about the orphanage and certainly not Herve's attempted rape. She was fearful of what might really have happened to Father Charles and Dean, why they had been lost before the border. Herve was capable of anything.

"They don't have a cell phone," Grace said. She snapped off the lid and gulped the water. She felt herself getting better.

"Right. You told me that," Nelson said. Before they had gone to sleep, he had offered to drive her back to find them. "Well, give the word and I can suit up."

Nelson stood in his boxer shorts and a worn muscle t-shirt that stretched across his small belly. But he seemed younger, more robust than his years would suggest. She smiled at his willingness to help her whatever the cost to him. Nelson acted like the parent she never had.

"We could miss them," Grace said. "If they are in the van."

She remembered Herve's threat to use the ferry to transport the children from Jacmel to Petrale at the border. Its safety record was infamous, but people still took it because few had any options. If the van had, in fact, broken down, she feared Dean and Father Charles might have tried to get a berth.

"They might have taken the ferry."

"Ferry? That's a worn-out cargo boat at best. Well, they would be dumber than I am. That thing drops more people in the ocean than carries them."

Grace found a chair and lowered herself gingerly to the seat. She still felt fragile and weak from being sick. She also had a growing fear for the lives of the men. Again, she pictured Herve's sleight of hand at the border. The bills concealed in his outstretched hand. The way the money was snapped up by the border cop. Could it have been a payment to have the American detained? Or worse? Herve was more than capable. He would do whatever was necessary to protect his business.

"I need to go talk to Herve," Grace said.

"To Leogane? You just spent twenty-four hours in his company."

"Could you drive me?" Grace asked.

DEAN NOTICED THE BOAT HAD SUNK DEEPER UNDER THE ADDED WEIGHT OF THE EXTRA PASSENGERS AND GROWING CARGO. There were bags and boxes and containers of all sorts, piled haphazardly in the back, on the sides, under those lucky enough to sit. When Dean saw a film of water slide over the wood rails and into the boat, he became alarmed. He considered getting out. But where would he go? He looked for Father Charles further down the gangway.

The outboard engine belched and spewed a puff of oily smoke, seeming to groan as it pushed the giant, floating bathtub forward. Dean swallowed and put the fear out of his mind. The loud chatter around him sounded like tourists on a cruise as the boat heaved over the gentle swells. A woman laughed happily when a baby wave splashed her.

Dean spotted the priest clinging to the boat, staring into the darkness. He worked his way through the crowd to sit alongside Father Charles. The priest smiled grimly at his arrival. They didn't speak. Dean did not understand why the priest was helping him. His orphanage and the trafficking business were better served by having Dean disappear one way or the other.

"Where's the van?" Dean asked, wanting to break the silence.

"Please?"

"Your van," Dean repeated. Both watched the passing shore as if there were something worth seeing in the scrub grass and scattered dwarf trees.

"It had no gas."

Dean thought it funny that he'd come back simply because he had somehow run out of gas. Sometimes, the reason we do things has a more simple and pragmatic reason than we think.

The priest's dark eyes appraised him.

"Everything happens for a reason," Father Charles said.

"The hand of God at work?" Dean asked.

"We are always at his mercy, yes?"

"No. We're not."

The priest raised his thick eyebrows.

"We're not at his mercy, Father, because whatever happens we choose how we react to it. That's not God. That's us, for better or worse."

The priest looked away into the brightening shore. The sun had risen without warning, burning away the morning clouds at the horizon and lightening the pale sky.

"You must be a lonely man, Mr. Dean. With no God, you are alone in this world."

Father Charles wiped away a spray of sea water from his bald head before splashing it on his cheek like after shave. Dean felt the sudden warmth as well. He pulled off his damp t-shirt and made a shawl out of it, protecting his face from the burning rays that would soon follow.

There was a time when he believed in God. He was younger and embraced the idea and the feeling that the Lord looked over this universe and his life in particular. But as disappointments grew, and as he witnessed and wrote about the endless crime and thoughtless cruelty perpetrated every day, he lost faith in the idea that a god could preside over our worst impulses. He had been lucky in some ways, too. But luck was not religion.

By late morning, the sea was a deep, translucent green that recalled the color of Grace's eyes. He hoped she would be worried about their absence by now. Unless she was somehow involved in all this business. He didn't want to consider that idea, but he couldn't help his own suspicions. They were part of the trade.

"Water?" Father Charles offered a liter plastic bottle to him.

"Repurposed?" Dean asked, remembering what the priest had told him back in the slum.

The priest smiled sadly. Dean felt poorly for asking as it recalled how good he had felt about the priest when they first met in the slum. The water appeared clear. He was aching for some of it. But he had come this far. There was no need to take unnecessary chances.

Father Charles handed off the water to a matronly woman with a rainbow-colored African headdress. She took it greedily and chugged the water. Beads of sweat dripped down her wide, deeply wrinkled neck. Dean watched, envious, and worried he had made the wrong decision not to drink it himself. Perhaps he would pay for it.

"Your face," Father Charles warned.

Dean touched his skin, which was dry and leathery and warm to the touch. Despite the homemade shawl, he was likely to burn. The sun was reflected off the water, intensifying its power.

"How long to Jacmel?" Dean asked. He couldn't help but think of himself and Grace there. It seemed ages ago.

Father Charles checked the near shoreline. The boat had hugged the coast for the entire trip. There had been a few of the tin and wood shanties scattered like junk yards along the coast. But there were no towns or villages.

"Not long," Father Charles said.

Dean pulled his knees closer to his face in a semi-fetal position, anxious to hide as much of his exposed skin as possible. The shadows created from some of the passengers sitting or crouched around him had seemed to help for a time. Now the sun was nearly overhead. Dean groaned inwardly.

No one else was complaining. It was an attitude he had seen time and again in Haiti. He was impressed and humbled by it. It was remarkable given the outsized woes they had to contend with from one end of the struggling republic to the other.

Survival was everything. By whatever means necessary without complaint or anger at their predicament. The *restavek* system was evidence. No boundaries, no limits. Whatever it took. Where was God?

After a time, the sunlight began to dim into a grayish haze. Dean was grateful for the breeze that had suddenly picked up. Any relief was welcome, and the gradual cooling made the ride more bearable.

A sudden roar of applause rippled across the boat with the force of a crowd cheering at a stadium. Dean followed their collective attention to the hills in the distance, crowded with nice homes or hotels. He was relieved. The town was within reach. Slowly, he felt the change in the air temperature. He thought he could smell rain.

Dean lifted himself out of his crouch and looked over the packed boat to the horizon. Coal black storm clouds billowed high into the grey sky like oil smoke. The brooding clouds frightened him. They were moving far faster than the bloated boat.

The chatter around him rose as the outskirts of Jacmel harbor appeared. Dean, however, was fixated on the storm at sea. It was moving still faster. A grey curtain of rain was falling. The sea below it churned with frothing whitecaps. The boat bobbed severely. No one else seemed to notice. The movement was just a boat in water. The wind was stronger, too, blowing ahead of the rain. The faces around him were fixated in the opposite direction, some smiling at the blue walls of the town. Dean felt a need to warn them. But no words came out.

A sheet of water exploded over the bow as the boat slammed into a growing swell. A few cries went out from the unexpected drenching. The sea had turned a dark pewter. The side of the boat was taking water already. His instinct had been good. It was too heavy to be seaworthy. Now it was a sitting duck.

"Father Charles?" The priest looked up from his seat, attentive but not reflecting any concern.

"Yes?"

Dean checked the packed cargo, looking for anything that might float.

"Don't you see the storm?"

The mood of the crowd on the boat had already changed. The happy chatter had subsided, followed by a queer, pregnant silence. Everyone looked to the horizon, where a wall of rain was marching across the open ocean, rolling toward them with inexorable force. Dean felt the terrible power. They were in the path of the storm and it would hit them long before they reached the safety of the harbor.

"Dear lord," Father Charles said. He clasped his hands together.

Now, sheets of water were flying off the bow, as the boat hit the roiling water. There was a sudden chorus of wailing around him. The wall was advancing, and they could hear the rain bang the water as if the drops were pounding metal.

The loud noise acted like a cue. There was a rush for the cargo pile as people scrambled to find a way to safety, something that might keep them afloat. The wind whipped around the boat, blowing trash and loose bags into the water. Dean braced for the coming impact like a car about to be hit.

The wind and rain slammed across the boat like a hurricane, pushing it hard leeward. Seawater poured into the boat as the bullets of rain exploded in a ferocious, heavy downpour. Dean gripped the side, struggling to see through the harsh rain. Jacmel had disappeared from sight. The storm cut them off from the land. He fought his own panic. They were close enough. He might swim, if necessary.

Cargo boxes went flying past as water crashed into his back and neck. He was shocked to glimpse passengers tossed into the sea with boxes. Stalks of sugar cane floated around them. Another wave followed and slammed Dean in the head and shoulders. But he hung on to the side. Others screamed for help in the sea.

His hand felt strange. He looked down to see it underwater. They were taking on more of the sea. The boat slowed, shuddering from the swells. Dean thought he stood a better chance in the boat than the open water. He had no idea what kind of currents or eddies could be swirling out there. He checked for Father Charles, hoping he was thinking the same.

The priest was gone. Dean searched the sea frantically, chaotic with arms and heads and screams. There was no way to identify who was who. He searched around him for life buoys but, of course, there were none.

The boat slowed further, trying to drag itself through the heavy water. Those in the water were slowly, agonizingly, drifting away. Dean suddenly remembered the look on the priest's face at the shore. Father Charles couldn't swim.

Dean searched the open sea through the veil of rain for the bald head. But there was almost no visibility. There was panic now. Passengers were rushing to the bow of the boat, the only part above water. The boat was filled with ocean water and rain, but the exodus of passengers and cargo had lightened the load and actually saved it from sinking. The hull remained buoyant, pitching slightly but churning through the leaden water toward the harbor.

48.

THE RAIN WAS FALLING IN THICK SHEETS, POUNDING THE BLACK STREETS OF LEOGANE. Nelson clung to the steering wheel. Grace perched nervously on the passenger seat. She would get the truth out of Herve, whatever it took to get him to confess what he had done. Grace felt a dread she could not shake.

"What's the number?" Nelson repeated. "I can't see anything."

Grace glimpsed one number through the reflection from a store window and stopped. They were close. Then she spotted his all too familiar green door. She remembered the bedroom, nearly empty of furniture except for the king-sized bed.

"Stop here," Grace said. She had the door open before he came to a complete stop. She leapt out into the rain and ran to the door.

"I'll wait here," Nelson said from his lowered window.

Grace hesitated at the door, oblivious to the warm rain. She was soaked instantly, her clothes clinging to her like a wetsuit. Water banged the top of her head. She made a tight fist and rapped the door, one blow after another, as if she were beating the wood itself. Grace felt the heavy water on her bare shoulders in the booming silence. She hadn't even considered the fact that he might not be home.

"Let me call him," Nelson called. He had taken out his cell phone. But before he could dial, the door opened.

Herve stood in the lighted entrance, shirtless. He stared at Grace and smiled.

"You change your mind, baby?"

"What did you do, Herve?" Grace demanded. She held both arms at her sides, her hands still bunched into fists.

"Who drove you here?" Herve motioned to the Land Rover. It was impossible to see anyone. He turned his attention back to Grace.

"Did you pay them off at the border?"

Herve sobered, looking from Grace to the Land Rover.

"They ain't back?" he said. "Is that Nelson? Shit, woman."

"What did you do, Herve?" Grace shouted the question this time.

He leaned back as if the question was an object hurled at him.

"Watch it, baby," Herve said.

"Just tell me."

Herve peered at the Land Rover, the exhaust puffing in the rain. The driver's side window slid down.

"Herve?" Nelson shouted. "For God's sake, let her in."

"Hi, Nelson." He waved and made a gesture for Grace to enter. But she wouldn't move, ignoring the rain.

"Tell me!"

Herve pursed his lips. He looked at her body wrapped in the wet clothes. Someone moved behind him. She wore a t-shirt that stopped far before her waist. The young woman sauntered to the bathroom, oblivious to the commotion at the door.

"They'll show up, baby." Herve said as his lover of the moment closed the door behind her.

"You bastard," Grace said. She spun around and ran back to the car.

"Your boy ain't no hero," Herve yelled after her. He slammed his door shut.

Grace sat upright in the muggy car, ignoring the water sliding from her head, along her cheeks. The realization hit her hard. Herve had somehow arranged for Dean to disappear at the border.

"What is he talking about?" Nelson asked after closing his window. "What hero?"

"Herve did something with Dean," Grace said and took a meek breath.

DEAN SPOTTED JEROME THROUGH THE WINDOW OF HIS STUDIO. He felt a flush of relief. Jerome would keep him from being alone. He felt the crush of survivor's solitude, the angst of all that happened. Dean noticed the late morning sunlight streaming through another side window, the dust glittering like specs of gold. It was unworldly, like a dream. Jerome answered the door after Dean finally knocked.

"My friend, you return," Jerome said. Dean stared back, suddenly not sure why he had walked here from the dock. What was he thinking?

"What happened?" Jerome asked soberly.

"It was bad. A storm came up."

"Where?"

"At sea."

"You were out in a boat? Why?"

Dean felt the coarse dryness in his throat.

"You have some water?" Dean asked.

He remembered trudging away from the boat, off the wharf, and had gazed up the hill to the top where he and Grace had sat only a day earlier. Only a day.

He took a sealed water bottle from Jerome, snapped open the cap, and drank greedily. He felt some of the water slip out of the corners of his mouth, unable to swallow properly.

"Why were you on a boat in a storm, may I ask?"

Dean swallowed more water, his stomach filling.

"Escaping a jail."

"You were arrested? Why?"

Dean moved to the bed where he had made love to Grace. He hesitated to sit down on it. The mattress was low on the floor and it would have been a challenge for him to easily sit. He looked at Jerome, who was watching him intently. He was surprised to remember a part of their conversation on the long tap-tap ride from Port au Prince, could hear it verbatim in his mind like it had been recorded. At the time, Jerome's talk had sounded like New Age babble. Not anymore.

"You were right, Jerome," Dean said.

"How?" Jerome.

"You told me on the bus that what I came here for would find me. It did."

Jerome waited.

"You don't remember saying that," Dean said, feeling foolish.

"Why were you in jail? Never mind. Let me give you some food. You need food," Jerome said. He hurried to the corner of the room where the hot plate rested on a low wooden box. He opened a green Tupperware container and sent the smell of peppery beans into the small room. Dean thought of Grace's body, unclothed here, smelling of mandarins.

"Here. *Mange*," Jerome said. Dean took the plastic container and the plastic fork that was handed to him.

"*Mange*," Jerome ordered. "There is a chair outside."

Jerome darted outside. Dean could smell the sea and hear the screeching of the wandering seagulls.

"Sit," Jerome said, returning with the blue canvas captain's chair.

Dean followed Jerome's orders.

"Where is your beautiful friend?"

Dean inadvertently glanced at the woman-in-progress on the canvas behind Jerome. He thought he recognized the regal shoulders, the narrow waist. The eyes were closed.

"We went to the DR. She drove back with someone. It was only the priest and I on a boat to Jacmel."

"The priest?"

Dean's story came out in a gush, out of sequence, back and forth, zigging and zagging, from Grace to the orphanage to Herve and, finally, the priest. Father Charles. He stopped abruptly when he described his head above water, the terror in his eyes.

"How did you know he could not swim?" Jerome asked. He was poised cross-legged like a yogi on his mattress, across from Dean.

"He told me."

Jerome took a long, strained breath and exhaled slowly.

"I am sorry, my friend," Jerome said.

Dean studied the canvas again.

"You are painting her?" Dean asked. "Grace."

"An idea of Grace, yes. Not her. I am painting from my imagination."

Dean wanted to see her and knew that he would. He had survived. But when he did see her, he suddenly understood that he would have to hurt her deeply. He would have to say what had happened to Father Charles. He would be informing her that a parent had drowned.

"Why were you arrested, my friend?" Jerome asked.

"They thought I was smuggling children out of the country."

"Were you?"

Dean stared back at him. "I was with the people who were."

"This was your story," Jerome said.

"I didn't choose it," Dean said. "I told you."

"My friend, Dean. We choose always."

A heavy, brined breeze blew and gave an instant of relief. As he climbed the steep hill that rose up over the docks, he saw the green and sapphire water and was struck by its beauty. There were still people milling on the wharf. But there was also freight arriving on hand-pulled carts. On the boat, a crewman was directing where they should be placed. The boat was loading up for its return trip.

Dean climbed to the summit and walked past the cafe where he had sat enraptured with the woman sitting languidly across from him in the shade. She made him nervous and uncomfortable and alive. He was at the start of something, the edge of a future he could not see or imagine. Now, it seemed like a long time ago, already fading like the lost grandeur of this watercolor city. He heard the rumble of the tap-tap as it approached.

THE ROAD TO COLUERS WAS DARK AND WET AND SMELLED OF THE RECENT DOWNPOUR. The night air was cool as Dean climbed out of the nearly empty bus and walked the rest of the way to the community center. There were no lights on, but the white brick building glowed faintly as did the half moon and stars behind the clearing sky. He was bracing himself to confront Grace with the news of Father Charles.

Dean smelled the pungent, spicy tobacco as he approached. The tip of the cigar grew fire red for a moment before grey smoke rose in a cloud in front of Nelson's face. His eyes appeared to be taking Dean in.

"You didn't walk all the way back," Nelson said. He drew on his cigar.

"Where is Grace?" Dean asked sharply. Nelson seemed surprised by his tone of voice and took a moment to answer.

"She passed out. Exhausted," Nelson said. "Worried when Father Charles and you didn't show up. Especially you."

Dean glanced into the darkness. He closed his eyes for a moment, thinking he might have to wake her up, which would make his telling even more difficult.

"We learned you weren't expected back," Nelson said. "So, I am mighty glad to see you."

"Thanks, Nelson." Dean felt outside himself, as if he were a ghost, invisible even to himself. "I wasn't sure I would get here either."

Dean crouched down to his ankles so that he and Nelson were directly eye to eye across from one another. The tobacco smoke was comforting.

"Father Charles wasn't so lucky."

Grace stepped out of the building. Her eyes lit up when she saw him. She smiled, and tears dripped down her cheeks like rain in the ghostly light. She ran to him. Dean caught her and held on, hugging her like his own life depended on it. Yet, he knew she couldn't have possibly heard the words he had just uttered.

"Thank God," Grace said, her eyes shining with a depth of affection that both startled and frightened him. Her concern and love humbled him.

"What happened?" Nelson asked.

Dean slowly backed away from Grace. She looked at him in confusion.

"Father Charles and I got the ferry boat," Dean said. He paused, searching for the best words to continue, to reveal what he was afraid to reveal.

"To Jacmel?" Nelson asked.

Dean nodded. He looked into Grace's eyes, wanting to stop and not say anything. But he couldn't.

"He didn't make it to Jacmel."

"Didn't make it?" Nelson asked.

Dean looked at Nelson.

"He drowned in a storm."

"Drowned?" Her voice sounded to him like a shriek.

Dean studied the ground ahead of him. The moon lit it like a bare lightbulb.

"He fell overboard, Grace. He couldn't swim."

Grace shook her head several times. The tears returned. Dean moved toward her to comfort her, but she held up her palm for him to stop.

"Did you see him?" Nelson asked.

"There were no vests. He was too far away already."

"Too far away?" Nelson asked.

"Too far to swim to him," Dean said. "Too far."

Dean hated how he sounded, overcome and weak with emotion. He wanted to be stronger.

"He came to save me," Dean said, "That's why we were on that boat. But I couldn't save him."

Grace turned away. He wanted to hold her again. But she walked away slowly, dumbly, like a sleepwalker.

"I need to lay down," she said without turning around.

The cicadas roared somewhere in the empty darkness. It sounded to Dean like people screaming, angry.

"Why did you need to be saved?" Nelson asked from behind him.

Dean turned.

"I was in a holding cell being interrogated."

"A holding cell?"

"I was being charged with child trafficking. Or something."

Nelson took a long draw from his cigar. The smoke rose up into the silvery light like the screen at a cinema. Both of them stared at the pungent cigar cradled in Nelson's three fingers.

"Herve is going to be pretty surprised to see you," Nelson said, finally.

"I bet."

Dean looked down at the dark mud beneath them. It was thick with clay. He remembered Herve's expression at the roadside breakfast in the DR. They were talking about the photojournalist who had visited the orphanage. Dean was all but certain that Herve had planned his disappearance, too.

"I'm sorry, Dean," Nelson said. He took a nervous puff of the cigar before flicking the nub away, where it disappeared into the mud with a hiss of smoke.

DEAN LAY NAKED AND SPENT IN HIS BUNK. Two mosquito coils smoked like foul-smelling incense sticks on either side of him. He was drenched in his own perspiration and exhaustion. It felt like he had a fever. The dark sea continued to swell in his mind, the crests boiling over as the heavy rain pelted the surface like a fusillade of bullets. He saw the priest. At least he thought so. It was so brief, a flash, and he thought he witnessed the arms of the man flailing against the roiling water, trying desperately to keep his head from sinking below the surface.

He might have jumped into the ocean to save the man. Dean was a good swimmer. He might have reached the man in time and locked him in rescue hold. The boat pilot might have seen them bobbing in the water and returned to pick them up.

Now there was no way to know. He looked for the man through the pelting rain. But there was only the dark water and colliding swells and angry spray.

Father Charles was gone now.

Dean sat up suddenly, remembering the balding priest strolling across the black canal. He was walking on water. Charles urging him to follow, as though the miracle was common, something anyone could perform. Dean heard the warm laugh, bellowing at him as he1 struggled through the walkway of sinking sewage and fell to the ground on other side.

Dean got out of bed and stood on the cool, cement floor. Everyone in the bunks remained asleep. He felt sicker when he spotted Grace, curled in a fetal position on her single bed across from him. She appeared sound asleep. He knew she would wake up to the pain again, the loss of a father and protector. It was not his doing. Dean understood that. But he felt responsible in spite of it.

Dean grabbed his soiled chinos, stepped into each pant leg and snapped them closed at his waist. He slipped on his shirt, having to pull parts of it across him as the cotton clung to damp skin. He began buttoning from the bottom. He had never concentrated so deeply on the simple act of getting dressed.

Dean was grateful he was leaving to return to New York. It had been planned. He could not face Grace when she woke up. He didn't want to hurt her anymore. It was best that he left.

DEAN WALKED ABSENTLY TOWARD THE ORPHANAGE. He remembered Grace walking alongside him that morning, which seemed a lifetime away. The smell of her, the presence. But he was doing what he had planned, what he had to do. Dean was due back in New York. He had a story to file. He laughed to himself, a mirthless, humorless laugh. His story, when printed, would do more than expose the trafficking. It would be another strike against Grace and what she loved. Yet, he had to do it just as he had to leave.

He stopped at the edge of the forest. The voices of children drifted through the air. They were awake, but who was caring for them, he wondered. Father Charles would not have left them unattended while he was gone.

Dean considered walking down to the compound and finding out. But what did it matter? He could do little about it anyway.

When he returned to the community center, Dean found everyone had gone. The Land Rovers had driven off, the visitors gone. His walk had lasted much longer than he realized. But, still, he looked for Grace. Her bunk was empty.

Dean walked up the short hill to the bakery. The high, bruised mountains seemed to climb over one another well into the distance. The bald ridges were like shoulders jostling for their place in the sun. He could imagine future forests of lush moringa blanketing the range, an island returning to what it once was, centuries ago. Why not?

The sun was rising quickly, beating down on him as always. He didn't fight it or complain to himself. He would be out of it soon enough. He found Grace hiking down the hill toward him, as if she knew exactly when to come. He smiled dumbly, thrilled to see her. She wore her red bandana, the dirty apron. Her face was dabbed with flour.

They both stopped a few feet away from one another.

"I was told you were leaving."

Dean nodded.

"This morning?"

Dean nodded again. He should say something, but no words came to mind.

"Well isn't that just fine."

"I don't like goodbyes," Dean said. He did have a habit of not saying goodbye, even in casual situations. He often left parties without a word to the host or other guests. He felt it formal and unnecessary. Mostly, it made him uncomfortable.

"Too bad."

"I was coming to see you."

"You saw me."

She glared at him.

"I'm sorry."

"You said that already," she said, her lips hinting at a sneer that took him by surprise.

"Grace, look..." He moved toward her. She backed up.

"Don't. Don't you get anywhere near me," she said. "You got your story. Go home."

Dean was stunned by her palpable hate.

"I don't want to leave."

"Yes, you do."

Dean never imagined there would be reason to stay. As he studied her familiar face, the lines of aging and sorrow endearing her more to him, he was reminded again that his own journalistic ambition threatened to destroy the progress she and others had made in Coluers. The exposé of the orphanage would bring scrutiny to the village and the region and could threaten the funding that kept things going.

They heard the whine of the bus gears in the distance. The tap-tap to Port au Prince was climbing the hill on the other side of the bakery. Dean checked the overlook platform, as bare as an altar. Grace followed his attention. They both lingered, looking silently at the platform like it was trying to speak to them.

"I am so sorry about Father Charles."

"You said that, too."

The tap-tap crested the hill, trailing a familiar cloud of tan-colored dust. It rumbled to a stop just beyond them. A few passengers trundled out of the front, unhurried. The ropes on the side were empty. He could see that Grace recognized some of her bakery staff. They waved to her and glanced warily at the *blan*.

"I'm coming back," Dean said. He had no idea he was going to say it. But spoken out loud, he knew it was true.

"You have what you came for," Grace said. Her eyes had softened, her face drawn and tired.

"I don't think I do," Dean said. She smiled with her lips, saddened with the same intensity he'd witnessed last night.

"Di m' ki sa ou renmen, m'a di ou ki moun ou ye."

"Which translates?" Dean asked.

Grace leaned back.

"Tell me what you love, I'll tell you who you are," she said.

Dean nodded, knowing what he should say, what he needed to say. But he didn't. He stood mute and didn't move when Grace turned around and sauntered back up the road toward the bakery.

THE PRESS RELEASE ARRIVED IN HIS MAILBOX THE DAY AFTER DEAN EMAILED HIS ARTICLE TO THE *NEWSDAY* EDITOR. The cheaply xeroxed letterhead had originally been embossed with the organization's name, Moisson, with sprigs of harvested wheat crossed together like arms. He hadn't known the NGO possessed a logo. The face of the organization in his mind was Nelson. He was the blue-eyed, white-haired lawyer riding bareback on the plodding mule in the endless hills.

The short PR note, written in the journalist style common to the genre, made Dean feel even more removed. The note described a midday memorial at the orphanage chapel, the same chapel where he and the priest had talked. Now, thousands crowded into the compound, many traveling for miles over the mountains to pay their respects. Father Charles was a hero of the poor, it stated unequivocally, a champion of the young needing care and longing for a family life.

Dean stood up from his desk in the corner of the living room and looked outside into the brown garden of late fall. He listened to the mid-morning traffic rumbling down the towering canyon of drab apartment buildings that lined both sides of West End Avenue. He wondered why he had ever believed New York City was a place he would want to live.

Dean had considered not writing, or at least not submitting, the story. He'd done enough damage. He feared he'd taken the role of most journalists who came to Haiti: hunters looking for deadly game that could boost or even make a career. Jerome had said it once on the tap-tap. Reporters came not to tell the story of Haiti but to use the country to make their own mark.

Even worse, he understood that what he would report would sully the great priest. Grace would be hurt even more, like losing her beloved father twice.

But, despite the doubts, Dean wrote and submitted the story. He felt a responsibility to report the truth. It was the allegiance that mattered. He could not worry about the consequences. Still, the story had come at the expense of others.

He imagined Grace mourning the bald priest. She loved him as a father and a savior, a personal savior, the man who rescued her from a life of servitude and horror. Dean expected Grace would hate him for exposing his trafficking orphanage to the public. It would be like admitting to the world your father wasn't the man you admired. His boast, his promise, that he would return to Haiti felt presumptive, naïve.

DEAN WAS PROUD OF HIS STORY DESPITE HIS MISGIVINGS AND HOPED TO BUY TWENTY COPIES OF THE PAPER FROM THE NEWSSTAND ON 96TH STREET AND BROADWAY. The physical presence of his story impressed him beyond what he expected. It wasn't an article on the web. He could pick this up, feel it in his hand. It felt substantial.

The newsstand was a steel hut positioned near the subway entrance where thousands hurried past. The Hispanic vendor standing inside had objected to the large purchase since it would nearly wipe out his supply of the Saturday paper, which the owner believed would discourage customers from stopping at his business. So, they settled on ten copies.

"Why do you have so many?" he asked. His dark eyes were intelligent and suspicious.

Dean pointed out his article and, especially, the bold black byline. He had to admit it felt like having his name in lights.

"You?" he asked, impressed.

Dean was reminded how so many foreigners still respected the written word. It remained as intrinsic to their cultures as cable TV was to Americans.

The vendor scanned the headline, shaking his head.

"All for money," he said "Always, yes?"

Later in the day, Dean was happy to get emails from friends and acquaintances who praised his article. But he wasn't encouraged. He knew stories about events in foreign countries didn't raise much interest except maybe in New York with its legions of immigrants.

Dean kept in close touch with the newspaper editor over the next weeks, pitching stories. But nearly all of their brief and cordial email conversations ended with the same line.

"Let us know when you have something else to share with us."

Dean's story came and went in the hyper-paced news cycle. The media beast was omnivorous. The revelation of an orphanage trafficking in children was a minor headline for a few hours (world news section, page 4), then was swept off the ledger by new ones. Dean had hoped for more reaction, outrage perhaps, or simple interest. The story was amplified by a few web sites that picked up the exposé, but the reporting couldn't keep up with the beast that demanded new news.

There was one attentive reader. A week after the article appeared, Dean received a handwritten note forwarded by the newspaper's editor. It was posted and dated from the rented New York office of Moisson.

Greetings Dean!

Not the PR we were looking for. But I read your article with considerable admiration and sadness. You offended many people—including our board of directors—but none more so than those closest to you. I am sorry. But you wrote what you were obligated to write. It is your calling. I thought it might be mine once, but the law found me first.

Dean could hear Nelson's warm voice. He absently rubbed the edge of the paper between his finger and thumb, fascinated at receiving a genuine, physical letter. He didn't know anyone who wrote them anymore.

I am writing to you also to tell you. Herve Frenois has not been seen for weeks. He did not attend the funeral. Even without an official inquiry, the publicity couldn't have gone down well with an apparatus used to operating in the dark. May God protect us all.

Regards,

Nelson

Dean had quoted Herve in the article after he claimed all he and Father Charles had undertaken was within the law, sanctioned by the government and other agencies. It was a bald-faced lie, of course, but Herve shrewdly guessed no one would commit resources to investigate the suspected child laundering.

No one cared. Dean felt angry as if he had been conned. This story was supposed to matter, to make a difference. He did much more harm than good and for what? He'd fooled himself, he thought bitterly. Grace may have been right with that Haitian saying. He'd shown what he loved and now knew who he was, and it wasn't pretty.

HERVE SKIPPED THE FUNERAL. He didn't need to go. The sad rites were for the comfort of the living, not Poppy. The priest was gone to his Savior. Poppy preached that the next life was the goal of the living. There he would join with the Father, Son, and Holy Spirit. But, for Poppy, he would stand with the Son of God, the man come to earth to suffer for all.

Herve didn't believe a word of it. There was plenty of suffering to go around, and no one man, no one crucifixion, was going to change that. It was crazy to think a person would voluntarily suffer for anyone else. People just didn't do that. Self-interest ruled.

As he strolled down the dark, unlit street toward the parked Mercedes, he heard a couple bickering loudly, their voices bouncing off the facades of the cinder block houses like gunfire. Tensions got bad on a hot, muggy night like this one. The air was dead still.

Herve was planning to drive to the community center in Coluers. He'd been going every night since the boat accident. Grace had taken over the administration for the time being and was always there to talk. They both missed him. But Herve was surprised how much Poppy's death bothered him. For weeks, he avoided talking with anyone. He bought a few women to ease his sadness. But he couldn't feel that either.

Herve lived a waking dream where he kept seeing the nervous, smiling priest who loved rare steak, but also the chubby kid who was his only friend when they were boys. His only one. Now he was gone. But the finality would not touch him. In his vision, Herve would watch as Poppy stumbled into the community center, smiling, telling him how God rescued him from the sea.

"You need to believe, Herve. One day you'll have to," Poppy had lectured him more than once.

"Why is that?"

"Because you'll have no choice."

Herve stopped alongside the front door of his car, noting the dirt caked on the front tire rims. Annoying. He'd paid one of the neighborhood kids to wash and wax the car. At least the smooth paint glimmered like a woman's torso in the faint starlight. Herve liked to think of his car as a woman, and he slipped inside with relish.

He knew life would be difficult without Charles. There was no replacing him as a friend. But the orphanage was going to need someone. He liked the idea of Grace. She was a *restavek.* Kids got sold for good reasons. When she got a good, sweet whiff of the money in it, any objections would blow away like smoke. Women loved money more than anything else. It promised comfort and security and endless clothes. Grace was no different.

Herve still wanted her badly. Her body could be brought around, too. She couldn't hold out much longer, especially with the *blan* gone. Same old. The white man took what he came to get and left a mess behind for someone else to clean up—or not.

Herve heard the sound of a car approaching behind him. He turned as the headlights appeared. It was moving fast, faster than he'd ever seen in sleepy Leogane. Herve froze in momentary confusion, but he knew. It was a fear that dogged him as it did so many. It was as much a part of their history as freedom.

The old car squealed to a stop, just missing a collision with his car's back end. He glimpsed the men inside. One wore sunglasses. Herve inserted the key and turned. There was still a chance to get the car started and escape. They wouldn't be able to keep up. But nothing happened. He turned the key in the opposite direction and the locks popped open.

Car doors opened behind him. Footsteps echoed like gunshots. Dogs barked desperately in the distance. Herve turned the key to start the engine. The doors all flew open. He started, shocked by the blow against the back of his head, then everything was white before he lost consciousness.

CYNTHIA'S EYES NARROWED COOLLY AS SHE OBSERVED HIM. The voices of the other diners in the cafe mixed with the subdued clatter of plates and silverware. Both sat silent and pensive in the shadowy light of the table candle. Dean knew something was coming.

"Did you meet someone over there?" Cynthia asked.

The question was casual, not confrontational. It was voiced in the same tone as if she had asked if the mosquitoes were bad in Haiti.

Dean was honest to a fault. But he believed this was one time he shouldn't tell the truth. There was no point. Grace would never leave Haiti, and he was back home. He didn't want to have a confrontation anyway.

"I met a lot of people," Dean said.

"I'm sure you did," Cynthia said, glancing at the uneaten dinner on her plate. The glaze on the grilled tofu had cooled and hardened.

"Why?"

"Because you've been acting differently since you've been back," Cynthia said. He could see she had been thinking about it for some time. "With me," she added.

"I started a new career, for Christ's sake," Dean said. He told himself he likely would have felt differently even if he had not met Grace. But he also had not stopped thinking about her, remembering the scent of the miracle tree blossoms that drifted off her into the humid, soft air.

"Yeah, a new career," Cynthia said and took her silver fork and cut a piece of the tofu. Dean could smell the soy sauce, an aroma that seemed to emanate from the vegetarian restaurant as a whole.

"I am aware you don't approve," Dean said. She had been livid when he announced he was quitting the firm and going back to the work he had always loved most.

"Who knows, maybe you'll be able to make a living this time around."

"It's an honest living."

"Is that what these exposés are?"

Dean was silent. He understood his article had helped to shut down the orphanage and the lives of many desperate children. They had nowhere to go. He had turned so many back into starving orphans.

"The truth will set you free," Dean said. It was flippant, and he didn't really believe it, but it was too late.

"Free? Do you feel free, Dean?"

Dean didn't have an answer. He felt guilty that his reporting had put an end to the only home those children knew. There would be no one to feed them or house them or take care of their lives. Of course, they wouldn't be sold like slaves either.

"You're right. I need to do something," Dean said. He looked down at the kale salad he had ordered. The sesame oil on the dark leaves glistened, smelling of sweet smoke. He had yet to taste it.

"Like?"

"I should do something," Dean repeated, wanting to convince himself. "Not just report. Get involved."

"Oh my God, Dean. Now you're going to be a social worker?"

Dean shrugged.

"You sound like a kid. And you're a long way from that."

"I should go back," Dean said. He couldn't help but think of Grace.

Cynthia's face went taut with surprise. She took her bite of food as if her throat were dry and she had trouble swallowing. Finally, she looked at him, her eyes strained and on the verge of crying.

"You met someone," Cynthia said. "You shit."

Cynthia sat in cold silence. A few moments later, she suddenly laughed. It was dark and sardonic.

"You know what's funny? I'm not actually sad. Just angry that you lied and tried to cover up what you can't."

"I'm sorry," Dean said.

"Shut up," Cynthia said. "Just shut up."

DEAN MOVED OUT OF THEIR APARTMENT A FEW DAYS LATER. He found a studio sublet in the East Village with one window that opened onto a fire escape. Light filtered in at midday but only for a few hours before it became dim inside, then darkness. There were times he felt as though he were living in a tomb. But his new venture as a fulltime freelance reporter kept his spirits up. He had become what he once was, what was supposed to have been his calling. Yet it felt like an empty achievement. He wasn't any happier than he'd been before. He was beginning to feel lost. The new road he was driving down wasn't the way.

CNN's talking head was chattering from his flatscreen on the wall as he logged onto his computer. Pungent steam poured out of his hot morning coffee that sat alongside. He'd dropped an English muffin in the toaster, which he knew he was unlikely to eat, but it had become his routine. His inbox was flooded with junk mail despite the filters. He was looking for responses to the emails he'd sent last night about his new story. Meanwhile, news headlines and stock market ticker tapes flowed across the TV screen, switching to shrill commercials in midstream then back again to the headlines. What was strange was the announcer repeating the date, January 12. Okay, Dean thought, so it's January 12.

Then the news reader said something he wasn't sure he'd heard correctly. It was a familiar name. The second time Dean heard it right: Leogane. He looked up at the screen. It looked to be some kind of refugee camp. Then, the repetition started. Leogane was the epicenter of the earthquake. Of course. Leogane. The name of Herve's home exploded in his mind. An earthquake had hit. Towns flattened. Thousands killed among collapsing homes and buildings.

Dean turned from his desk into the tiny living room to see the images. It wasn't the same country. Shanties blown into a vast, sprawling sea of bricks, dirt, and rubble. Hills wiped clean. Towns blasted like they had been the target of an air assault. Faces dejected, crying. Corpses in the street.

Leogane had been hit harder than Port au Prince. Coluers, he knew, was less than a half-hour's drive away. Easily encircled in the earthquake zone. He guessed Grace had likely been at the community center or her bakery. He pictured her there, her face brushed with white flour. Dean felt as though he were in some dream, not really understanding what was happening around him.

Dean grabbed his cellphone. He called Nelson's number at the NGO. But it was busy, likely jammed with other calls. Dean paced in his narrow hallway. He called the Haitian Embassy in midtown. An answering machine picked up. He had to find out what had happened to Grace. He pictured the flimsy orphanage, the ground rising, terrifying the children, the walls flattening like dominoes.

THERE WERE NO COMMERCIAL FLIGHTS TO HAITI. Nearly a week passed before Dean was able to talk his way onto a seat on a charter flight with Catholic Relief Services. He shared the small, narrow prop plane with career helpers who were accustomed to flying into disaster zones. They slept through the unstable air that yanked the plane up and down like a yo-yo.

A Red Cross staffer had warned him Haiti remained chaotic since the "*bayat la*," as the people called it. *The thing*. The terrifying rumble of aftershocks were continuing.

Dean hired a driver to take him directly to Coluers and bypass the city, or what was left of it. He would report on Port au Prince later.

In Coluers, Dean was startled to see there were no ruins, no suffering from the earthquake. Instead, there was the bustle and hum of progress. Women from the bakery, still wearing their white aprons and baseball caps brushed with bread flour, grinned as they hurried past the *blan* to the bus. There was a burst of laughter from the interior of the tap-tap where the workers had disappeared.

Dean climbed onto the cement veranda outside the bakery. Some mud flew off his shoes, scattering on the toothpaste-white concrete, and he was sorry he had soiled it. A new picnic bench had been set up nearby, looking like a rest stop off the Connecticut turnpike. He heard a radio chattering from inside the bakery, then the burst of rock Kreyol, familiar sounding, like any pop station blaring from a bodega on the streets of New York.

As he approached the squat building, as white as the veranda, he saw sacks of flour stacked nearly to the ceiling. Bare light bulbs dangled from the concrete ceilings, illuminating the broad, stainless-steel ovens. Dean was impressed with how much progress had taken place at the bakery in the months he'd been away. It was functioning completely now and better supplied than any shop he'd ever seen in the country.

He walked apprehensively into the oven room, next to the sacks of flour, searching. A cheap, unseen portable radio was playing a ballad in Kreyol. He turned the corner before he glimpsed the woman he had traveled to find. Even then, he wasn't sure what he would do.

Grace stood at a stainless-steel table, kneading dough. A red bandana covered her head like a veil. Her proud cheekbones gleamed with perspiration; a streak of white flour spread on one like make-up. Grace was working hard, utterly focused on the task. He studied her without a sense of time, admiring her familiar beauty with wonder.

Grace turned to look at him. Her eyes barely registered for a moment. Dean thought he had made a terrible mistake returning. He had misjudged her feelings for him, assuming they were exactly as vital as his. He didn't know what to do.

Suddenly, Grace's old self returned, her eyes lit brightly with affection. Her pressed lips relaxed, then grew into a wide smile. She beamed at him, and he felt himself grinning like a young boy. He had not misjudged her feelings at all.

As he walked toward her, she checked the dough in her floured hands. Her eyes welled with tears when she again met his.

"I had to come back," Dean said, as if some explanation was needed.

Grace's lips trembled as her face strained with such intensity that veins were visible at her temples. He thought she was either going to scream at him or collapse. Dean moved closer but stopped just out of reach, fearful he might upset her more.

"The bakery is fine," he said, bewilderment in his voice. "Coluers?"

She tensed when he touched her shoulder with his hand. Dean withdrew his hand but watched her closely, fearful.

"Gone," she said. "The orphanage is in bad shape, but none of the children were even hurt."

"A miracle," he said, amazed. Dean could not imagine the plywood barracks could have withstood the force of the moving earth.

Her eyes shone with a despair he'd never seen before, not even after the loss of Father Charles. Dean moved forward, feeling desperate. He had returned to be with her. But he could not summon any words to express himself. He was overwhelmed.

"You came back to report?" Grace asked, coolly.

Dean felt the separation, quiet but quivering beneath them like an earthquake. She was moving away from him. Dean shook his head as he met her questioning gaze. But still, the words would not come.

"I have to get back to work," Grace said, wiping her hands across her soiled apron. "It is all we can do now."

Grace stepped away, mechanically, knocking the breath out of him. Dean couldn't believe what he was allowing to happen. It was like watching an accident in slow motion, a glass falling from a table moments before it shattered on the floor.

"Grace," he called. She stopped and slowly turned around. She seemed merely curious, as if he wanted to ask some trivial question.

Dean felt foolish, humiliated. He had returned to sweep her off her feet, but when the moment came, he couldn't do it. Instead, he stood in the mud on an empty road with nowhere to go.

The whine of a distant engine broke through the silence. Grace turned back to the bakery without a word.

The bright tap-tap appeared around the bend, the sunlight bouncing off the exuberant graffiti. Dean stepped forward like a sleepwalker as the bus slowed and squinted inside for a seat. As the bus lurched forward, he stole one last glance out the window.

Grace was coming toward the bus. Dean was not even conscious of how quickly he lurched out of his seat or his shouted command to the driver to open the door. He leapt out long before the tap-tap even slowed so that he bounced off the road as soon as he hit and tumbled over his shoulder. He pushed up off the road and hurried toward her.

They halted a few paces from one another as if there was a dividing line. The distance between them was small, but it seemed to widen with each moment of hesitation and confusion. Dean struggled to catch his breath, seeing her neck and chest heaving, straining under the thin shirt.

"Why did you come back?" Grace asked, finally, tears dripping across her dusty cheeks. "Can't you tell me? Why?"

"For you, Grace. Only for you."

The words spilled out of him. He felt a sense of triumph and also fear, a vulnerability he didn't like, pulling him forward. He was caught up in an unknown current now, feeling his life changing, sweeping forward whether he was ready for it or not.

They stepped into each other's arms. Dean held on, feeling their bodies bound together without a thought to ever letting go.

They watched the cloud of dust swirl after the tap-tap, around the corner and down the bare mountain. They were left alone on the sun-beaten road. A hot breeze stirred then collapsed, and they were surrounded by the roar of cicadas.

He kissed the side of her head closest to him, tasting her damp hair, smelling her sweat. He felt her heart racing, shuddering against his ribcage. He smoothed her hair reflexively, wanting to calm her. He was surprised to suddenly feel his own chest beating as rapidly as hers.

After a long moment, Grace slipped away, taking both his hands as she did so. They looked at one another and laughed.

"I love you, Grace Mouzon," Dean said. He felt exposed and alone, as though he were sharing a secret.

"I know," Grace said.

Dean glanced over the hill at the community center perched on the hilltop. He remembered how he had started when he met her coming out of the shadows of the hotel doorway, thrilled and then frightened, as though he had met something more than a lovely woman on a dark and rain-swept porch. It was something like fate. The question then, as now, was whether he was open and strong enough to embrace it.

"I want to stay here with you," Dean said.

"Here?" Grace said, her lips forming an embarrassed smile.

"Yes, here," Dean said.

"You are in love," Grace said.

She leaned over and met his open lips. They kissed tenderly; their tongues entwined like their damp fingers. When they finally pulled back, an unexpected breeze touched them. They held hands, facing one another.

Her lower lip betrayed a slight, almost imperceptible tremble. He studied her, reminded of her past, the feelings of unworthiness that rose up in her in equal measure to her general self-confidence.

"I love you, Grace."

"You said that," Grace said, smiling, her eyes gleaming, fever bright. She reached behind her and untied her white apron. She slipped the shoulders off and let it fall to the road. She pulled off her red bandana and shook her hair, which bounced into life with a flirty air that made him laugh.

"What are you doing?" Dean asked.

"Going on break."

She stood in front of him, her long arms at her side. Her pose and expression made him imagine the gangly twelve-year-old Grace, standing outside the church where Father Charles would rescue her and give her the promise of new life.

"What about New York?" Grace asked.

They turned together as if by habit and began walking in the direction of Coluers. A quiet sobriety descended over them like the light fading over the day.

"The center is gone," she reminded him.

"But the orphanage," Dean said. "Who is caring for the children there?"

Grace didn't answer. Dean felt awkward alongside her, looking at the empty country road. He felt her hand in his, suddenly, and relaxed.

DEAN WOKE WITH A SHIVER. The morning shade was cold and damp. There was no window glass, only a cutout for one. The plywood hut made it feel like they were camping and just passing through. He rolled out of the empty but still warm bed and noticed the sunlight striking the grassy square, tinged with a smoky vapor. He took a quick breath, relishing the sweet moisture. Soon it would be hot enough. Already, he found he liked it.

The children were still asleep. But the jungle around them stirred with the cry of unseen birds and the chatter of insects. Dean walked across the plank landing, the newly treated wood streaked with green arsenic, and down the two steps to the grass. He thought about the painting scheduled to begin today. He'd picked up the supplies himself days earlier from a warehouse at the airport.

The sound of the jet engines and the smell of benzine clinging to the humid air at the airport had brought back unexpected memories. Most prominent was the familiarity, the feeling of travel, of starting fresh. Maybe it had been only the routine of arriving at a new airport in another city, but there was the unmistakable feeling of possibility even in that.

Grace had woken early and hiked to the center to get supplies for breakfast. Food was scarce for another day until the truck came from Leogane. Dean was working to change the delivery system and even the food itself. Rice and beans were not enough. They could do better. The children deserved it.

"*Blan!*" The sharp feminine voice startled him. Dean spun around to find Katrine standing behind him, her hands on her tiny hips, staring up at him. She was the most vocal and strident child at the orphanage, a fact he didn't always like. Katrine could be a pain.

"*Bewn jou*," Dean said. "You are up early."

"I am hungry, *blan*."

Dean nodded. He walked to her and scooped her up in his arms. Her dark eyes peered at him.

"I am hungry, too, Katrine. We'll eat soon."

The little girl nodded, pleased.

"What?"

"What do we eat?"

"Food."

"Porridge? Fruit?"

"Moringa maybe," Dean said. He'd grown to like the miracle beans when mashed and spiced hot.

"That's all?"

Dean didn't know what kind of food Grace would bring back to the orphanage. He also hoped there might be baguettes from the bakery even if they might be days old and a little hard. They tasted wonderful with the butter from France, a staple sent from a Paris-based NGO.

"A feast, Katrine," Dean said, smiling. He rubbed his nose on hers until she giggled. She suddenly put her tiny hand on his damp face and left it there, studying his skin.

"I think I will call you Poppa," she said.

"No more *blan*?"

"Poppa Blan," she said and giggled.

Dean grinned and walked with her into the spotlight created by the sun. It warmed him instantly. He loved holding the little girl as if she were his own daughter. He ignored the mosquito that bit him in the neck. It was, like the incessant heat, a part of life in the high mountains.

Also by **WILLIAM PETRICK**

In a remote rain forest in Belize, a filmmaker risks everything to get the story.

THE FIVE LOST DAYS

"....makes me grateful for all the close calls I avoided in a lifetime of reporting documentaries....utterly believable and downright scary."
– BILL MOYERS, LEGENDARY JOURNALIST AND WINNER OF OVER 30 EMMY AWARDS

An obsessive videographer jumps to film his own skydive—with just one fatal mistake. The father of a condemned killer takes on an ambitious reporter anxious to make her career. A corporate spin doctor learns that sometimes the absolute truth is the most effective lie. Stories of life in the media of mirrors.

VIDEO VÉRITÉ & OTHER STORIES

"... powerful tales will give you much to think about and will remain with you long after you've put the book away."
– SEATTLE POST-INTELLIGENCER

Visit **PearhousePress.com**

www.ingramcontent.com/pod-product-compliance
Lightning Source LLC
Chambersburg PA
CBHW060602310726
48982CB00008B/1207/J

* 9 7 8 1 7 3 4 7 1 1 9 3 6 *